MW01123710

He'll
Find
You

Final
Justice

He'll
Find
You

Final
Justice

LAINE BOYD

Copyright © 2017 by Laine Boyd. All rights reserved.
No part of this publication may be reproduced, stored in a
retrieval system or transmitted in any way by any means, electronic, mechanical, photocopy, recording or otherwise without
the prior permission of the author except as descriptions, entities, and incidents included in the story are the products of the
author's imagination. Any resemblance to actual persons, events,
and entities is entirely coincidental.

Cover and interior design by Marquee Publishing
Library of Congress Control Number: 2017902222
Marquee Publishing
3901 Berger Ave.
St. Louis, MO 63109 USA
Published in the United States of America

ISBN-10: 978-0-9985017-3-4
ISBN-13: 0-9985017-3-5

1. Fiction/Suspense/Thriller/Crime Fighting/Family
2. Fiction/Mystery/Suspense/Police Family

Also by Laine Boyd

Unharmonious
Dinner and a Murder
He'll Find You: 'Till Death Do Us Part

To the brave men and women who daily put themselves in harm's way to protect our country, whether at home or abroad, past and present, with my deepest respect and gratitude for your service and your sacrifice. Thank you.

Acknowledgments

I am beyond grateful to several wonderful people, without whose specialized knowledge and insight this book would be rife with inaccuracies. Sandi Hafner, R.N., has been my faithful medical expert for four books, letting me know when I'm killing people incorrectly, or treating their illnesses with too much creativity. Her patience knows no end and is a good match for my persistence. Lynn Walker Furgerson, R.N., is a valued addition to my expert medical resources and provided helpful information with specific details. St. Louis attorneys John H. Goffstein, Gary H. Lange, and Timothy P. O'Mara, addressed legal queries; I always enjoy talking with them. Leland Boyd, retired St. Louis County Bomb and Arson Squad detective, answered endless questions as to investigative techniques, and explosive devices. Mike Rhoads, a security expert, provided enough details to warrant another book! His training in surveillance and other security-related questions was fascinating. I deeply appreciate the patience and willingness of these special people in sharing their expertise and experience in their fields.

If I have not been as accurate as I should have been, or taken too much liberty with certain scenes in this story, it is my fault alone and not the fault of any of my experts who were so generous with their time and willingness to provide me with their perspectives.

Gloria Harrison, Kris Hillen, Sandi Hafner, Renee Dyer, Bethany Fisher, Rick Rodriguez, and Lynn Meyers provided support as my beloved test readers. I value their input and honesty, and am very grateful for their help and the time they invested.

CaSondra Poulsen was my fantastic editor, and her insight was, as usual, spot-on! I'm so happy to be working with her again!

Finally, I would like to thank Marquee Publishing, LLC, for their publishing and graphic services and their efforts to keep my first two books, *Unharmonious* and *Dinner and a Murder*, from going out of print, as Ballad Publishing closes.

I am deeply grateful to all of these terrific people who have been a source of help, information, encouragement, and support.

November 10, 2016
St. Louis, Missouri

Day 1

3:43 p.m.

Carson Hollister whistled a cheerful tune as he locked his car, and strolled with long, light strides from the parking lot to the offices of Medical Staffing Remedies, Inc., where he was employed as a junior accountant. He opened the door and walked to the receptionist's large, curved mahogany desk situated by the foot of the staircase, overlooking a spacious lobby and waiting area.

"Hey, Lizard Wizard," he said, grinning at the receptionist. He leaned over the counter, rendering it impossible for her to not see him.

Lizzie Wise raised her eyes from the computer screen without moving her head, and spoke to him in a flat voice. "You're late, Carson. We all get one hour for lunch. It's nearly four o'clock." She looked back at the computer screen and ignored him.

"I worked until two-thirty without a break, so I took a late lunch. Had to run a couple of errands. Anyway, Mr. Carmody isn't in this afternoon, and he doesn't care when I go to lunch as long as I get my eight hours in. Hey! Wanna grab a burger and a movie Friday after work? C'mon, Lizard Gizzard, it'll be fun. You can pick the movie…and the restaurant." He leaned further over her desk, his eyebrows raised in vain hope, still sporting a goofy grin, smitten with the unshakeable Lizzie Wise. Blonde curls fell gracefully from a pile of long hair arranged in a loose bun on top of her head, framing her wide-set, blue-green eyes and turned up nose. Carson's heartbeat quickened every time he saw her. He knew if Lizzie would just give him a chance—one little chance, he could win her over. However, subtlety was not his strong point and if Lizzie Wise was attracted to suave and debonair men, then Carson was out of luck.

She turned her lovely eyes toward Carson and blinked. "Heavens to Murgatroid is coming. She's been looking for you ever since you were seven minutes late," she warned him in a deadpan voice. She leaned forward and glanced to her right, down the hallway. No one was coming. Lizzie looked back at Carson. "And no, I have no interest in anything resembling a date with you. If you don't stop bugging me, I'm going to file a harassment complaint." She again returned her gaze to her computer screen. In spite of her repeated turndowns, her tone was never harsh and Carson could not detect that Lizzie was ever offended. Not really. She just needed to give him a chance. Until he had reason to believe she was truthfully upset at his attempts to win her affections, Carson would never stop asking. He was determined to win the heart of the beautiful, but very hard to get Lizzie Wise.

Carson heard the quick drum-rolling footsteps of Miriam Murgan, the one-woman HR department and self-appointed judge and jury, approaching from down the hall, the clackety-clack of her heels echoing ominously on the polished hardwood flooring as she neared the reception area. The staff at MSR referred to Miriam as Heavens to Murgatroid, a woman so talented, she could make an entire mountain range out of a miniscule molehill. One tiny infraction of her ever-expanding nonsensical rules would inspire Heavens to Murgatroid to write a new company policy, ensuring that the offending employee would not only be embarrassed to death over a simple mistake, but the rest of the staff would have a new edict pronounced upon them, however ridiculous, written in stone, forever and ever amen. Once, an unfortunate mouse found its way into the sleek, contemporary office building over which she ruled with iron fists. An exterminator was summoned at once, paid extra for the same day visit, and Miriam banned each and every staff member from keeping food in their desk drawers and eating at their desks, since it was obviously their carelessness in dropng crumbs that attracted the little rodent. The revered recruiters, however, could continue to do as they pleased. The crumbs that fell from the desks of the sacred recruiters, of course, could never attract a mouse—only those crumbs dropped by the staff who served them were suspect. Everything was a monumental deal to her, and thus, to all the employees.

Carson, like the rest of the staff, avoided the woman like the plague. At the first sound of her heels, he darted around the reception desk, keeping his head low, and dashed up the twenty-four-foot staircase, taking the steps two at a time, toward his office on the second floor. Halfway up the staircase, Carson heard Lizzie tell Murgatroid that he had returned from lunch some time ago, and no, she didn't know why Murgatroid hadn't seen him. Carson laughed to himself and continued to sneak up the staircase. *Thanks for the cover, Lizard. She does like me. I knew it!*

Five years before Carson landed a job at Medical Staffing Remedies, Inc., the firm purchased a two-story historic corner building in the fashionable Central West End neighborhood of St. Louis. The firm was situated halfway between the Washington University-run Barnes-Jewish Hospital and the SSM-run St. Louis University Hospital, providing recruiters with an ideal location. The inside of the building had undergone a complete rehab, and although the turn-of-the-century façade was historic in appearance, to blend in with the rest of the neighborhood, the interior was swank and ultramodern. The office décor screamed that loads of money had been spent to attract the best and brightest medical personnel from all over the world. MSR, as the business was referred to among its employees, was a high-end recruiting firm that matched surgeons, specialists, and sub-specialists with the many major hospitals in the St. Louis area.

Carson Hollister was not a recruiter. A newly-employed junior accountant, Carson considered himself lucky to have landed a sweet position with a successful firm. Grateful for the job, and being employed a mere five months, he wanted to make a good impression on the powers that be. The senior accountant and managing partner, Edmond Carmody, would be retiring in the next few years, and if Carson proved himself worthy, he would be promoted to senior accountant. As he worked under the careful eye of Mr. Carmody, Carson believed Mr. Carmody liked him. Carson was a good worker and a quick study, picking up the way MSR liked things done. It was his first real job that didn't involve asking if anyone wanted fries with their order, and he was eager to impress. He had succeeded so far, unless your name was Lizzie Wise or Heavens to Murgatroid.

Lizzie was friendly to everyone, and cordial to Carson. He had tried charming her, but she fell for none of it. Carson wasn't bad looking, he knew. Tall and slender, fair-skinned with dark hair and eyes, Carson had had his share of girlfriends. No one special, but he'd never had anyone behave as actively disinterested as Lizzie. It didn't help that every time he spoke to her, he lost his composure, ended up saying something stupid, and felt like he'd been transported back to junior high school.

Being the most recent hire and in a subordinate position, Carson was given the last, lone office in the back of the maze that sprawled over the second floor. His office was not much bigger than a closet, with a single window that overlooked the flat, tarred rooftops of the adjoining buildings, most of which were single-story storefront offices. The large parking lot that MSR shared with the neighboring businesses lay below. Even the secretaries had a better view from the atrium hub, where their work spaces were set in a starburst pattern. But Carson didn't care. The job came with benefits and the pay was good for a first-year employee. He had recently moved into a one-bedroom apartment and was soon able to buy a new bed, new sofa, second-hand end table, TV, and nightstand. Nothing matched, but it was functional, and except for setting aside money to treat Lizzie to a date, the remainder of his paycheck went toward student loans.

As Carson reached the top of the long winding staircase, he heard the front door below open. It was not customary for interviews to begin this late in the afternoon, and he was curious as to who the late arrivals were. He turned and peered over the banister. Two hooded figures dressed in black and carrying semi-automatic weapons rushed in with their guns pointed at Lizzie. They said something to her that Carson could not make out. He heard Miriam Murgan's footsteps start and stop. Her shrill voice demanded to know what they wanted. *Does she not see the guns? I can see them from here! That woman is out of her mind.* Then, they began shooting. The shots echoed through the air. Terrified screaming, followed by more gunshots, reverberated throughout the building. Carson froze, staring in disbelief over the top of the banister, no longer able to see Lizzie, then fled to his office as he heard heavy footsteps stomp through the downstairs offices and then ascend the staircase, the rat-a-tat-tat of their weapons ringing out. *Is Lizzie shot? Did she fall backwards? Is she hurt?* Carson couldn't tell.

On the second floor, pandemonium reigned as secretaries, recruiters, accountants, and other staff ran in different directions, tripping over each other, screaming. Over the din of stampeding footsteps, panicked voices shouted, "Call 911! We're under attack!"

"Terrorists!"

"They're shooting everybody!"

"Help!"

"Run!"

As Carson neared his office at the back of the last hallway, he heard windows breaking as his helpless co-workers jumped two stories to escape the hooded intruders thundering up the stairs. He ran into his office and climbed out the window, dropping onto an adjoining rooftop a few feet below. Running to the edge of the roof, he looked over the parking lot trying to ascertain the best route of escape. The back of the parking lot faced an alley, but a chain link fence blocked any exit that way. He would have to drive through the lot and out the main entrance, where he would be an easy target. It was the only way he could escape, unless he drove his car through the landscaped yards of the private residences on the street adjoining the lot. *Who attacks a recruiting agency for medical personnel? Competition may be cutthroat, but it isn't violent! Who* are *these guys?* Carson's heart pounded in his chest as he shimmied down the drainpipe and landed on the grass below with a thud. He ran as low to the ground as he could, through the rows of parked cars, weaving for cover between trucks and SUVs, winding his way toward his own car. *Stay calm.* He tried to control his breathing. He tried to dial 911, but his fingers shook so much they were useless. *Once I'm outta here, I can call for help.*

He fumbled around in his pocket for the remote starter his parents had given to him last Christmas, and grasped it, trying to steady his hands. Plotting his escape from the chaotic scene behind him, Carson decided it would make more sense to have his car started and running for a quick getaway. That way, he wouldn't feel like a sitting duck in case the intruders made their way into the parking lot and his car wouldn't start. Carson's car was not the most reliable of his limited possessions. A few more paychecks and he would have enough for a down payment on something newer with monthly payments he could afford. Looking over his shoulder, he crept toward his old Ford, still staying low, until he was two cars away. He glanced up at his building, and to his horror, saw one of the gunmen standing on the roof where Carson had stood only minutes before. Carson ducked between the cars and with fumbling fingers, pressed the button to start his engine.

A deafening explosion followed by a blinding light, and Carson felt his clothing plastered against his skin as though a powerful wind had caught him. The repercussion from the blast vibrated through Carson's body, flinging him backward until he lay flat on the ground, stunned and dazed. He saw the hood of his car blow higher than the rooftop, as the car doors blew outward in every direction. The concrete parking lot swam before his eyes in blurry waves as Carson struggled to understand what had just happened. Debris rained from the sky and he realized he couldn't hear anything. Something gritty was in his mouth and he tried to spit it out. He spat repeatedly, spewing concrete, asphalt, dirt, and other materials he couldn't identify. The world around him was silent, but for his heartbeat which throbbed like a jackhammer within his chest. Carson tried to sit up, but his body felt as though it was made of jelly and he fell back onto the ground. His nostrils filled with a noxious odor, and his car was engulfed in flames. Thick, black smoke billowed, covering the parking lot, stinging his eyes and nose. Several other cars in the lot sustained damage. The cars closest to his would be totaled. Carson pushed himself up once more into a sitting position and leaned against the car behind him, trying to collect his thoughts. He put his hand to his head. Blood ran down his forearm as he pulled out a section of a side view mirror that had lodged in his forehead over his eyebrow. Car parts and shards of glass lay scattered, and the smell of toxic smoke sickened Carson. His scalp and hair were gritty with debris.

That was meant for me. Those men are after me*! What's going on? Get outta here. Gotta get outta here. Now!* Carson struggled to stand, pulling himself up along the back fender of the car on which he was leaning. Glancing back to the roof of his office building, he saw the gunmen's back as he retreated through Carson's open window. He dug grit out of his ears and rubbed them. His hearing began to return, although faint, as he detected muted sirens wailing in the distance, and the blast of fire engine horns. He shook his head to try to clear it and unplug his ears, but it only made his head hurt. Muffled sounds threw him off balance and Carson felt dizzy and sick to his stomach. *What's happening? Lizzie! Get out! Get out!* Carson stumbled to the edge of the parking lot. His clothes were torn and he was dirty and bleeding, but shock blocked any pain he might have felt. He tried without success to walk away from the scene as though all was normal, staring straight ahead.

Carson hid among the tall shrubbery that lined the lawns of the homes on the side of the block behind his office building, and watched the fallout scene unfold. He continued to spit out gravel and grit. Running his tongue over his teeth, he felt the rough layer coating them and wished he had some water to rinse his mouth. *Get out!* He'd always thought the tall bushes that lined the front yards of the stately brick homes on this block in the Central West End were ugly, but this afternoon, he was grateful for the cover they provided as he crept away from the parking lot, away from his office, in search of safety.

Carson needed to think, needed his head clear. But his head was throbbing and while his hearing was returning, sounds were muffled, and a high-pitched ringing noise whistled through his head like a train, causing him to trip every few steps. He continued walking, stumbling as though drunk, behind the tall shrubbery until his office building was no longer visible. Still in shock and unsure of where he was, Carson saw a bus stop sign ahead and walked toward it. He fumbled in his pocket for his wallet. He didn't know which bus line it was or where it might take him, but he didn't care. *Anywhere away from here.*

Carson lived in an old apartment in Maplewood, a working-class suburb abutting St. Louis, on the second floor of a three story, six family brick building. It was only fifteen minutes or so from work by car, but he didn't know how long it might take by bus, or if he was even on a bus line that would take him toward home.

The sun would be setting soon and the temperature was starting to drop. Carson pulled his torn jacket around him. He was alone at the bus stop, which meant it wasn't yet five o'clock. He figured it couldn't be much after four, but it seemed hours ago that he was asking Lizzie out. He hoped he could catch the last bus before the public transportation got crowded with commuters leaving work for home. *Home.* Carson sighed. He wanted to be home, take a hot shower and lie down in his new bed. Miss Buttons, his sweet kitty, would come and snuggle with him and everything would be fine. This would be a bad dream and he would wake up in the morning in his own bed with Miss Buttons telling him she would starve if he didn't feed her, and he would go to work like he had been doing for the past five months. Next month, he would get another car. *This is just a bad dream.*

A cold gust of wind hit Carson's face, returning him to his present dilemma. He looked down the street and saw a bus approaching. He squinted to read the signage across the top. As the bus neared, he saw Maplewood Station flashing and breathed a sigh of relief. When the door opened, the bus driver looked at Carson with wide eyes. "I don't want no trouble on my bus," the driver started.

"What?" Carson asked, confused, then realized his appearance must have startled the driver. "Uh no, man, no trouble. I was in an accident. Just wanna get home."

"Any trouble, boy, I call the police," the driver warned. Carson put his hands up. "Promise, man. Just wanna go home, that's all."

"Two dollars." The bus driver looked Carson up and down in clear disapproval.

The bus was nearly empty, occupied by a couple of university students reading with their headsets on, and a handful of older folks, a few of whom had fallen asleep. Carson nodded, satisfied. *Nobody likely to remember me.* Carson took a seat behind the side door exit and glimpsed his reflection in the window. He looked even worse than he felt. His hair was tousled and his face was covered in black smudges. The cut on his forehead above his eyebrow from where the car mirror landed looked bad. Smaller cuts over his face would heal without scarring. His lip was cut and his clothing looked like he'd been in a fight with a pack of wolves. His hands were scraped and raw. A large hole in his slacks revealed a chunk of glass embedded in his thigh. *Too bad Halloween was two weeks ago. I'd have won first prize for Walking Train Wreck.*

Carson smoothed his hair with his hands and went to work to remove the glass wedged into his leg. The bus hit a bump in the road, causing Carson to cut his finger on the glass. He flinched, and then gingerly pulled the chunk of glass from his leg, wincing as the air hit the open wound. He applied pressure with the torn edge of his slacks and after a few minutes, the bleeding stopped. He examined himself and could find no additional injuries that needed immediate attention. Carson reached into his pocket and pulled out his cell phone. It was broken. No surprise.

I'm so sleepy. Probably from being hit in the head with the flying mirror. The bus stopped and the students got off. At the next stop, an elderly woman struggled to exit the bus. Carson wanted to help her, but thought his appearance might frighten her. He thought of his mother, and how she now depended on people to help her. His parents had raised him to be considerate of others, but he couldn't decide whether it would be more considerate to assist the woman or to prevent a heart attack by not scaring her to death. He wasn't prepared for a situation such as this one. *If this lady was my mom, I'd want someone to help her. Maybe her eyesight's not all that great.* He rose to help her. She accepted his assistance and when she looked up to thank him, she shook her head and said, "I'd sure like to see the other guy!"

Carson smiled at her in spite of his pain. "Wish I *had* seen him," he answered. He returned to his seat and watched the woman turn and walk down the block, leaning on her cane. His stomach tightened. He hoped the people at Cloverlawn Memory Care Center, where his mother was living, were kind to her. They were always nice when Carson visited. He'd never seen signs of abuse. His mother had fallen once, but they had called him right away. She was shaken, but fine. There would be more falls. It was inevitable. He missed his dad. As independent as he was, Carson felt an intense need for his parents after the events of this afternoon. He put his head in his hands. *Don't fall asleep. You'll miss your stop.*

When Carson lifted his head, he saw his stop up ahead. He chided himself for dozing off, but then thought maybe he should go a block or two further and walk back. The brisk air would wake him and keep him alert. *What if these guys know where I live? Am I being paranoid?* Carson's head was pounding. He longed for a hot shower and a comfortable bed.

He exited one bus stop past his own and walked back to the quiet side street on which his apartment was situated. A strange car with no license plates was parked outside his building. Two men were sitting in the front seat. One of the men was looking up toward Carson's apartment with binoculars. The hair on the back of Carson's neck stood up as fear gripped his heart. He shivered. *They're gonna shoot me when I get home. I should run—get out of here. But Miss Buttons! I can't do that to her. The back way! Careful!*

Carson cut through the alley to the rear of the apartment, and took the back fire escape steps to the second floor. It was getting dark. He crept toward the back door and suddenly stopped. Chips of paint lay scattered around the outside ledge of the kitchen window. Carson never opened that window and he could see it was unlocked. He peered into his kitchen window from the landing outside and gasped. Someone had been in his apartment. He saw a wire running along the baseboard of the far wall. He assumed the wire meant that his apartment would blow up when he entered, just like his car had when he pushed the remote starter. *What is going on? Who are these guys and what do they want with me?* His heart began to pound. *Miss Buttons! I can't leave Miss Buttons!* Carson thought of the little white and orange cat that had adopted him the day he moved in. That same kitchen window had been left open the day he took the apartment and a friendly stray cat had wandered in and made herself at home. Carson had asked the neighbors, but they said she was just another homeless stray, and if he was going to keep her, he would have to have her spayed, or there would be a lot more than one cat living with him. A line of orange spots dotted her white chest, so he named her Miss Buttons, got her spayed and vaccinated, and she seemed as happy to stay with Carson as he was to have her. She waited for him every evening at the front door and never allowed him to oversleep.

Carson sat on the steps to the fire escape. He tried to think over the throbbing pain in his head. If he opened the door, it would be certain death for him and Miss Buttons. If he called the police, he figured they could probably disarm the bomb. But how would he answer their questions? He had no idea, and he had plenty of his own questions he wanted answered. Carson needed rest. He couldn't think clearly, and as the shock wore off, the pain set in. He pulled out his wallet and counted. Forty-one dollars. He had only four hundred twenty dollars and eighteen cents in his bank account. Carson didn't like to use the ATM at night and darkness was descending as the last rays of sun began to vanish. He went down the stairs and walked through the alley, away from his apartment, thinking.

Suddenly, a yowl disrupted his thoughts and a weight landed on his chest, knocking him off balance and scaring him.

"Miss Buttons! How did you get out?" He hugged his kitty and she purred, butting him with her head burrowed into his neck. "We gotta get outta here, Miss Buttons."

Carson carried the cat, holding her close against his chest and began to walk, not certain where he should go, other than far away from his own apartment and in the opposite direction of the strange car parked in front of his home. He was glad he'd eaten a late lunch. He walked for over an hour, staying off the main streets. A lump formed in his throat as he thought about Lizzie. He hoped she hadn't been hurt.

3:58 p.m.

Sam Hernandez fidgeted in his car, stuck in traffic. Normally a patient man, the job he was now working was running against an impatient clock. He didn't know how much time his client had left before the condition that was shutting down his lungs would claim his life, but Sam was determined to finish the job as soon as possible. He sucked at his bottom lip and thumped on the steering wheel as he inched toward the Kingshighway exit, bringing him closer to completing his mission at glacial speed.

Sam was driving past the BJC hospital complex, a behemoth medical center, when he heard a loud explosion and felt his car shake. He switched on his police scanner, but before he could discern the chatter from the static, the wail of sirens screaming from several directions surrounded him. An uneasy feeling churned in Sam's gut and he tightened his grip on the steering wheel. Once past the medical complex, the traffic eased up and Sam headed toward the office in the Central West End. When he'd left home over an hour ago, he was smiling at the thought of finishing this job with its anticipated happy ending, but now, the sounds of the explosion and sirens concerned him and he couldn't shake his apprehension.

Three blocks from Medical Staffing Remedies, Sam's stomach tightened into a tangled knot. As he drove toward the building, the air was alive with the noise of emergency vehicles, police cars, fire trucks and ambulances, and Sam could see thick black smoke covering his destination. He turned and parked four blocks away and walked toward MSR. The scene sickened him. Dead and wounded lined the sidewalk in front of the office building as paramedics performed triage, separating the critically wounded from those whose injuries stopped short of life threatening. A crowd had gathered to gawk and postulate uninformed theories on the unfolding drama. Sam mingled with the crowd in an effort to pick up conversation. Murmurs of terrorist attacks, masked gunmen, office workers being massacred by gangs and random attacks floated through the crowd, which the police were pushing back with minimal success. Sam was queasy. *This is no coincidence. No terrorists, no gangs, and certainly not random. They were after Jordan. I hope they didn't get him. If I'd just been here sooner!* He cursed the traffic. He removed the photo he'd taken of Kenton Farraday's son and studied it. It wasn't necessary. Sam had the young man's face memorized. He scanned the scene, straining to see if he recognized any of the victims. Some had already been whisked away to area hospitals. Barnes-Jewish and St. Louis University Hospitals were the closest, and Sam guessed half the victims were going to each.

More police arrived and the crowd was pushed back farther. News crews appeared from all the major stations in St. Louis. There was no point in staying. Sam left. *What am I going to tell Kenton? They got there first? How?*

Sam hurried back to his car and called Kenton Farraday's house. Vivienne Simonet, Kenton's nurse and housekeeper, answered the phone. "Hi, Vivienne. It's Sam Hernandez. Kenton's not watching television, is he? Good. No, no. Don't wake him. Listen, when he does wake up, don't let him turn on the news. Yeah. You could say that—it's very bad. Listen, my job just got a little tougher, but I don't want him to worry. I'll stop by later today when I have more information. Uh huh. Uh huh. No proof, you understand, but I'd bet my last dollar that Pamela and Richard are behind this. If the TV won't wake him, then you go ahead and watch so you're prepared. It'll be on all the news stations. I don't want Mr. Farraday getting upset when we don't have any facts yet. Well, yeah. Besides the obvious."

Sam turned the scanner back on and tried to glean whatever information he could from it, but it told him little he had not already ascertained.

4:14 p.m.

Detective Adam Trent sat in his office at the Clark Street Precinct finishing paperwork when the call came in. Gunfire, explosions, possible terrorist activity in the Central West End. He rose from his desk and called to his team. "Bo, Connor, Samantha. We got a big case. Central West End. Grab your gear and let's go. Earpieces, everyone. I'll catch you up on the way. Bo and Connor, you're together, Samantha, you're with me." The team headed down the stairs to two squad cars, flipped on the lights and sirens, and headed toward Medical Staffing Remedies.

The streets were barricaded for a two-block radius around the crime scene. Adam and Bo parked their cars and the team met in front of the building. Bomb and Arson Squad and uniformed police officers were already busy working the scene. Adam asked one of the officers who was in charge, but before the officer could answer, Felix Santos, of Bomb and Arson, approached Adam and shook his hand.

"Adam," he said, nodding to Adam's team.

"Felix. Not surprised to see you here." Adam shook his hand and gestured to his partners. "This is Bo, Connor, and Samantha, my team. I see you've got your screens in place already. What've we got?"

Felix motioned for them to follow him to the parking lot. The techs had covered the parking lot with several layers of screens to filter down their search for bomb parts, wire, residue, and other evidence, to determine the type of bomb. "A lot of gunfire inside the building, but no explosives or fire inside. Parking lot's a different story. I can tell you right now, by the smell, they used C4. I don't need no screens to tell me that." He shook his head. "Too many years in the Army to ever forget the smell of C4."

Adam, who had served as a Marine, agreed. He surveyed the damage and whistled. "Wow. Lots of work for *your* team, huh? What do you know so far?"

"Hard to believe, but all this mess was caused by one explosive device in one car. Old Ford. Registered to Carson Hollister, twenty-five, white male, new employee on the job five months. No priors, no record of any kind. Graduated *cum laude* with an accounting degree. This place is his first big boy job, as far as we know."

"Disgruntled employee?" Bo asked.

"Investigation's just started, but as far as we've been able to ascertain, he liked his job. But that's for you and yours to determine."

"Okay. Kinda looks like someone didn't like him," Adam said, looking over the parking lot littered with burned out wreckage. "No way could someone survive this."

"Except there's no body," Felix answered.

Adam raised his eyebrows.

"Any body parts?" Connor asked.

"Nope. Nothin' to say anyone was in the car when it blew. Looks like the car was empty when the bomb went off. When we're finished up here, I'll send you my full report. Somethin' ain't kosher in the deli." Felix sucked on the inside of his cheeks and squinted his eyes. "When my investigation is finished, you can take the lead on this. Meantime, you oughtta check inside."

"Lookin' forward to your report. Good seein' you, Felix." Adam and his team walked to the front of the building. A stretcher with a body bag was being taken out by two EMTs and loaded into the last ambulance. A uniformed officer recognized Adam and spoke.

"Detective Trent. That's the last victim." He shook his head. "We see all kinds of things on this job. Ain't never seen nothin' like this before, though."

"Body count?" Adam asked.

"Sixteen people work here total. Three confirmed dead, two hanging on by a thread, six more with various degrees of injuries, all on their way to the hospital, four unaccounted for and three with minor injuries and likely needing a change of underwear."

"My math says that's eighteen," Connor said.

"One of the badly injured was a doctor who was interviewing for placement by the firm, and one assailant dead. No ID yet on him."

"How many assailants were there?" Adam asked.

"Pretty sure two. The witnesses are really rattled. Their stories are confused, but it looks like we got two perps, so one's in the wind."

"And the four unaccounted for?" Bo asked.

The officer consulted his notes. Head honcho, Edmund Carmody. Took the day off to see his granddaughter's school play. Not confirmed, but no reason to doubt it. Big family man. Danita Jefferson, a recruiter, Jalisa Moore, a secretary, home on medical leave following surgery, again, unconfirmed, but no reason to doubt it, and Carson Hollister, guy whose car blew to smithereens. Missing. No idea."

Adam nodded as he took notes.

"Anything else, sir?" the officer asked.

"We'll take it from here. Good job, thanks." Adam reached for the door handle, but the officer held up his hand and shook his head.

"Sorry, Detective Trent. Evidence Techs are still in there. They should be done pretty soon."

"I see." Adam and his team peered inside the building through the wall of windows on either side of the front door. Three windows had been shattered. Gunfire had ripped holes throughout the lush interior. Pieces of drywall and glass shards mixed with wood splinters littered the floors, table tops, and furniture. Blood spatters and pools showed the location of the victims when they either sustained their injuries or breathed their last. "Who's in there?" he asked the officer.

"Elle," the officer replied. "Need to talk to her?"

"Please."

The officer opened the door. "Hey, Elle! Adam Trent wants to see you."

Evidence Technician Elle Canterbury stepped around the corner and came to the front door. "Hi, Adam. We're not done processing yet. Can we get back to you?"

"Sure. I should've realized you were still here. We're leaving. Can you send me your report ASAP?"

"You got it. We're gonna be here well into the night. But for you, since you asked so nice, I'll stay up even later, 'cuz who needs sleep, anyway?" She grinned at him. "You'll have my report first thing tomorrow morning," she called over her shoulder as she returned to the room she was processing.

Adam gathered his team and they walked back to their cars. "They're gonna be a while. I'll review their reports and prepare our assignments. Knowing Elle, she'll have her report to me tonight. Let's meet early tomorrow and plan our investigation. Go home, get some dinner and get a good night's rest. In my office, seven a.m. Anything changes, I'll call. Keep your cell phones on."

"Hey, Samantha Jane," Bo whispered to the newest member of the team. "Wanna meet me at Imo's for pizza?"

"Nope."

"How's about Pi?"

"Nope."

"What about the Fountain on Locust?"

"Nope."

4:32 p.m.

Sam Hernandez sat in Kenton Farraday's spacious living room.

"He'll be right down, Mr. Hernandez," Vivienne told him. "He's got one of those chair elevators so he can get up and down the stairs easily."

"Has he seen the news?"

"No, sir. He just woke up a few minutes ago. I hear him now."

Sam heard Kenton approaching and stood to greet him. The hum of his oxygen machine and the rolling of the walker as Kenton Farraday entered were unmistakable. His smile faded when he saw Sam's face.

"Sam, what's wrong? Did you find Jordan? What's happened?" Kenton began to cough. Vivienne left to retrieve his medicine.

"Please sit down," Sam answered, and helped Kenton to his chair before he resumed his seat. Sam leaned back in his chair and closed his eyes. Taking a deep breath, he opened his eyes and spoke in a controlled voice. "Mr. Farraday, there's no easy way to say this. Only a couple of minutes before I reached

Jordan, two armed men entered the office building where he works and began shooting people. There was an explosion in the parking lot, which turned out to be Jordan's car."

Kenton pitched forward and grabbed his chest. Vivienne rushed to his side and eased him back. She poured his medicine into a small cup and set it before him.

Sam continued. "We don't know anything for certain, but here's what I think."

Kenton looked up at Sam, his eyes brimming with tears.

"I think that when the gunmen began their killing spree, Jordan escaped and made it to the parking lot. I do know that no bodies were discovered in the parking lot, so I'm guessing Jordan may have had an automatic starter. I think he got away, but he may be hurt."

"Do you think Pamela and Richard have him? Or whomever they hired to do this?" Kenton asked.

Sam shook his head. "There's no way to know for certain. I won't stop until I find him, Mr. Farraday. I promise you that. The pictures on the news are going to be upsetting for you, so you may wish to avoid the newscasts. All I've been able to ascertain as of now is that Jordan was not among the dead or those taken to the hospital. One of the gunmen was killed. I would think that once their plan went south, they would have fled, and not attempted to take a hostage. I'm sorry. When I left to pick him up, I was sure this day was going to have a happy ending."

Sam stood. "The police are looking for Jordan as well as the gunman. Jordan's listed as missing. But *we* have a leg up because we already know who was behind this and why. We also know they are ruthless and will stop at nothing. I found him once. I'll find him again." He turned to leave. "I'll keep you posted. I can see myself out."

Frustrated, Sam drove toward home. His mind churned as he tried to understand how anyone could have found Jordan before he had. He'd been careful. He was positive he'd never been followed, never seen anything out of the ordinary or suspicious. Kenton had given him every assurance that Vivienne, his nurse and housekeeper, and Martina, his executive admin, were completely trustworthy. Nobody else knew. How could Pamela and Richard have known? *That's it!* Sam struck the steering wheel with the palm of his hand. There could be only one way! He stopped at a gas station to use one of the few pay phones left in St. Louis. His wife, Julie, should be home by now. She'd had symphony rehearsal earlier that morning and a vet appointment for the dog in the afternoon. Sam looked at his watch. Not quite five. *She's probably practicing and won't answer the phone.* He dialed Julie's best friend, Su Li Jernigan. Su Li picked up on the second ring.

"Su Li," he began.

"Uh-oh. I don't like the sound of your voice. What's happened?"

"Listen. I need a favor and I need it now."

"Okay." Su Li's reply was cautious.

"I'm not sure, but the house might be bugged and my cell phone might be bugged. If it is, then Julie could be in danger. I need you to go over there now, take her outside the house and tell her to pack a bag for herself and get Wolfgang's things as well. Can they stay at your place for a few days?" The urgency in Sam's voice was unmistakable.

"Of course. Always. I'll leave now. Don't worry. Be careful, Sam."

"Thanks."

4:45 p.m.

Julie Hernandez opened her door and immediately, Su Li pressed her finger to her lips. Su Li motioned for Julie to come outside, and continued to give her the silent sign. The women walked several yards from the house before Julie spoke.

"All right. What's going on?"

"Sam called."

"He called *you?*"

"He thinks you could be in danger and he thinks the house might be bugged. So we're talking out here. I'm just the messenger. When we go back to the house, he wants you to pack a bag for yourself and get Wolfgang's things and come stay at my house for a few days."

"All right. Let's go." Julie turned and headed toward the house.

"That's it? Let's go? No questions or comments?"

"Su Li, I know my husband. If he thinks I'm in danger to the point where I need to stay elsewhere, then I trust his judgment. Sam is so security conscious, so careful—if he believes there's been a breach of any kind, he won't rest and can't work on this case until he knows I'm safe. So let's get this done as soon as possible."

"Just like that?"

"Just like that. No talking when we're in the house."

Su Li helped Julie pack a few things. They rounded up Wolfgang's food, dishes, chew toys and other toys, and left the house in silence. Su Li's home was at the far end of the Hernandez property. Su Li had driven to save the twenty-minute walk between their homes.

Once inside, Julie said, "I need to let Sam know I'm safe."

"Did you bring your cell phone? Just give him a call." Su Li helped carry the bags upstairs. Su Li's oldest daughter, Hannah, was away at college, so Julie took her bedroom.

"You said he called you from a pay phone. He must think his phone is bugged, so maybe mine is, too. You know Sam. He's very careful. We need to give him a coded message."

The women sat on Hannah's bed. Su Li giggled. "You mean like the crow flies at midnight? The eagle has landed? Bugsy sent me?"

Julie grabbed her side and moaned. "Yeah. Something like that, but not so corny. What about telling him you brought the flowers in before the frost comes? I think he'll get that."

Su Li rolled her eyes and they giggled together. She dialed Sam's cell phone. "Hi, Sam. Just wanted to tell you that I brought your flowers inside before the frost comes."

"Wha—? Oh. Okay. Thanks, Su Li. Don't give them too much water. I'll be home soon."

"What'd he say?"

"He told me not to let you drink too much wine!"

"That depends on how much chocolate you've got in the house. So when do David and the kids get home?"

"David gets in around five, so any minute. The boys have practice, so they should be here in about fifteen minutes. We need to leave soon to pick up Becky at school. The kids are working late on the class talent show."

"Where's my little buddy, Noah? He's going to want to play with Wolfgang."

Su Li smiled. "Noah's visiting his grandparents today. David's sister moved to Springfield. Her husband took a job there, so my in-laws are suffering from grandchild withdrawal syndrome. Noah had his first overnight with them last night. They'll drop him by after dinner. He'll be thrilled that Wolfgang's spending a few nights."

Julie nodded. "I see. Smells like chili in the crock pot?" They started downstairs toward the kitchen.

"Nothin' wrong with *your* nose! I'll make cornbread when we get Becky home." Su Li checked her watch. "We should leave in about ten minutes. How about a cup of tea while we wait?"

"Sure. Did Sam say anything else?"

"No. But he sure sounds tense." Su Li put the kettle on and put the tea leaves in the basket of her teapot.

"He'll probably stop by here before he goes home, right?"

"I s'pose. The most important thing to Sam is that you're safe. I think he worries more about you than Samantha Jane."

Julie sighed and ran her finger around the rim of her tea mug. "Yes, my daughter, the homicide detective. I always dreamed she'd go into music."

The tea kettle whistled. Su Li poured the hot water into the teapot and set the lid on top to steep. "Kids need to follow their own dreams. Becky's more your daughter than mine, ya know!" Su Li laughed. "That kid practices as soon as her homework is finished. She'd rather play her piano than go outside and play. Tea's about ready. Spiced rooibos, okay?"

"Yum. I wonder what kind of chocolate goes best with that?" Julie asked.

"No sweets before dinner. Sheesh! What am I, your mother?"

"It's gonna be fun staying over here. Just like old times!" Julie stirred honey into her cup and sipped the tea. "Mmm. This is good."

5:37 p.m.

Sam knocked on the door of David and Su Li Jernigan's home. Julie answered.

"Hey, baby," he said, holding her close and running his hands through her hair. "You okay?" He kissed her and brushed her hair back from her face.

"What's going on, Sam? Is it this case? It didn't sound dangerous to me when you took it." Julie's azure blue eyes searched his brown eyes.

"I'm not sure, honey." Sam ran his hands down Julie's pale, thin arms and held her hands in his. "I think there's been some sort of breach." He shook his head. "I don't know how—I don't know *how* it could have happened, but something's going on, and I can't put you at risk." He pressed her to his chest and wrapped his arms around her. "We're working within a short time frame, so I think you'll be here a few days at best."

Julie looked down and nodded her head. She sighed. "I thought all this—this cloak and dagger stuff was behind us after you retired. You've been serving process and following cheaters for the most part. This case sounded pretty simple."

Sam lifted her head, cupping her face in his hands and kissed her lips. "Yeah. Well, it's gotten a little more complicated."

Su Li came to the door. "Hey, Sam. Don't just stand there. Come on in. Do you want to stay for dinner? Chili and cornbread."

Eight-year-old Becky ran into the room. "Hi, Uncle Sam! Stay for dinner. *Please?*"

Sam laughed and picked the little girl up for a bear hug. "I guess with an invitation like that, I better stay for dinner. But I'll have to eat and run. David and the boys home?"

"David called. He's working late. Again. The boys'll be home any minute. We can eat then and you can get going." She turned to her youngest daughter. "Becky, honey, why don't you get the table set? We'll need six bowls and small plates."

"Okay, Mom." Becky skipped off and called over her shoulder, "Then I can practice, right, Mom?"

Julie flashed a wide smile and Su Li shook her head. "Sure," she called to her daughter. She turned to Sam and Julie. "That girl sure loves her piano."

"It's good somebody does," Julie said. "She's my little buddy, and my most eager piano student. Do you need any help?"

Su Li laughed. "Not from you!"

Sam leaned over to his wife. "Baby, your cooking skills are legendary—the stuff nightmares are made of. Your best friend doesn't even trust you with chili."

Julie stepped on his toe.

"Ow!"

They heard a car in the driveway. Sam looked out the window. "Matt and Levi are home."

"Great," Su Li said. "Dinner in five minutes."

5:38 p.m.

Jenna Trent greeted her husband with a hug. "The library got some new books in and my favorite author was included. I already had dinner in the crock pot, so I got to curl up with a new book. Which reminds me—didn't get any laundry done." Jenna looked up at Adam. "You look tired, Adam. Dinner's about ready. Tough day?" She set a roast on a platter and surrounded it with potatoes and carrots and put it on the table before returning to the kitchen.

"You could say that. Have you seen the news?"

Jenna stopped, holding the bowl of green beans mid-air. Her shoulders slumped. "No. Why? What's up?" She swallowed and placed the bowl on the table, preparing for whatever crisis Adam had been assigned.

Adam filled his wife in on the afternoon's events. Jenna nodded, resigned. Late nights and weekends of working would become the norm until the case was closed.

Adam walked to his desk and flipped on the computer. "Elle Canterbury's the crime tech on the case. She's good and she's fast. I'm hoping to get her report tonight." He looked up and looked around the room. "Is Amy out taking Blue for a walk?"

"Yeah. She'll be back any minute. She always watches for your car." Jenna peered out the window. "Here she comes now."

The back door opened and Amy appeared with the large blue and white pit bull in tow. "Hi, Daddy! Blue was a good girl, of course." She bent down and kissed the dog squarely on the mouth and rubbed her head. Blue wagged her tail and waited for Adam to acknowledge her. He scratched behind her ears. Blue left and sat by her empty food dish, staring.

"Amy, I've told you not to kiss that dog on her mouth. It's germy." Adam shuddered.

"But I love her, Daddy! I've been kissing her my whole life. You're such a germophobe! Wanna kiss? I still have puppy love on me!" Amy came toward her father with puckered lips.

"Yuk." Adam looked at Jenna. "Did you teach her that word?"

Jenna giggled. "Name five people who don't know that my big, strong, hero-husband is afraid of little bitty germs."

"Little bitty germs can make you very sick. Or even kill you." He turned to Amy. "Blue's hungry. And wash your hands after you feed her, Amy. It's time for dinner."

"See?" Jenna teased.

Adam pointed his finger at Jenna. "Stop picking on me."

She wrapped her arms around him. "You gonna pout?"

He hugged her. "Maybe."

The family took their seats at the table and said grace. "Did you talk to Mom about Thanksgiving this year?" Adam asked Jenna.

Amy interrupted. "We always go to Gomer and Oompah's house for Thanksgiving. Aren't we going this year?"

Jenna patted Amy's hand. "Honey, Gomer and Oompah are getting older. You're already twelve! We thought that this year, we'd have your grandparents join us here at the house for Thanksgiving."

"Are they too old to drive? Union's pretty far."

"Daddy will go out and get them that morning and take them home later."

Amy was crestfallen. "But Gomer makes the best special Thanksgiving food!"

"Amy, your mother's a wonderful cook. And she's got Gomer's recipes." Adam took a second helping of creamed spinach.

"But Gomer's pumpkin pie. It has the black pepper in it," Amy whined.

"Okay, Amy. Her pumpkin pie is pretty special. How about if we ask Gomer to just make pumpkin pie? If Gomer does the whole meal, she'll be too tired to enjoy it. Thanksgiving is for everyone, right? And, Daddy's not working on Thanksgiving this year, *right?*" Jenna turned to Adam and raised her eyebrows. He gave her a thumbs up.

"Okay. I guess so. But it won't be like Thanksgiving at Gomer's house with the fireplace and my own pink bedroom and an upstairs and farm animals and Oompah's tractor rides."

"Yeah, honey. It's a real tragedy." Adam took a second helping of roast and potatoes. "If you wanted a pink bedroom so bad, you should've said something. I can paint it. Probably have it done before Thanksgiving."

Amy rolled her eyes. "No, Daddy. Pink is for *little* girls. I'm *twelve.*"

Adam stopped his fork halfway to his mouth and looked at his wife. "Did I, or did I not just hear the twelve-year-old whining about not having her pink bedroom at her grandparents' house for Thanksgiving?"

Amy groaned in exasperation. "Daddy! I'm too old for my own pink bedroom at our house. But at Gomer and Oompah's house, it's nostalgic."

Jenna suppressed a smile, as her eyes twinkled at Adam. "Oh, nostalgic, is it?" he asked his daughter. "There's another big word for a little squirt."

Adam changed the subject. "The mayor is chiming in on this investigation," he told Jenna. "Says it makes St. Louis look bad." He shook his head. "We've got crime out the wazoo, not enough cops on the streets, everybody leaving the minute they're eligible for retirement, no support from the public, and the mayor kowtowing to every special interest group that thinks it's wrong for the police to have guns. But now that there's been an attack on a swank business in the fashionable Central West End, we're somehow supposed to have this wrapped up right away."

"Do you even know who you're looking for?" Jenna asked.

"Nope. Could be a terrorist group. Could be a disgruntled employee. Could be just about anything."

"Why can't Gomer and Oompah spend the night?" Amy asked. "We always spend the night at their house."

"Because they have the farm to run. The animals need feeding." Adam stood. "Help me clear the table and then go get your homework done. Fantastic meal, as always, babe." He leaned down and kissed his wife.

After clearing the table, Adam checked his inbox. "Still no word from Elle." He flipped on the television. "Here, Jenna, my new case is coming up next. You can get back to your book in a couple of minutes."

Jenna joined her husband and watched the scene in the Central West End as it played for what seemed to Adam, the hundredth time. "How terrible! Does Captain Peterson know?"

Adam shook his head. "He and Melanie are deep in the Smoky Mountains, camping and getting away from everything. They won't be back for a week. And I'm not about to call and bother them on their first getaway in years. It's a big case, but he would've assigned it to me if he were here, so there's no difference."

6:04 p.m.

"Delicious, Su Li. That was chili my mom would've been proud of. Thanks for the invite. Sorry to eat and run." Sam stood to leave. Becky ran to him for a hug. "Thanks for letting Aunt Julie spend the night, Uncle Sam. This is gonna be so much fun!"

"Anytime, pumpkin," he answered. "You make sure Aunt Julie behaves like a good girl, okay? Keep an eye on your chocolate." He tweaked her nose.

Becky gave him a knowing smile. "You got it!"

The teenagers shook Sam's hand and Julie walked him to the door.

"I'll get to the bottom of this, babe. Don't worry. You could be in a lot worse places than your best friend's house. Where's Wolfgang?"

"Slept through everything. Still sleeping. Great watchdog, huh?" Julie kissed him goodbye. "Please be careful."

Sam drove the short distance from the Jernigan's home to his driveway. The light was fading, and Sam figured he had less than twenty minutes left to survey the exterior of their massive home if he wanted to finish before dark. No sign of tampering. He entered the house and climbed the steps to his office. He removed his bug detecting equipment from the closet and began a room to room search, beginning in the attic and ending in the basement. Still nothing.

The clock in the foyer chimed eleven times. Sam sank into a chair and rubbed his temples. He was sure that somehow, someone had heard him, followed him, *something*. He disassembled his cell phone but found nothing.

It was late and Sam was tired. He put the cell phone back together and thought. Jordan was out there, somewhere. Surely, the young man was bright enough to figure out he was in danger. But what would he do about it? To whom would he turn? And the most troubling question—would Sam lead Pamela and Richard's hired goons to Jordan?

Sam lifted his head. He had an idea. He took his detector to the garage and went over his car with it. The device began to beep, and as he moved it toward the back of the car, the beep grew louder and stronger. And then he found it. A tracker had been placed under his rear bumper. He removed it, crushed it under his shoe, and carried the debris to the bathroom where he flushed it. He returned to the garage and went over the rest of the car. The indicator beeped again, but Sam could find no bug. He opened the driver's door and the device's indicator became active. Sam realized that his Bluetooth had been compromised when someone managed to pair his cell phone. *That's how they listened to my cell phone without physically placing an actual bug in it. Remotely!*

6:11 p.m.

Pamela Farraday stretched out on her white leather sofa, kicked off her Louis Vuitton heels, and watched the news from the comfort of her penthouse apartment in Clayton. Her brother, Richard, sat in the chair opposite her, picking at his fingernails and smoothing his clothes with his hands.

Pamela swallowed her glass of Bordeaux in one gulp and flipped off the television in disgust, snapping the six o'clock news anchor to silence after the story ran about the Central West End attack. She reached for her burner phone and called the only number on it.

"You call that a professional job?" she spat.

"Cool it, lady. We got our guy."

"Oh, really? Seen the news tonight?"

"Whaddya talkin' about? My guy saw the car blow to bits. It was wired to do that when the engine started. Contract's done. Balance is due. Time to pay."

Pamela sucked at the insides of her cheeks. "Oh. So you *haven't* seen the news. Too many big words for you, I guess. The police are looking for the owner of the car. You *botche*d it. He's still out there."

"Cops are blowin' smoke. Alls they're doin' is shakin' the tree to see if anything falls out. My guy saw the car blow. No way could anyone survive it. And for insurance, since you paid for the best, I had two other guys watchin' the kid's apartment. He never came home. Even if he does, once he opens the front door, ka-boom. He's gone either way. Shaw Park. Tomorrow at noon. I expect the rest of the money."

"I have no assurance the problem has been taken care of. No tick-ee, no wash-ee." Pamela's fists clenched and unclenched as she spoke.

"All right, look, lady. I'll have my people watch his apartment a couple more days. If he don't show up, then time to pay up. Don't cross me, toots. We had a deal."

Pamela slammed the phone shut and tossed it on the coffee table.

Richard wiped perspiration from his forehead. "What'd he say?"

"He's an idiot," she answered. "He insists that Jordan's dead, but there's no proof. Not one ounce of proof that he didn't screw up completely."

"If he's dead, then why are the cops looking for him? And what about all those other people?" Richard stood and began to pace the floor, running his fingers through his hair. "Those people at that office, Pam—dead, injured, and the building all shot up. I mean, what the—?"

"Collateral damage, Richard. It's the cost of doing business."

Richard sat down with a thud. He pressed his fingertips into his temples and pulled at his hair. "We're in too deep, Pam. This never should've happened."

She snorted. "Nothing can be traced to us. One contact—through a burner phone. Grow a pair, would you? We have nothing to lose by continuing, and everything to gain. *Everything!*"

"What about all those people? Geez." He looked up at her, pleading.

"So what?"

"You're insane." Richard stood to leave. "I'm going home." Richard left in a hurry, while Pamela was still taking a breath to support her retort. But the door slammed shut before she could speak. She threw her shoe, hitting the door.

7:32 p.m.

The sun had set and Carson did not know how long he had been walking with Miss Buttons plastered against his chest. She had fallen asleep and felt like dead weight, numbing his arms. He didn't know where he was going and was unsure of where he was now, but he kept walking, putting as much distance between him and his apartment as he could. He was tired and every inch of his body screamed in pain. Carson paused under a streetlight trying to get his bearings. He thought he saw a familiar apartment complex. He searched his brain, trying to figure out where he was. Then he remembered. "This is where Jalisa lives, Miss Buttons! Maybe that's where we need to go."

Jalisa Moore was the secretary for two of the recruiters, Lindsay Liscomb and Kevin Bosch. She had always treated Carson well, showing him the ropes and introducing him to the complex world of office politics. Three days ago, Jalisa grabbed her side and doubled over in pain. Carson saw her fall to her knees and rushed to her side. He insisted on taking her to the hospital.

When the commotion reached her office, Heavens to Murgatroid appeared and demanded that they wait for an ambulance. It was company policy, even if Murgatroid had not yet written it. Jalisa was moaning and gasping in obvious pain.

Carson ignored Murgatroid. "Jalisa can't wait for an ambulance! Can't you see how much pain she's in? She needs help now!"

Turning to Jalisa and supporting her on his arm, Carson helped Jalisa to the front door of the building and seated her on the chair nearest the door. "I'll be right back," he told her, and ran to get his car. He drove her to the emergency room and she was rushed into surgery where her appendix was removed only minutes before it would have ruptured.

When Carson returned to the office later that afternoon, Murgatroid was fuming. "You disobeyed a direct order! I'm writing you up for this. It'll be a part of your permanent record. I'll not tolerate insubordination."

Carson shot back, "Minutes mattered, Miriam. They took her into surgery as soon as we got there. If we'd waited for the ambulance, Jalisa could have died, or at the very least, had a much lengthier recovery. Or maybe the life of an employee doesn't matter as much to you as your rules."

Murgatroid glared at him with bulging porcine eyes. "Oh, I'm sorry," she said, dripping with sarcasm. "I didn't realize you had a license to practice medicine." Having made her hateful point, she stalked off.

Carson lost all respect for the woman. "At least I'm not guilty of impersonating a human being. At least I have a soul!"

Murgatroid had set her sights on Carson from that day forward, looking for any reason to write him up.

Carson wasn't too concerned about the vitriolic office manager. Mr. Carmody liked him, and Mr. Carmody ran the show, in spite of Murgatroid throwing her ample weight around. The incident had made a friend out of Jalisa, at any rate. Carson visited her at the hospital and yesterday, had taken her home to settle her in her apartment to recuperate. He'd picked up some pre-made meals and asked Jalisa what else she needed, but she assured him her church would take care of her.

Now, Carson stood before the door to her building. Not knowing how Miss Buttons would react to an elevator, he walked six flights to the top floor where Jalisa's apartment was located, and rang the doorbell. He guessed it was after seven, and his appetite was returning. He heard shuffling behind the door and saw an eye looking through the peep hole. The door opened and Jalisa, clad in her pajamas and robe, stared at Carson.

"Carson Hollister! What are you doing here? *Look at you!*"

"It's kind of a long story. Can I come in?"

Jalisa looked up and down the hallway, but it was empty. "What's that?" she asked, pointing to Miss Buttons.

"This is Miss Buttons. She's my cat. Jalisa, you're not going to believe…"

"I know what happened. It's all over the news!" Her large brown eyes were wide and she looked up and down the hallway again. She opened the door and Carson stepped in. "The police are looking for you."

"The news? Really? Do you know how Lizzie is?"

"Did you not *hear* me? The police are looking for you. You're a person of interest." Jalisa took a step backward, eyeing Carson with suspicion and pursing her lips.

"What? Me? You gotta be kidding." Carson struggled to remain standing. The stairs took his last ounce of energy, and he felt done in.

"Do I *look* like I'm laughing?" Jalisa walked bent over to a recliner covered with a blanket and pillows. A TV tray was set up next to it. "I gotta sit down, Carson. It still hurts to walk." She sat slowly, arranging the pillows and blanket around her for support. "You got a litter box and food and all for that thing?" She motioned for Carson to sit.

"This *thing*," Carson started, setting Miss Buttons down and sitting on the sofa. "This thing is my kitty. I'll go pick up some things for her." Carson leaned back and closed his eyes.

"No need," Jalisa sighed.

Carson opened his eyes. "What? You got cat stuff?" Carson watched as Miss Buttons began to explore her new surroundings.

Jalisa snorted. "No, genius. You see a cat? The crazy cat lady next door has anything you need. Let me rest a few minutes and we'll go over there and get what Miss Buttons needs."

Jalisa aimed the remote and turned the television on. "It's on all the channels. What do you know about this, anyway? You involved?"

"*No!* Why would I destroy a place I loved working at? Why would I do *anything* to hurt Lizzie? Why would I risk my *own* life and show up here looking like this?"

Jalisa's face softened and she relaxed as much as she could with her pain. "Yeah, you're right." Her pursed lips turned upward. "One, you're too goofy, and two, I think you got a kind heart." Jalisa managed a smile. "I *know* you got a kind heart." She turned back toward the television. "Commercial's over. Here it is."

Carson cringed at the sight of the fire in the parking lot. "That was my car," he said, pointing to the burned-out remnant that only three days ago transported Jalisa to the emergency room. The camera switched to the front of the building where the dead and injured were being transported on stretchers to waiting ambulances. Police swarmed, thick as bees. "Did they say anything about Lizzie? What about the others?"

"Some dead, some injured. I think they have to notify family members first. Carson—what do you know about this?" Jalisa turned to face him, taking care not to pull her side.

"I don't know anything about this. Why would I do something so terrible? How does that make any sense?"

Jalisa shook her head. "It doesn't make any sense. Who shoots up a recruiting agency for medical personnel?" She took a slow breath and let it out. "Would you get me some water, please? I need another pain pill." She handed an empty glass to him.

Carson rose and took the glass from her. "Kitchen this way?" he asked, pointing around the corner from the dining area.

"Yeah. Thanks, Carson."

He left and returned with the water. He watched as she opened a pill bottle and swallowed the medicine. "How are you feeling, Jalisa? Are you in a lot of pain? Is there anything I can get you?"

Jalisa shook her head. "No. The pain comes and goes. It's worse at night. I'll feel a lot better in about twenty minutes or so. Aunt Mae is bringing me some dinner tonight. You can't be here when she comes."

Carson sighed and looked down. He rubbed his aching head with his fingertips. "I don't have anywhere to go. I took the bus home, for obvious reasons. When I got there, someone had been inside my place and I saw a wire running along the floor by the wall, like it'd been rigged to blow up when the door opens."

"How do you know someone was in your place? You could'a left a wire on the floor."

"I don't have any wire. I hardly own anything at all. There were paint chips on the window ledge where they'd opened a window that hadn't been opened in months, and Miss Buttons was outside in the alley. I don't ever let her out of the house, so she had to have gotten out through the window when it was open." He reached down to pet the cat who was rubbing her face on his legs. "Can I use your bathroom to clean up?"

"Yeah. You look awful. It's that way." She pointed toward a hallway. "Don't leave my bathroom a mess. By the time you're done, the pain meds will have kicked in. We can go next door and get some things for your kitty."

"Don't worry, I won't. Need anything else before I clean up?" Carson stood and headed for the bathroom.

Jalisa shook her head, and, pulling her pillows around her, leaned back in the recliner.

Several minutes later, Carson emerged from the hall bathroom. He had showered and combed his hair, but his clothes were tattered and dirty. He sighed. "This is as good as it gets. I need clothes from my apartment, but I'm afraid it'll blow up, just like my car. Whoever these guys are, they're not messing around."

Jalisa looked up and down at Carson and pursed her lips. "That place above your eye is gonna need stitches. You didn't leave the bathroom all dirty and gross, did you?"

"No way, Herr Commandant. You'll never know anyone was in there." Carson sat down on the sofa with a thud. He put his head in his hands. "I don't know what I'm gonna do, Jalisa. None of this makes any sense to me."

"You're sure they're after *you?*" She readjusted her position in the chair.

"Not at first, I wasn't." Carson looked up. "At first, I thought the same thing as everyone else. We were under some kind of attack—terrorists, gangs, something. Be glad you had appendicitis, or you could have been hurt—or killed. There was gunfire exploding everywhere, people were screaming and crying and running in all directions. It was total chaos. I had no idea what was goin' on. I just wanted to get outta there as fast as possible. I was at the top of the steps when it all started. Lizzie was downstairs at her desk…"

"Oh no, not Lizzie!" Jalisa's eyes widened. "Is she okay?"

"I have no idea! I'm worried sick about her!" Carson threw his head back against the sofa cushions and pulled at his hair. "I got out through my window and then off the roof. As I was going to my car, I clicked to start the engine and it blew sky high! Then I see my apartment's been broken into and it looks like it's wired to blow. So, yeah. To answer your question, I'd say it sounds like someone's after me!"

Jalisa knit her eyebrows together and studied Carson. "I gotta ask the obvious question. Why? I mean, it's not like—you know—you ain't nobody special that I know of. Old car, tiny apartment with almost nothin' in it, student loans. Really, Carson, you got a heart the size of Texas, but nothin' worth killing over." Jalisa shook her head. "I mean, you're just a nice guy and a good worker. It's real hard for me to imagine you got any enemies."

"I don't. Geez, I'm an only child, my dad died last year, and my mom's got dementia and is in a home. The small amount of money my parents did have I use for her care. Those places, even the low rent ones, are expensive! I have a separate account where I put the proceeds from the sale of their house, their investments, everything, and I write the place a check every month, plus the pharmacy bills and Mom's other medical needs. Yeah, there's some money there, but sure not enough to kill for!"

"Well, then, ya must've made *somebody* mad!" Jalisa sipped her water.

Carson laughed and leaned forward, lowering his voice. "I made Murgatroid angry when I took you to the hospital."

Jalisa started to giggle. She choked on her water, then grabbed her side and winced.

Carson jumped up and went to her. "Oh, Jalisa, I'm sorry! I didn't mean to make you hurt!"

She sat back and smiled at him. "I dunno. It was kinda worth it. Anyway, the painkillers are kicking in. 'Bout time."

Carson looked around the apartment as if noticing it for the first time. "This is an awfully nice place you've got here. MSR must be paying their secretaries pretty well."

"I wish. My brother, Malcolm, pays the rent and utilities." She pointed to a framed photograph on a shelf of a serious look-ing man in a military uniform staring into the camera, as though he were daring the photographer to take his picture. The man in the photo had the same full lips and large brown eyes as Jalisa, only his eyes lacked the softness of hers, and instead, held a determined steeliness. Carson thought Malcolm looked much larger than his younger sister. The entire section of the far wall paid tribute to Malcolm Moore with photos, medals, citations, and plaques. "Malcolm's in special forces—does top secret missions and stuff. I never even know where he is or what he's doing, but he's paid enough to keep this place. My brother's watched over me since I was fourteen and our mom died. He's a great big brother. He takes all the dangerous jobs and gets hazard pay. I never know when he's coming home, but his bedroom is on the other side of the bathroom, and you were using his bathroom. So it needs to be kept clean. Malcolm is a neat freak."

"But he didn't come home when you had surgery?"

"Nope. I got a number I can call where they can get in touch with him if there's an emergency. But I didn't call for this. I knew I'd be okay, and the people at church take good care of me. Which reminds me," she snapped her fingers. "Aunt Mae will be here soon with my dinner. *She cannot see you or your cat, understand?*"

Miss Buttons stretched on Carson's leg and meowed, asking to be picked up. He obliged.

"I gotta take you next door to the crazy cat lady and get you some stuff for your cat." Jalisa pulled herself up, holding onto the arm of the chair.

"What about my clothes?"

"You wanna borrow a skirt? You oughtta have a doctor look at that cut over your eyebrow. Hey! I got an idea. I got a bag of Malcolm's old clothes that I keep forgetting to take to Goodwill."

"Uh, Jalisa? Malcolm looks like he's about seven feet tall and four feet wide." He grinned at her. "I'd probably wear your skirt better."

"These clothes are ancient—before he started working out and bulking up. He's not too much taller than you are. These are his skinny clothes. From a long time ago." She walked toward a closet in the hall and opened the door. "See that big black bag? There might be something you could wear." She shrugged. "Anyway, it's the best I can do."

He rummaged through the bag and pulled out a pair of jeans and a sweater and disappeared into the bathroom.

"Close enough," he said when he came out.

Jalisa laughed. "You look like you raided your big brother's closet! Or a walking scarecrow."

He picked up Miss Buttons. "You're sure the cat lady won't mind?"

"I should prob'ly give you a little head's up."

Carson raised his eyebrow.

Jalisa sat. "Her real name is Katherine Katz. But she goes by Kitty Katz. No joke. She even started to have plastic surgeries until her doctor figured out she was getting cut to make herself look like a cat. Then her doc told her no more, and told her he was going to warn other plastic surgeons about her. So I think she quit pursuing the look. At least with surgery. But she's an odd one, and I don't mean just odd lookin'."

Carson's mouth opened and he stared at Jalisa.

She continued. "Anyway, Kitty's brother, Arnie Katz, owns this building and the rest of the complex—all the buildings forming the courtyard. He's retired military. Took a real liking to my brother, so he gave me and Malcolm a good deal on this place. In return, he asked that we keep an eye on his sister. He's a nice guy, but Kitty is the only other neighbor on this whole floor. All the adjoining apartments except ours are connected and she's got all of them. It means a lot to Arnie knowing me and Malcolm look after her. She's harmless, but could be pretty easily taken advantage of by others. Mr. Katz trusts me and Malcolm."

"Her place must be huge," Carson said.

"Uh, yeah. You'll see in a minute. Kitty has around seventeen cats. I guess the rest you'll have to see for yourself. She has one entire room that's filled with extra litter boxes, kitty crates, scratching posts, and bags of food and litter. Enough toys to stock a pet store. She's got a living room, dining area, kitchen, and bedroom. Plus a few bathrooms, since it's combined apartments. All the other rooms are for the cats."

"Holey Moley!"

"You know that phrase, you can't save every puppy in the pound? Well, Kitty's mission in life is to rescue every cat she sees. It's pretty out of control." Jalisa straightened her posture a little, the pain killers having taken effect, and motioned for Carson to follow her. "C'mon."

The two friends walked to the door at the end of the hallway and rang the bell. A middle-aged woman with flaming orange hair fried from overuse of chemical dyes, opened the door. She wore no make-up, except for black eye liner, applied to extend the corners of her eyes, in an attempt to make her appearance more cat-like. High-arching eyebrow pencil exaggerated the feline effect. Her ample figure sported a brightly colored floral caftan and pink sandals adorned her feet. "Jalisa! It's nice to see you out of the apartment. How are you feeling?"

"Better every day, thanks, Kitty. This is my friend and his cat."

"Oh, look at the beautiful baby!" She took Miss Buttons from Carson's arms and cradled her like a baby.

"That's my cat," he whispered to Jalisa.

"What a sweet little girl! Where did you get her? Oh, where are my manners? Come in, come in!" She opened the door wide to admit them and proceeded to ignore her visitors in favor of cuddling Miss Buttons.

Carson stopped short just inside the door to Kitty's apartment. The large living room held a sofa, chair, coffee table, and a small entertainment cabinet with a television on it. Every piece of furniture bore scratching marks. The rest of the room was packed with floor-to-ceiling kitty condos and scratching posts. It looked like a jungle of carpet-covered trees, on which were perched more cats than Carson could count. Black cats, white cats, calicos, striped tabbies, orange cats, gray cats, black and whites, and tuxedo cats. A variety of kitty toys littered the floor. The pungent odor of ammonia made Carson take a step backward.

Jalisa suppressed a smile as she watched his eyes tear. She had tried to warn him. "She was a stray that my friend took in. Kitty, I was just wondering, do you think you might be able to spare a litter box, some litter, food, and a scratching post?" It was a silly question, of course, asked out of consideration.

"I'd be delighted to help! I'll be right back." The orange-haired woman planted a sloppy kiss on Miss Buttons and returned her to Carson. She let out an excited "Mew mew," and left the room, returning laden with as much feline paraphernalia as the imagination could contain.

Carson knew he didn't have enough money in his wallet to cover what Kitty brought, but he took out his wallet with a promise to get her the rest when he got to the ATM.

"No, no. This is on me," Kitty insisted. "You did a wonderful thing to give a home to a homeless animal. I'm happy to help." The cat woman leaned forward and whispered, "I have two rooms full of cat supplies. You never know when you might need them. I always tell my brother, Arnie, that, and now, I'm right! See? This is my gift!"

Carson began to object, but Jalisa cut him off. "Thanks so much, Kitty. You're very kind. We appreciate it, but we have to go before my pain meds wear off."

"I understand, dear. Come by and see me again. And bring that darling kitty with you so I can smooch her pretty little face!"

When they returned to Jalisa's apartment, she eased herself into her big recliner. "I've been sleeping here, in my chair. You can take my room for the night until we figure out what to do with you. I'm getting tired." She motioned toward the opposite end of the hall from Malcolm's room.

"What about your brother's room? You said he was gone most of the time."

"No way. Open his door, but don't let the cat in."

Carson did so. The room was pristine.

"See how that bed is made? You can flip a quarter right off of it. Can you make your bed so tight a coin bounces?" Jalisa didn't wait for Carson to answer. "Didn't think so. Everything in that room is perfect. It's perfect when Malcolm comes home, and it's perfect when he leaves. My brother is six foot four and two hundred pounds of solid muscle. He knows over a hundred ways to kill a person. And you want to sleep in his room?"

"Guess not. Can I set up Miss Buttons in your room? You don't mind?"

Jalisa sighed. "If I wanted a cat, I'd go next door and borrow one. But there's no other place, so just keep my room clean. I won't be using it until after these stitches come out next week and I can get comfortable."

They heard the elevator ding outside the apartment and Jalisa's eyes widened. "Carson! Hurry up and get that stuff to my bedroom! Now!"

"Why?"

"That's Aunt Mae! She better not find you here, or you're dead! Me, too!"

Carson scooped up Miss Buttons, shoving her and the items he got from Kitty into Jalisa's room and closed the door, just as the bell rang. He squatted behind the bedroom door and peered through the keyhole. *Surely, Aunt Mae cannot be more frightening than those killers after me!*

Jalisa opened the door to a mammoth-sized woman in a flower-print dress, carrying a casserole dish. The aroma announced that lasagna was for dinner and Carson's mouth watered as he inhaled. "Aunt Mae, that smells wonderful," Jalisa said. Carson couldn't take his eyes off the woman. He remained with his face glued to the keyhole. He wasn't sure if he found her or Malcolm more frightening, but he hoped he would never run into either of them in a dark alley. He'd had enough excitement and danger today to last a lifetime.

Aunt Mae's thundering voice shook the walls as she brought the casserole in. "Have you seen the news, honey?" She set the lasagna dish on the table. "Your operation was a blessin' in disguise, child! What a terrible thing. I thanked the good Lawd you was safe. Does Malcolm know?"

"I don't think Malcolm needs to worry about anything besides his mission. I'm fine. You're feeding me as though every meal's my last. I'm safe and healing up just fine. No sign of infection, and I'm taking my medicine like a good girl. I don't want to bother Malcolm unless there's a true emergency. You understand, Aunt Mae?"

Aunt Mae folded her thick arms in front of her ample chest. Her nostrils flared and Carson was reminded of an angry bull preparing to charge. "And in what universe is emergency surgery not a true emergency? And then a vicious attack by terrorists at your office? I suppose that's not an emergency either?"

"Aunt Mae, I'm *fine*. I'm healing and a nurse calls me every day to check on me. I've got good food, thanks to you, and I'm getting plenty of rest. This is a distraction my brother doesn't need. Anyway, if his team's mission is accomplished, he might get to come home for Thanksgiving. Maybe even stay through Christmas. Wouldn't that be great? But if he came home now, when you're taking such good care of me, we might not have him for the holidays."

Aunt Mae's face softened as she removed the foil from the lasagna pan. Carson guessed that the slight upturn of the woman's lips constituted a smile of sorts. She went into the kitchen to get a plate and utensils and began to cut a piece of lasagna for Jalisa. "Of course. I'd love to see you two together for the holidays. I just think he should know, that's all."

"I'll tell him when he gets home. I promise." Jalisa held up two fingers. "Scout's honor."

Carson watched what he could from the keyhole. Most of the view was obscured, but the smell of the lasagna was driving him crazy, exacerbating his hunger. His stomach growled, and he pressed his hand against it, hoping Aunt Mae didn't hear the rumble.

"This is delicious, Aunt Mae. Thank you."

All of a sudden, the woman's eyes got so big, the whites gleamed, and she came bounding into the hall toward the door behind which Carson was watching, terrifying him. "What's *this?*" she demanded, bending down and picking up a small handful of cat hair. Her nostrils were flaring again, and Carson was reminded of a raging bull. All she was missing were horns, and maybe a ring in her nose.

Carson gulped and held his breath.

Jalisa got up and walked toward the woman, overdoing the limp. *Nice touch.* "Oh, one of Kitty's cats got loose and ran in when I opened the door. It was only in here a few minutes, but I guess it left a calling card."

"Humph!" Aunt Mae put the cat hair in the trash can, brushing her hands together to remove it all. "Now, *that* woman—she ain't right in the head. All them cats! I'm sure she's breakin' some kinda law. No tellin' what kinda germs are livin' next door to you."

"She's not hurting anyone. She checks on me every day since the surgery."

"Oh, Lawdy! That woman ain't bringin' you no meals, is she? You'll get some kinda cat sickness if you eat anything she made!"

"She offered, but I told her you were taking good care of me." Jalisa pushed her plate away. "I can't eat anymore. It's delicious, but my appetite isn't very good. I'm really getting tired." She yawned.

Aunt Mae patted Jalisa on her shoulder and her voice softened. "You just let me clean this up and I'll put the leftovers in the fridge for your lunch tomorrow. I'll get goin'. You need your rest." She cleared the table and washed the few dishes. "The whole church is prayin' for your recovery, honey. You just concentrate on gettin' better. Aunt Mae will take good care of you."

"Thanks for everything. I'm better every day."

"You lock up behind me. Those crazed killers are still on the loose. Not only that, but that co-worker who took you to the hospital? He's missin' and they think he's involved. Don't you open that door to anyone, you hear?"

"I'll be careful, Aunt Mae. Goodnight." Jalisa shut the door and locked it, making as much noise as she could, since she knew Aunt Mae would be listening. The elevator door dinged its arrival, and Aunt Mae was gone. Jalisa called to Carson. "You can come out now. Coast is clear."

Carson tiptoed into the living room. "Is she on your mother's side or your father's side?"

Jalisa started to laugh, then winced in pain. "She's not my

real aunt. She's everyone's Aunt Mae. The whole church calls her that. Anybody's sick or hurt, she shows up with dinner. You hungry? There's enough to feed a small country in the kitchen. Be sure you clean your dishes. If she comes back tomorrow, she can't know I've got company. Especially man company."

Carson didn't need a second invitation to dinner. He fixed his plate and crammed the food in his mouth as fast as he could.

"You'll enjoy that lasagna more if you bother to chew it first."

Carson slowed his pace. The rich tomato sauce and cheese was perfectly seasoned and the noodles firm enough to be slightly chewy. Carson felt better as the warm food settled into his stomach and coaxed away the hunger pangs. "First off, we're friends, so I don't count as man company. I couldn't do that to Lizzie, anyway."

Jalisa rolled her eyes. "Like Lizzie cares."

"So—you know I like her?"

Jalisa snorted. "The whole office knows you like her!"

Carson blushed and shoveled another forkful into his mouth. "Second, how can the police possibly think I'm involved? It was *my* car that got blown up!" He chewed and swallowed. "You got a car?"

Jalisa raised her eyebrows and looked at Carson with her head cocked. "Uh, yeah. But you can't have it, the operative word being *my* car." She folded her arms across her chest.

"I need to get to an ATM and empty out what little money is in my bank account. If the police think I had anything to do with what happened today, they may freeze my money."

Jalisa shook her head. "Carson, I am not giving you my car. No way."

"I just need to go to the ATM. I'll be right back, I promise. Geez—where else am I gonna go? Jalisa, I'm stuck! Nowhere to go and no way to get there. You can't possibly think I'm mixed up in whatever this is that's going on. I'll bring your car right back."

"Nu-uh."

"Okay. I know you aren't able to drive yet. What about if I drive and you sit in the passenger seat? Jalisa, all I got is forty bucks. That's it."

Jalisa pursed her lips and thought. "Okay. But those ATM's—they've got cameras and I am not about to get charged with aiding and abetting if you turn out to be some type of kind-hearted criminal."

Carson rolled his eyes. "I didn't ask for any of this. And I didn't *do* any of this!"

"I'll sit in the passenger seat, and you park a block away and walk to the ATM, then walk back to the car and we come straight back here. Got it?"

"Fine. We'll do it your way. First, I gotta know about Lizzie." Carson wrung his hands.

Jalisa's eyes softened. "You're pathetic. How 'bout I call and see what I can find out?"

Carson leaned back and closed his eyes. "Thank you."

Jalisa reached to the end table and picked up her phone. "First I'll call Lizzie's cell and see if she answers." She dialed and Carson leaned forward, waiting.

"No answer, Carson. Just voicemail. Hand me that big phone book down there," she said, pointing.

Carson did so and sat with his elbows on his thighs, listening for news as she dialed. "If Lizzie was hurt, she'd either be at Barnes or SLU. I'll call Barnes first."

"Yes, hello? Can you please connect me to a patient's room? Her name is Elizabeth Wise. She would have been admitted today. Thank you." She paused and covered the mouthpiece. "She's checking," she whispered to Carson before returning to the call. "Oh, uh, I see. Can you tell me how she's doing? Um, yes, of course I'm family. She's my cousin, and I'm out of town." Carson stifled a choking sound. "Okay, well, thank you." Jalisa hung up.

"What? Tell me!"

"Lizzie's in ICU. She's critical, Carson. I'm sorry. The lady wouldn't give me any more information. She may not have believed I was family." She wrote on a piece of paper.

"But she's alive! I gotta see her."

"That ain't gonna happen, Carson. ICU is family only. I heard the lady mumble a room number."

Carson nodded, deep in thought, and took the paper from Jalisa. "Thanks for making the call. I appreciate it. Can we leave for the ATM now?"

Jalisa dressed in loose fitting sweat pants and sweatshirt. They took the elevator to the basement level garage and left in her car.

"Park here. There's no cameras. And hurry. My medication is starting to wear off."

Carson looked around. The street was empty. He hurried to the ATM, pulling his hood around his head and face, and withdrew the four hundred twenty dollars he knew was in his account. The extra eighteen cents would have to stay. A math whiz from early childhood, Carson could figure complex equations in his head and keep the numbers straight. He always balanced to the penny. Grabbing the money, he ran back to the car.

Jalisa winced when Carson got into the car. *She needs her pain medication.* "I got it. Now we're going home. Thank you. Thank you for everything."

"I wasn't really worried, Carson. I knew you were a good person the day you came to work for us. I could just tell. You risked a lot by taking me to the hospital, but you saved my life. It's just that, wow—what a weird and awful day this is. I'm totally freaked out by it all."

"*You* are! How do you think *I* feel? These guys are after *me!*" He started the car and they headed back to her apartment.

Jalisa changed the subject. "So did you balance to the penny, Mr. Junior Accountant?"

Carson laughed. "I'm sure I did. Didn't even check the receipt. I wanted to get you back as soon as possible." They stopped at a red light and he pulled the receipt out of his pocket. He gasped and Jalisa turned her head and looked at him.

"What's wrong? Geez, Carson, you're white! I mean, well, you're always white, but you are *really* white!" She took the receipt from him and her eyes popped. "Whoa! That's kind of a lot of money! That's a whole lot more than four hundred bucks!"

Carson took the receipt from her hand and stared at it. He shook his head. "There's gotta be some mistake. The bank made an error, but as soon as whoever this money belongs to finds out there's a hundred grand missing from their account, they'll find it in my account. Too bad, though." He shoved the receipt back into his pocket.

They returned to Jalisa's apartment. Carson helped her out of the car and into the elevator. Her pace had slowed and she was walking bent over again. "I need another pill, and I need to go to sleep. It's after nine already. We've both had a long day. You take my room. I like to sleep in my recliner. It doesn't pull on my stitches so much."

Carson fixed a cup of herbal tea for Jalisa and brought her a large glass of water to put on the stand next to the chair while she changed back into her pajamas and robe.

He was uneasy sleeping in her room, but she was right— they had to figure out where he could go until everything was straightened out. He lay back in her bed. Miss Buttons jumped up and parked herself on top of his chest. He closed his eyes as the events of the day played through his mind, tumbling like clothes in a dryer. *Odd timing for the bank to make such a huge error. I gotta get a car. Lizzie...Lizzie...Lizzie.* Carson petted the purring cat, curled in a ball with her head tucked under his chin. Soon, they were both fast asleep.

Day 2

5:00 a.m.

Sam Hernandez rose early, filled his gas tank, and drove west-bound on I-44 to a truck stop at the Cuba, Missouri exit. He parked his car and went inside the diner, taking a seat at the counter, surrounded by several truckers lining the counter and seated in the booths behind him. He ordered coffee and a light breakfast, and sat, eavesdropping on the conversations around him. He ate quickly, but lingered over his coffee.

A patient man, Sam listened while pretending to read the newspaper, until he overheard the conversation he was hoping to hear. The truckers were recounting where they were coming from, where they were going, the gut-wrenching accidents they'd witnessed, the loose women they'd picked up, and the truck stops with the best and worst food. Many of them were local or bi-state, delivering goods only throughout Missouri and Illinois, or Missouri and Kansas. One of them, proud of the artistic paint job on his rig, was a cross-country, Maine to California driver with a voice that needed no amplification.

Sam paid his bill and left the diner. Finding the colorful cross-country truck, he took his cell phone and duct-taped it underneath the carriage. Returning to his car, he continued west-bound until he got to Springfield, where he exited and drove to a house on a quiet residential street.

He walked to the back door and rang the bell. A large, burly man wearing a Cardinals jersey, a frown, and a two-day beard answered, wiping breakfast from his mouth with the back of his hand. But when he saw Sam, he broke into a wide smile, grabbed Sam and hugged him.

"Sam! Why in the world didn't ya tell me you were here in town! Come in! Want some breakfast? Pancakes. Right outta the box." The man opened the door wide and ushered Sam into a small, messy kitchen. "So what brings you to Springfield so early in the morning? That purty wife of yours git tired of seein' your ugly mug and finally told ya to hit the road?"

Sam choked. "Julie pulls something like that, she'll have to learn to cook. That'll never happen. No." Sam shook his head and chuckled at the thought. "She's stuck with me for good. Wouldn't have it any other way. So, how's things, Bull?" Sam took a seat at the crowded kitchen table and Bull poured coffee, piled a plate with pancakes and set it in front of him with a fork that may or may not have been washed that month.

"Same ole, same ole. Lonely since Betsy died. Been seven years, now, since cancer took her." Bull paused and sighed. "I ain't the housekeeper she was," he said, waving toward the rest of the house, which was in the same shape as the kitchen. "Retired from the force last year. Doin' a little PI work now and then, nothin' big, supplements the pension." He shoved a forkful of dry pancakes into his mouth.

Sam took a bite of the pancakes and drenched them with syrup, hoping to make them edible. "And your *other* business?"

Bull flashed a smile, showing partially chewed pancake between his teeth. "So, I take it, this ain't no social call. 'Splains why ya didn't bring me no flowers. Wanna tell your ole partner what's goin' on?"

Sam leaned back in his chair and pushed his plate forward. "Bull, I'm in the middle of the case of a lifetime. It sounded safe and easy when I took it, but the stakes are high and I underestimated the opposition. My fault, there. My cell phone's been paired, and as far as I can tell, my Bluetooth is corrupted. Can't take any chances. Right now, my phone's on the underside of a cross-country truck. Wiped the memory, but I can at least send the bad guys on a wild goose chase."

Bull nodded and became serious. "Is your house safe? Where's your wife?"

"Julie's safe. She's staying somewhere else. My bug detectors indicated the house was clean, but my car and my cell phone are a different story. I need a burner phone from you and a clean car until this case is over. I also need to store my car someplace safe. These guys have access to military explosives and they're not afraid to use them.

Bull leaned forward. "This got somethin' to do with that big explosion y'all had in St. Louis? Whoa!"

Sam nodded.

"How're you tied up in all that, Sam?" Bull leaned back in his seat and studied his old partner.

Sam took a drink of his coffee, forced himself to swallow, and set the cup next to the unfinished pancakes. *This stuff is worse than the diner's. Bull's lucky to be alive.* "It's a long, involved story. Right now, I can't break a confidence, but it's big, Bull. Really big. When this case is over, how about you come out for a nice dinner and I'll tell you everything?"

"I'll hold you to it. C'mon down to the basement and let's get you what you need. Then you foller me ta where you can leave your car and I'll get you all set up." He stood. "You wreck it, you bought it, though. We good?"

Sam laughed. "Bull, there's so much money involved in this case, your ugly bug eyes would fall outta their sockets. I wreck it, I'll replace it with any car you like."

"In that case, there'll be interest. Starting with when ya rang my doorbell and interrupted my gourmet breakfast."

Three hours later, Sam was ready to return to St. Louis.

"Thanks for everything, my friend. Can I buy you some lunch before I go?" The men shook hands.

"Nah. But thanks. I do a little volunteer work down at the children's cancer ward downtown. I need to get ready. The kids love me and I don't want to be late. You be careful, and I'll look forward to that home-cooked meal when you return the car. I'm thinkin' maybe a Bentley if you wreck the Chevy. Seems fair."

Sam hugged his former partner. "Trust me. My client could buy you a Bentley with his pocket change."

6:40 a.m.

Adam, Bo, Connor, and Samantha arrived at the Clark Street headquarters early the next morning to prepare for the investigation into the attack at Medical Staffing Remedies. Adam brought a box of donuts from Donut Drive-in, Connor brought a coffee cake his wife had made, and Samantha carried in a box of bagels and flavored cream cheeses.

"I see we alls had the same idea this morning," Connor said. His large frame filled the doorway as he lumbered in and set the coffee cake on the table by the far wall of Adam's office. "'Cept Bo, there. 'Cuz he's too busy bein' a cheapo mooch."

"Really? I'm hurt." Bo grabbed his chest. "Wounded, even. So you think we needed four different kinds of simple carbs around here? Ain't y'all never heard of a moment on the lips, forever on the hips? Besides, I'm watchin' my girlish figure. Good lookin' guy like me, I gotta be careful," Bo drawled in his thick Tennessee accent. He wiggled his hips and snapped his fingers in the air as he turned around in a circle, grinning at Samantha.

"Maybe Samantha there's got a dress yous can borrow." Connor snorted.

"Maybe Samantha just lost her appetite," Samantha chimed in. She put her bagels and cream cheese next to the coffee cake.

"Donuts for dessert, I guess," Adam said. "Bo, if the simple carbs are that big of a problem for you and your girlish figure, you could've brought bacon and eggs for protein. Or some fruit, if you prefer complex carbs."

"Or maybe yous woulda preferred some kale, egg whites, and hummus. Or maybe some of dat tofu crap." Connor's south St. Louis dialect drove the team nuts, but he was a dedicated cop, and a team player with a heart of gold, so they overlooked it and refrained from correcting his atrocious grammar. He cut a large chunk out of his wife's coffee cake and shoved it into his mouth. He stared at Bo. "Mmmm. My Kathleen's a great cook," he said with his mouth still full.

"I'll just start with some dessert," Bo said, reaching for a chocolate Long John.

"What about your girlish figure?" Samantha asked.

"Thought you'd never notice." He winked at her and she rolled her eyes. Bo scooted his chair closer to Samantha. Samantha scooted her chair away from him.

Adam passed out packets of materials to his team as they pulled up chairs around his desk. "Feel free to file a sexual harassment complaint against Bo, if you like," he said to Samantha in a flat voice. He shot Bo a dirty look. "He's not only being stupid—he's being stupid in front of witnesses." Adam took his seat.

Samantha pressed her upturned lips together. "The likes of Bo do not scare me. Some little boys never grow up."

Bo grabbed his chest. "Wounded again. Such a tough crowd." He grinned at Samantha and winked again. She continued to ignore him.

"Ain't yous never serious 'bout nothin'?" Connor asked. He thumbed through the folder Adam had passed around.

Adam cleared his throat with more drama than necessary. He knew Connor and Bo would lay down their lives for each other, but Bo loved to give Connor a hard time, and Connor rose to the occasion, every time. It was good-hearted fun on Bo's part, but Bo didn't always know when to quit. "We have four murders to solve here."

"Four?" Connor asked.

Adam nodded. "Yeah. One of the critically wounded was a client who was interviewing in the first floor conference room. My understanding is he was a vascular surgeon that MSR was recruiting for MoBap. He lost his fight late last night."

"Who's the other critical victim—the one that's hanging on?" Samantha asked.

Adam consulted his notes. "The receptionist, Elizabeth Wise. She's out of surgery and in the ICU with a guard outside her door," Adam answered. He looked up at his team. "We're not taking any chances here. She's got no family in the area that we know of, and there's already been a call asking about her from someone claiming to be family. As far as anyone knows, her family hasn't been contacted yet."

"She gonna make it?" Bo asked, reaching for a cinnamon twist.

"Nobody knows at this time." Adam shook his head. He shuffled the papers in front of him and continued. "You've got the latest reports. Felix, from Bomb and Arson, sent me his report on the explosion in the parking lot. It appears that the explosive device was centered on the left side of the transmission housing under the driver's seat. Not enough left of the car, an old Ford, 2003 Escort ZX2, dark blue, to make a definite determination. Blew the car to bits, and damaged dozens of other cars in the lot, totaling the ones in its immediate proximity. Vehicle's registered to Carson Hollister, twenty-five-year-old white male, employed at MSR five months, last seen just before the shooting started, and who is now missing."

Samantha flinched. "Could he have been, um, you know—vaporized?" She shifted in her seat.

"Good question. The blast was very powerful, much bigger than what would've been necessary to kill a man. As you can see in the report, Felix thinks the bomber was a pro, or at least someone with an extensive knowledge of explosives. C4 is military and not available to the public, so that means someone stole it from the military. Could'a been Scott Air Force Base, Fort Leonard Wood—that's Felix's department, not our concern. But we believe Mr. Hollister survived the blast. Blood was found in the parking lot, along with tatters of clothing, so it's possible that Carson Hollister was injured and could even be wandering around dazed, or lying in a ditch somewhere. Nobody's seen him or heard from him. We've got uniforms canvassing the area and also checking abandoned buildings, in case he sought shelter. Although we believe he's injured, someone could think he's homeless, especially if he passed out. We don't have any evidence that he's dead. We don't know much about him and we need to talk to him."

Connor spoke. "Could also be, this Hollister guy is behind the attacks and blew up his own car, and we need to be lookin' at him real close-like."

"So, Mr. Hollister could be the victim, the perpetrator, or the perpetrator trying to look like the victim, but any way you slice it, he's involved somehow," Bo added. "Did Felix and his team find any explosive devices on any of the other cars in the parking lot?"

Adam shook his head. "No. Only Carson Hollister's car was wired to blow. We don't know if someone was targeting him, or if he blew up his own car to cover up another crime. There's an APB out on him. We need to find him. Whether we arrest him or protect him remains to be seen. Right now, he's simply a person of interest. A lot of interest."

Adam pulled out a green folder from the reports and waved it for his team to see. "If you'll take a look at Elle's report, we don't have anyone's DNA. All employees at MSR have to pass a background check, but it's pretty minimal—just the basics."

"What about military service or anyone who worked in a government position? They'd have prints for sure, and probably DNA." Bo shoved a handful of sugar donut holes into his mouth."

"Dat's some girlish figure yous are watchin'," Connor mumbled under his breath.

Adam nodded. "And so, we come to our jobs. Connor, as can be expected, you're on computer and cell phone duty. I want to know every e-mail, business or personal, every phone call, every website visited, and every query inputted from each employee. I also want you to run background checks on each one of them for military service, government, or security jobs. And, do a more thorough criminal check than the basic stuff for employment. Whatever fingerprints or DNA you can find, submit it, if for no other reason than to exclude the innocent. Report back here tomorrow morning when we meet again." He handed Connor a printout of the employees' names, known e-mail addresses, and phone numbers.

"Samantha and Bo," Adam gave them identical sheets. "Employee interviews. Find out if anyone had any hard feelings, beefs, any dirt, motives, whatever you can find. The uniforms are conducting preliminary witness interviews. If they find anything promising, they'll turn it in to us for follow-up. Except for the receptionist, the other victims should be going home soon or at least before Thanksgiving, I would think. Oh, and one more thing on that receptionist, Elizabeth Wise. Check to see if anyone has tried to visit her. I don't like that somebody claiming to be family called to ask about her, when, like I said, her family's not been notified. And while you're on it…"

Bo and Samantha looked up at Adam. Samantha had been taking notes and paused.

"While you're on it, see why in the world her family has still not been notified. Out of the survivors, Ms. Wise is the most seriously injured."

"Yous thinkin' this was an inside job, Adam?" Connor asked.

"Not particularly. But until we can rule out everyone that works there, we're keeping an open mind. I'll be coordinating with Felix, Elle, and the coroner, if necessary. When we meet tomorrow, we'll review and move to the next level."

Adam made eye contact with each member of the team. "Questions?"

"We're good, Adam," Bo said, reaching for a bagel.

"On it," Connor answered. He snapped his notebook shut.

Samantha gave a thumbs up.

"See you tomorrow. Dismissed."

8:54 a.m.

Carson tossed and cried out as his recurring nightmare interrupted his sleep. He gasped and woke to find Jalisa staring at him.

"That's quite a dream you were havin'," she said. "I had to come in to make sure you were okay. If you were four years old, I'd ask if you had night terrors."

Carson sat up in the bed and rubbed the sleep from his eyes. "Yeah," he said. His voice was deep and hoarse. "I have it a lot. Same dream. Makes no sense. There's babies and young children, dirty, and crying. They're in a cold room with bad lighting. I hear cries and then all goes silent. I see babies and toddlers staring ahead as though they're looking at nothing." He shuddered. "I don't get it."

Jalisa wrinkled her face. "That's just creepy, Carson. Why would you have such an awful dream? Sounds like too many onions on your pizza before bed!"

"Except I had lasagna last night," he answered. "And I've had this dream for years—as long as I can remember. I don't know what brings it on."

Jalisa shrugged. "Don't look at me. I sleep like a rock. Clean conscience, ya know."

"I'm sure the pain killers help." He looked at her and frowned.

"What're you lookin' at so funny?"

"How do you get your hair to look so good like that so early?" Carson asked, still rubbing sleep out of his eyes.

Jalisa laughed. "This? The braids? It's a Senegalese twist, goofy. I don't do it every morning."

"Oh. Well, it's pretty. I always wondered how long it took you to do your hair. What time is it?" He reached for the alarm clock on the night stand. "Nine o'clock! Oh no! How could I have slept so late?"

"I'll leave you alone. I came in because you were making a ruckus while you slept. I was worried maybe you were having dreams about...you know...yesterday and all."

Jalisa closed the door behind her and Carson heard her making noises in the kitchen.

Miss Buttons demanded breakfast. Carson gave her food and fresh water, and hurried to the bathroom to shower and change into Malcolm's old clothes which hung on him like a football player's clothes on a figure skater. He joined Jalisa in the kitchen.

"You got anything for breakfast or some coffee, maybe?"

"I got cereal and leftover lasagna. No coffee, though. Sorry."

"That's okay. I'll grab some at the hospital." He put on his socks and shoes. "I don't suppose you'd let me borrow your car?"

Jalisa rolled her eyes. "Carson, you know they aren't gonna let you in to see Lizzie."

"Yeah, so you told me. It's a long walk from here. I'll bring the car right back. Promise."

She glared at him, but fished her keys out of her purse and dangled them.

"What time does Aunt Mae get here?"

"That lasagna is big enough for at least two nights, even if you eat it, so she won't come until tomorrow. What are you gonna do, Carson?"

"I won't be gone long. Thanks, Jalisa. I owe you." He took her car keys and started for the door.

"You bet you do."

10:41 a.m.

Carson walked into the hospital lobby and looked around. The maze of hallways, elevators, towers, and departments for every kind of medical specialty under the sun was dizzying and made him feel small. He knew Lizzie's room number. When he'd brought Jalisa here only a few days ago, he had become somewhat familiar with the layout. He strolled down the hallways becoming better acquainted with his surroundings. The wall clock read ten forty-five—time for the eleven o'clock shift change. When he saw a group of men and women arriving, he followed them down a hallway and through a door marked STAFF ONLY. He found exactly what he was looking for.

Minutes later, Carson, clad in a white lab coat with the name Bradley Evers, M.D. embroidered on it, sauntered toward the elevator and pressed the button to the sixth floor where the Intensive Care Unit sprawled over the south wing.

It was easy enough to find Lizzie's room in the ICU. It was the only room with a police officer sitting outside a closed door. Carson swallowed hard, pulled his damaged cell phone out and checked that his stethoscope was hanging like he'd seen on the real doctors. He took a deep breath and walked with confidence to her room. He spoke into his dead phone with solemn authority as he approached. "Double the dose for the first twenty-four hours, and call me with any changes." He nodded to the officer guarding Lizzie's room, while continuing to bark orders into his phone. The bored cop glanced up at him, nodded, and returned to his magazine.

Carson stepped into the room and shut the door behind him. His knees buckled when he saw Lizzie. She lay on the bed, pale and motionless. A thick endotracheal tube protruded from her mouth. Long tubes draped from her IV, and wires ran from her chest, plugged into machines that beeped and flashed numbers Carson didn't understand. Her head was wrapped in a large bandage. Scrapes and bruises covered her face and arms. Carson's heartbeat quickened. He knew she had been injured in the attack, but he was unprepared for the sight of his beloved Lizzie—so terribly hurt—so vulnerable and helpless.

Carson pulled a chair next to her bed and sat down. Her left hand was free of tubes and he held it tenderly in his. "Lizzie." His soft voice was just above a whisper. "I'm so sorry. This is all my fault. I don't understand what's going on. Please get well. Please get better. I love you so much, I'll even leave you alone if you want me to go away. You gotta fight. Fight with everything you've got. Fight to wake up. Fight to come back." He paused as his voice caught. "Please come back." He searched her face for some kind of response, but there was none. The machines kept beeping. The ventilator continued to wheeze as it pushed air into her lungs. But Lizzie Wise lay still as stone.

Carson stood. He bent over and kissed the small part of her forehead that showed beneath the bandages. He reached into Dr. Bradley Evers' coat pocket and pulled out a small teddy bear he'd purchased in the gift shop on his way upstairs. It was wearing a tee-shirt that said "Get Well Bear-y Soon" on it. "I got this for you." He tucked it under the covers next to her. Choking back tears, he left the room and returned to Jalisa's apartment.

12:03 p.m.

"I'd get you your own key, but I'm hoping you're not staying that long," Jalisa told Carson as she opened the door and let him in. "So what took you so long? I told you the hospital wouldn't let you see her."

"I saw her," Carson said, as he sank down onto the sofa. He put his face in his hands. "She looks bad." Carson choked as he spoke. He lifted his head and his eyes brimmed with tears.

Jalisa softened. "I'm sorry, Carson. How awful. Poor Lizzie."

Carson stared straight ahead. "She's got tubes and machines everywhere. Her head's all wrapped up. Why didn't I go downstairs and save her? I *ran*, Jalisa. I heard the shooting when I got upstairs, and I ran. She's just lying there. Didn't open her eyes, didn't tell me to get lost, nothing!" Tears spilled over his eyes and dropped onto his lap.

Jalisa got up and limped toward Carson, holding her side. She sat by him and patted his back. "If you'd have run back downstairs, those men would've killed you. You were the target in the first place. Lizzie's not gone yet, Carson. We just got to pray. It sounds like the doctors have done everything for her. We got to pray that God pulls her through." She went to the kitchen and returned with a glass of water for him.

Carson took a sip and set the glass on the end table. "I'm the one who should be getting you water. Thanks. You know, Jalisa, I miss my parents. I wish I could talk to my dad. But he's gone. Heart attack. Real sudden. Dad always had great advice. And my mom…she was always so wise."

"I'm sorry about your dad," Jalisa said. "And your mom. How is she?"

Carson sighed and leaned back into the sofa. "Sometimes she knows me, but most of the time, no. I see her every weekend and usually once or twice through the week as well. I read to her, and if the weather's nice, take her outside for walks. Sometimes, it seems like she's fine and I think the doctors don't know what they're talking about. But other times…"

"Wow, Carson. That's tough. I don't know what to say. Isn't she awfully young for Alzheimer's?"

"My mom's seventy-eight. Her symptoms started a few weeks after Dad died."

"*Seventy-eight?* Carson, you're only twenty-five. Your mom would've had to have been fifty-three when she had you!"

Carson nodded. "I know. She was. I was their miracle baby. My parents couldn't have children. Twice, they tried to adopt, but both times, the birth mother changed her mind. My mom was heartbroken, and they finally gave up. She went to the doctor, thinking she was going through, you know—"

"Menopause?"

"Yeah. And the doctor told her she was pregnant. They were overjoyed, and here I am. People used to always ask me why my grandparents came to all my school functions, but they were my parents. It was different having older parents. My friends' parents were always active and super busy, but my mom and dad were more mature and got tired faster. None of that made any difference to me. They loved me a lot. And they always had time to spend with me. Dad would take me fishing on the weekends. Mom retired from her job halfway through the pregnancy and poured herself into being a great mother. I've got no siblings. They were really devoted to being good parents. I was doted on a little bit, but I turned out okay, I guess. I just know that if they were here, they'd know what I should do." Carson's shoulders slumped. He turned to Jalisa. "So enough about me. How are you feeling? It looks like you're getting around better."

"Pain levels are dropping and I'm feeling a little stronger, thanks for asking. Look, I know you're worried about Lizzie. I am, too. But I gotta tell you, while you were gone, the police paid me a visit."

Carson's eyes widened. "What'd they want?"

"Whaddya think? My recipe for brownies! Carson, they're investigating the attack on our office, the bombing, and boy, they are looking for *you!*"

"What'd you tell them?" Carson swallowed.

"First, they wanted to confirm why I wasn't at work when the shooting started. Someone had told them I'd had an appendectomy, so I could confirm that. But then they started asking all kinds of questions about you. I just told them you were kind of new to the office and our paths didn't cross that much, and I didn't know much about you. I told them you seemed like a nice guy and I couldn't imagine you being involved. They left their cards and said to call them if you contacted me. I wish you'd call them. Maybe they could protect you." Jalisa handed Bo and Samantha's cards to Carson.

He studied the cards. "Or maybe not. Jalisa, I'm sure they have lots of questions. They can't possibly have more questions than I do, and I have no answers. I don't know who these people are, why they're after me, or anything else. You know that hundred grand in my account? Well, it's still there! I can't answer that, either, but it sure makes me look bad."

Day 3

7:02 a.m.

A dam and his team gathered in his office. He opened the boxes of goodies left from the day before. "Nothing like day-old bakery," he said as the team took their seats.

Bo reached for the donuts. "Not too bad," he announced with his mouth full.

Connor took the last slice of his wife's coffee cake. "Kathleen'll be hurt this didn't get eaten when it was fresh."

Samantha put up her hands. "No thanks."

"I s'pose day-old goods ain't quite good enough for the team princess, huh?" Bo drawled, tapping her on the shoulder, grinning.

"You can have mine, Bo," Samantha answered. She sat up straight and put her nose in the air. "I woke up in time to enjoy a nourishing breakfast. Protein, you know."

Adam went to his whiteboard and wrote MSR Employees across the top, listing each by name. Most days, he would join in on the light-hearted banter between his team, but he felt the pressure of being in charge of a major crime while Captain Peterson was away. The media and the mayor's office were screaming for results, while employees working at city-owned businesses were calling in sick in droves, and hotels complained of record-high cancellations. Fear was a great motivator, Adam knew, but he remained stoic and serious. If the mayor was so concerned about crime, he should have added more police to the force. Adam would not accept responsibility for a drop in tourism or work productivity. He had the best team on the force, but they weren't miracle workers.

He pressed his fingers into his eyebrows and rubbed them together. "Connor, why don't you start and let us know what your phone and e-mail search turned up."

Connor cleared his throat, washed the last of the coffee cake down with coffee, and wiped his mouth on his sleeve. "The partners, Edmond Carmody, the senior partner, George Magruder and Phoebe White, are all clean. Their e-mails are strictly business-related, 'cept Mr. Carmody gets a lot of stuff from his grandkids. I know everyone says he's getting ready to retire soon, but I think he's already got one foot out the door. Never misses a play, a concert, a game, anything his grandkids are doing. Ms. White occasionally e-mails her husband, but nothing out of the ordinary. She seems to buy a lot of shoes and purses, but with her income, I suspect it's no big deal. Same with their phones. Far as I can tell, the partners had everything to lose and nothing to gain."

Bo spoke. "Samantha Jane and I also talked to the partners, and we agree with Connor. This was their firm that they all built from the ground up. They spoke highly of their employees. Edmond Carmody was personally overseeing Carson Hollister, our missing employee, and he had nothing but good things to say. Plus, they even took out special insurance coverage in case of disaster, so the employees would continue to receive their paychecks and health insurance. 'Course, I think when they did that they probably had fire, tornado, or flood in mind, but the coverage also applies to this incident. That's one employer who takes real good care of their employees."

"From all appearances, this company was, for the most part, happy, healthy, and solvent—lucrative, even," Samantha added. "We interviewed the partners separately. All of them were shocked at what's happened, and none of them believe any of their employees could have been in any way responsible."

"So are we okay with removing the partners' names at this time?" Adam asked.

The team nodded, and Adam erased the names of the partners from the board.

Connor gulped down his coffee and walked to the snack table for a refill. "Helen Vargas, the executive secretary, has been there since the company started. She's Mr. Carmody's personal assistant, and she also does a little work for the other two partners. Her e-mail and phone are even cleaner than her bosses'. Divorced with a grown daughter in Atlanta, Ms. Vargas seems to lead a pretty quiet life. She has a lot of responsibility at the firm, and from what I can tell, she's valued and appreciated. Good salary and as much vacation as she wants. Never calls in sick and goes about her business with a minimum amount of fuss. Well-liked by all, but an introvert, so she doesn't socialize much with the other employees. Her records are spotless." He wagged his finger to Adam to erase Helen Vargas from the board.

"Helen Vargas and Phoebe White were the only persons in the office who escaped without injury," Bo interjected. "When Samantha Jane and I interviewed her, she said there was a back emergency exit leading out of Edmond Carmody's office. She and Ms. White went out that way when the shooting and screaming started."

"What about George Magruder?" Adam asked. "Why didn't he get out that way? Or the other employees?"

"Mr. Magruder was talking with another employee, Robert Shoemaker, out in the main area and got caught in the melee," Samantha said. "As to the others, they likely didn't know about that exit. It was an additional fire escape in case people were trapped on the second floor, and the partners figured there'd be time to direct people out that way. Nobody ever figured on the kind of panic that an attack like this one would set off."

"All right. Were you able to get through any more, Connor?"

"Oh, yeah, Adam. I got through all but one, actually. Most of these was pretty easy." Connor consulted his notes. "Miriam Murgan, the office manager. Married to the firm. Strictly business, all the way. A lotta her e-mails to the employees take a real nasty tone, so's it's my guess, she had her share of enemies. Nobody ever threatened her, nothin' like dat, but nobody was askin' her to lunch or parties, neither."

Samantha cleared her throat. "Nobody may've threatened Ms. Murgan, but you're right about one thing, Connor. Nobody liked her either. I'm not so sure anyone was all that upset at her death, but from our interviews so far, I think it's a stretch that anyone would have gone to the lengths they did just to kill her. As far as her culpability for the attack, though, she loved the firm. It was all she had in life and she was devoted to it. Sad."

"We heard plenty of stories about her—none of 'em good. She was a lonely, bitter middle-aged woman whose life revolved around her job," Bo said. "The people we interviewed described her as incapable of giving a compliment, and no matter what anyone accomplished, Murgan would find something to criticize. There ain't nobody missin' that woman."

Adam erased Miriam's name. "Was there any one in particular that had a beef with her—above and beyond her usual hatefulness?

Samantha shook her head. "Not that I could tell. She was an equal opportunity hater. She thought everyone was cheating the firm, slacking off, lying about something, you name it. Accused people randomly without cause. Even watched the clock when you had to use the bathroom. Came in early, stayed late. The folks I interviewed were certain she lay awake nights thinking of how she could make someone else as miserable as she was."

Adam shook his head. "It's a wonder they didn't have a revolving door of employees, there."

Bo answered. "She tended to leave the recruiters alone. They're the golden children, bringing in a ton of money. The rank and file employees, secretaries, receptionist, accountants, and the like caught the brunt of her wrath, but the recruiters certainly *saw* what was going on. I think folks stayed because the pay and benefits were really good and nobody wanted to let one bad apple spoil it all. Plus, with the exception of her, everyone else seemed to get along pretty well. Speaking of apples..."

Bo reached for an apple fritter from the donut box. Samantha made a face as though she was getting sick.

Connor glared at Bo. "May I continue? The secretaries, Madison Fontana, Callie McKnight and Jalisa Moore, don't raise no flags, neither. Ms. Fontana is havin' some trouble financially, and is working a part-time second job to make ends meet. And she gambles some, so she's not that smart about her money. But she's willing to work to dig out. They all do a little Facebook and some personal e-mails from work, but not much. They get the work done, anyway. I was able to trace through to their personal e-mail accounts, and except for Ms. Fontana's credit issues, there's nothin' that stands out there—just that she owes a lot and tends to be late on her payments." Connor checked his notes before continuing. "Callie McKnight is a world champion texting queen. But it's all a bunch of silliness, nothing worth talkin' about. Jalisa Moore has an account that's got some type of secure lock on it, as well as an untraceable number. That's got me wonderin'. Plus, her address is pretty fancy for what money she makes."

Bo interrupted. "Jalisa Moore's got a brother in Special Ops. His assignments are top secret missions in very dangerous places. My guess is anything classified and locked up would be more related to the limited contact she gets with her brother, than anything else."

"Yeah, Jalisa was out all week because she had her appendix out," Samantha added. "We talked to her for a little bit. Church goer, no boyfriends. She seemed to be a straight shooter, answered as many of our questions as she could. Still having some pain from her surgery, so we didn't stay too long. But she talked a lot about her brother. They're very close. She's got pictures of him all over the place. He pays for that real nice apartment, as well as her utilities. Whenever he does come home, he stays in the second bedroom. She showed it to us. Military spit polished! Keeps his door closed so her cat doesn't get in. She lives a rather quiet life. Kinda surprising for a young, attractive, single girl. Mother was a drug addict and died when Jalisa was a teenager. Father abandoned them when the kids were young. Jalisa's on the straight and narrow. But like I said, we didn't talk to her very long, due to her post-surgical pain. We'll go back in a couple more days."

"Jalisa's next door neighbor's a real whack-a-doodle. Has what looks to be hundreds of cats and makes herself up to look like a cat. I tried to get a little info from the crazy cat lady, but she mews a lot and wasn't all that helpful. I don't think there's much on the secretaries, Adam," Bo said. "Callie broke her ankle jumpin' out the window. Madison followed and landed on her, breaking her wrist. Both ladies should be getting released from the hospital today or tomorrow. Callie's the youngest, still living at home with her parents."

"So, we erase the secretaries?" Adam asked.

"I think we can get rid of Callie. Maybe move Jalisa to the bottom of the list with Madison just above her," Connor suggested. "Just in case something else comes up. I don't expect it will, but when there's financial troubles, sometimes people use bad judgment. If Jalisa's situation with her brother became known, she could be a blackmail target. Yous just never know."

Bo and Samantha shrugged, and Adam did as Connor requested.

"The receptionist, Elizabeth Wise," Connor began. He looked at his notes again. "This one's interesting." Bo and Samantha looked up and leaned forward in their chairs. Connor finished his coffee and went for a third cup, grabbing a donut hole. "Most kids her age are on Facebook, Twitter, WhatsApp, you name it. She don't even have an account. On anything. She's got no personal e-mail, her cell phone is a pay-as-you-go plan, and she has nearly all her original minutes. She ain't got no saved numbers on the phone, 'cept work. No friends, no family, no nothin'. I'd call that strange."

"I'd call that running away and hiding from something— or someone," Bo said.

Connor continued. "Ya think? This girl don't shop online, don't pay bills online. No electronic footprint outside of her work computer, which is mostly intra-office. Sometimes she e-mails clients and her co-workers, but it's all work-related. Except for one." Connor paused and looked at the team.

"Ya waitin' for a drum roll or to see if the suspense might really cause our untimely deaths?" Bo smirked at Connor.

"Dramatic effect, not that yous would notice," Connor answered. "The only personal e-mail she ever gets is from Carson Hollister, the missing guy."

"What do those e-mails say?" Samantha asked. "We obviously haven't interviewed her."

"Looks to me like Mr. Hollister is kinda sweet on Ms. Wise. Looks to me like it's not a two-way street."

"How so?" Adam asked. "Do her replies sound like she's offended, or does she get nasty? Has she threatened to take it to HR? Or does she simply say she's not interested."

"Most of it's just no thanks," Connor answered. "She don't sound angry or offended, just not interested."

"Have any of Hollister's messages sounded creepy, or threatening?" Samantha asked.

Connor shook his head. "Nope. A little love-sick, a little more persistent than I'd care for, but when yous are interviewing the other employees, yous might ask if this was just an office flirtation, or if he was as smitten as he sounds. Carson Hollister is the one person we know the least about and need to know more about."

"I'm leaving Elizabeth Wise on the board. Sounds like we need more information. Anything else on her or her family?" Adam asked.

"Not yet." Connor sipped his coffee. "But I think the reason her family ain't been notified is likely because there's no information available."

Adam frowned and paced in front of the whiteboard. He stopped, put his hands together and pointed toward Connor. "Miriam Murgan should have an emergency contact list, if she's the office manager, or whatever passes for an HR department. That information—some kind of emergency contact, should've been in her computer."

Connor nodded. "Yeah, she had that list. The contact on Elizabeth Wise's employee sheet was for Minniver Rodenta—*Minnie Mouse,* right? And the phone number was the time and temperature line."

"You can track her through her social security number, Connor," Adam said.

"Yeah, I know. But I didn't want to do dat without discussing it with yous guys." Connor popped the donut hole in his mouth, wiped his sticky hands on his pants and looked at the team. "Clearly, Ms. Wise is hiding from something, someone, whatever. What if it's an abuser, a stalker, someone who would do her harm if they could find her, and what if that someone is a family member? She ain't got no criminal record. Far as I can tell, she ain't hidin' from the law, so maybe we should protect that privacy she's tried so hard to secure. I think we oughtta wait this out and see if she wakes up and can answer a few things herself. She's been through a terrible ordeal here, and I think da last t'ing we oughtta do is put her in more danger. Assuming, of course, dat our assumptions is right."

The group cringed at Connor's assassination of the English language. Samantha winced and Adam shook his head.

Bo tapped Samantha on her arm. "Big difference between South City and *the* South," he whispered, with a wink.

"All right. We leave her on the board, and wait until the rest of our investigation is completed. Who else have you finished checking?"

Connor rearranged his notes before he spoke. "The recruiters are Lindsey Liscomb, Michael Grant, Robert Shoemaker, Danita Jefferson, and Andre Melton. Danita Jefferson was not at work. There's nothin' suspicious on her phone or computer, but she's pretty well addicted to Spider Solitaire. She keeps her personal calendar on the computer, together with her business calendar, and according to dat, she had a doctor's appointment." He pointed to Bo and Samantha. "Yous guys will have to confirm that." He returned to his notes. "Andre Melton, unfortunately, was killed in the fray, but there ain't nothin' on his computer dat raised no flags. He visited some on-line joolery shops. I'm guessing he was gonna propose to his girlfriend, based on what he was lookin' at, but yous guys can determine dat." He nodded to Bo and Samantha again.

"We haven't gotten as far as interviewing the recruiters, yet," Samantha said. "Lindsay Liscomb took a bullet to her shoulder and is expected to recover and go home, likely tomorrow or the next day. Michael Grant and Robert Shoemaker were badly injured by gunfire, and, although expected to pull through, they're still in serious condition and may be facing additional surgeries. Michael Grant has a gambling problem. Lots of credit card debt at the casinos. He makes good money at the firm, but at the rate he gambles and loses, it won't be long before he's in trouble."

Adam nodded as he took notes. "All right. We leave the recruiters on the board pending interviews. So, besides Carson Hollister, we've got Armand Teller. What do we know about him?"

"Armand Teller, the IT guy—I didn't get to research him, yet," Connor answered. "If he's involved, he'd be able to hide it better because he knows more about computers. I want plenty of time to look into Mr. Teller, to be sure I uncover all there is."

"And," Bo added, "Mr. Teller was also seriously injured. He's in no shape to be interviewed yet, either."

"And Carson Hollister, our missing guy?" Adam asked. He refilled his coffee cup and drank half of it in one gulp.

Connor took a deep breath and let it out slowly. He stared at his notes and twitched his nose left to right. "Carson Hollister is one confusing dude. I spent a longer time on him on account of him bein' a person of extreme interest." He cleared his throat and looked at the snack table, but remained where he was. "Carson Hollister's phone is clean and so is his computer. He's got a pack of student loans, but has never missed a payment. Lives frugally with one credit card only, and charges for emergency car expenses. Nothin' else on the charge card. Pays his rent and utilities on time. Phone records show he calls a memory care home in South St. Louis, Cloverlawn Memory Care Center, and he's got calls for pizza and Chinese, mostly." He pointed at Bo and Samantha. "Yous may wanna see if he's got a grandmother or aunt at dat place. He's got a couple buddies he calls every once in a while. Looks like they was in college together. Seems like a nice, quiet boy. So's he looks squeaky clean, 'cept for the matter of a deposit into his bank account for a hundred gran'."

"Whoa!" Bo and Samantha shouted together.

Connor nodded his head. "And here's the funny thing about dat. Late dat same night, a withdrawal was made from his account for some four hundred twenty dollars, leaving a balance of exactly a hundred gran' and eighteen cents. So's, whaddya make of dat?"

"That makes no sense at all!" Samantha said. "If he lives so frugally, why not use that money to pay off the student loans, buy a decent car, and maybe live in a nicer neighborhood? And if he's on the run, why not take the money and run—*really* run!"

"How long did you say he had that much in his account?" Bo asked.

Connor flashed a knowing smile. "The deposit was made the day before the attack. Not dat I'm sayin' dat's suspicious in no way."

Bo shook his head. "Did *Hollister* make the deposit? How was it made?"

"You and Samantha will need to find that out," Adam answered. "And you'll need a warrant for the bank. We need to know who made the deposit and how, and who withdrew the smaller amount of money, and from where."

"Hey! Need any help, here?" A woman's strong voice asked, causing the team to turn around. K-9 Officer Kate Marlin stood in the doorway with an enormous German Shepherd at her side.

"Kate!" Adam said. "Come on in. You know Bo and Connor. This is Samantha Hernandez, our newest team member. Samantha, Kate Marlin and her new partner, um…"

"Boris," Kate answered. "Robo was retired and is at my house livin' the good life! Boris just got his first drug bust, and it was a doozy! We've had playtime, and we're off for the afternoon. I was kinda hopin' you'd get the bombing case, and maybe, you'd need a little help?" The tall, muscular redhead beamed at Adam.

"Feel like running down some warrants? That'd help Bo and Samantha out."

"So Samantha gets paired up with Mr. God's-gift-to-women, huh?" Kate asked. "Whaddya got against her?"

Connor snickered. "Hey, Bo. If you want any more donuts, you better get 'em now. Looks like Boris' nose figured out we got food. He sure is a pretty dog, Kate."

Boris stared at the boxes of donuts and bagels with his ears forward. He licked his chops, but remained seated at attention beside Kate. Bo got up and stuffed one more donut hole in his mouth. Boris followed it with his eyes. "Can he have this stuff, Kate? I know you're picky about what you let your fur babies eat."

"How much is in there, Bo?" she asked.

"Two bagels and a cake donut."

Kate shrugged. "He's been a real good boy today. I'll make an exception."

Adam handed her the box and she set it on the floor before the dog. The dog remained still, looking up at Kate. "Get the treat!" she told him. The goodies were gone in three seconds. Boris sat back at Kate's side, licking his chops. She scratched behind his ears. "Such a good boy." Kate turned to Adam. "Let me have the warrant requests and I'll run them down for you."

"Just the one, so far, but let's get your contact info to Bo and Samantha, and they can text you, if you don't mind."

"That's fine. One last barbeque before Thanksgiving?" she asked Adam.

He laughed. "If the weather gives us a break. You'll have to bring Boris and Robo, or Amy will pitch a fit."

"Deal." Kate smiled. "See ya. Nice to meet you, Samantha. You'll love bein' on this team." Kate left with Boris at her side.

Samantha leaned back in her chair and stared at the whiteboard, deep in thought. "You know, it almost sounds like Carson didn't know the hundred grand was in there. It sounds like he did go to clean out his account, and, let's just assume for a minute, since he *is* an accountant, that the four hundred twenty dollars and change was all he *knew* was in there, and he withdrew it."

"But he would've had to have seen the balance." Bo said.

"I'm sure he did. But if he knew he only had the four

hundred and something in there, he would have known the rest didn't belong to him. Edmond Carmody swore to us that Carson was honest and trustworthy. Maybe he's being set up." Samantha countered.

"Interesting. Could be. Find this guy. We need some answers. The more we look, the more he's involved in something—maybe victim, and if so, why? Maybe perpetrator and weaving a web we aren't seeing with any clarity—yet. Anybody need a break before we continue?" Adam asked.

They all shook their heads no. Bo got up for coffee and returned to his seat.

"Our uniformed officers have reported in on the interviews they conducted in the neighborhood," Adam continued. He sat on the edge of his desk. "There's nothing of interest to report that we don't already know. Most of the neighbors were at work. A few were at home, but nobody heard or saw anything until the car blew up. Same with the neighboring businesses. And by that time, everything they saw was after the fact. We got a couple of reports from folks that said they saw the gunmen enter the building, but no license plates, no descriptions, no help."

"Wasn't one of the assailants killed, Adam?" Bo asked.

Adam sighed. "Yep. Finger prints were filed off, which tells me he did this for a living, and his DNA is not on file, so apparently, the guy was never caught prior to this incident. No ID, of course, so we're running him through facial recognition, and still nothing. But Elle's on it. You know her. Dog with a bone, so at some point, she'll figure out who he is."

Adam stood and faced his team who remained seated. "You've all done excellent work. I'm proud of you. A lot was accomplished in a short time. Connor, I'd like you to continue on Armand Teller and see if there's anything there. Keep digging on Carson, and I wanna know more about Danita Jefferson. Also, dig a little more on Miriam Murgan—see if anyone might have hated her enough to stage this. Maybe it just got out of hand. I think it's a long shot, but she seems to be the only one in the firm nobody liked, and she sounds like a person who had a lot of enemies. Also—and tread softly here—see if you can look into Jalisa Moore a little deeper. I think those locked accounts are likely military and related to her brother, but let's just be sure that's the case. Same with her apartment. But like I said, tread *softly.* We don't want to step on military toes or do anything that might call unwanted attention to a Special Ops soldier or his family."

Adam turned to Bo and Samantha. "You two covered a lot of ground in just one day. Be sensitive to those who are injured. They're all at either Barnes or SLU, so see if you can finish your interviews without making the nurses angry. Try to determine whether anyone knows if Carson and Elizabeth Wise have a personal connection. And *find Carson Hollister.* Kate'll get that warrant to you soon, so get some answers from the bank. Questions, anyone?"

Samantha raised her hand. "What about the second assailant? Any information on him?"

Adam shook his head. "Still working on it. Elle's team is done at the scene, so if you need to visit the site, go ahead. Her team is working this case at the lab, now, so we'll just have to wait for them to finish. Some of those tests take a while." He looked back and forth between his team and snapped his notebook shut. "Okay. That's it for today. See you tomorrow morning at eight. Dismissed."

The detectives filed out of the building. "I'll drive," Bo told Samantha. "My cruiser's parked at the back of the lot."

"I could drive, you know," she answered.

"I'm the senior detective, and I choose. If you want to drive, you'll have to go to the movies with me this weekend. My treat. Whaddya say?"

"I say you can drive, but nice try."

"Do I detect a note of sarcasm, Detective?"

"Wow, Bo. Not much gets by you. Easy to see why *you* made detective."

They reached his squad car and Bo stopped short. "You hear somethin', Samantha Jane?"

Samantha stopped and listened. She gasped. "It's coming from the dumpster! Quick!"

They scaled the fence surrounding the parking lot and ran to the dumpster on the other side. Bo flung it open and peered inside. "Aw," he said. He hoisted himself up, reached in and brought out a puppy.

"Oh, no!" Samantha moaned. "Who could do such a thing? He's hurt!"

Bo cradled the puppy in his arms. "Looks like his leg is broke and someone used him for an ashtray. Boy, I'd like to get my hands on the creep that did this!" The puppy wagged his tail and licked Bo's hand. "Okay, little guy, let's get you some help." He looked at Samantha and said, "Looks like you get to drive after all, but we're still takin' my car. I'll tell you where to go. And I'll hold him so he doesn't hurt himself any worse. Tempting to use the lights and siren, but we better not. We'll be there soon."

They walked to his car and Bo sat down carefully, keeping the puppy still. "Okay turn left here and keep going for a while."

After a few more turns, they reached a small animal hospital. "Make a right here. This is my vet. They'll take real good care of our little friend, here." He bent down and kissed the puppy on his head.

The receptionist looked surprised when Bo walked in. "Hi, Bo. Is Penelope okay?"

"Hey, Maggie. Penelope is fine, but this little guy isn't. Found him in a dumpster. Looks like a broken leg and some nasty burns. Will you have Dr. Benton take good care of him? Send me the bill, whatever it is. I want my new buddy here to get the best. And if you can find him a new family, I'll pay for his shots, neutering, anything, as long as he goes to a loving home."

"Sure, Bo. Actually, now that you mention it, I've got a family in mind. Had to say goodbye to their pooch a few weeks ago. Cancer. They may be ready for a new pup, and if so, this little guy will be in seventh heaven."

Bo winked at the receptionist. "That's what I wanna hear, Maggie. We gotta go." He gently handed the puppy to her and rubbed its head. "You're gonna be all right, little feller." The detectives left as Maggie walked the puppy to the back to see the vet.

In the car, Samantha was quiet.

"You okay there, Samantha Jane?"

She nodded. "Yeah. That was real nice of you. Maybe you're not as big of a jerk as I thought."

"Well, golly gee, thanks a lot!" He looked at her sideways. "So does that mean you'll go to dinner with me tonight?"

"Who's Penelope?"

"My cat." Bo pulled into traffic and headed toward Barnes Hospital. "Purty little white thang with blue eyes. Found her soaking wet in a downpour. She was hiding under my car, shivering. I picked her up and she just clung to me like flies on dung. I took her home and dried her off and brought her to that vet we just left. I'd met Dr. Bentley a few weeks earlier, when I'd answered a call about a break-in. I was impressed with the way she treated her patients and how much she cared for animals. They said it was easy to keep a cat because they don't need the time and attention a dog does. I had to leave her with them to get checked over and spayed, so I had a couple of days to think about it. Bought a litter box, food, toys, a couple of scratching posts, and before you could say meow, I had me a cat."

Samantha nodded her head and looked out the window.

"Why were you working a break-in? We're homicide."

"I was on my way to breakfast after an all-night stake-out and when I heard the call, I was right in front of the animal hospital, so I just answered it."

"Mmm-hmm." Samantha continued to look out the window.

"And you didn't answer my question, you know," he prodded.

"I know," Samantha answered. "Okay."

"Okay?" Bo sat up and his face brightened. "*Okay?*"

"Okay on one condition," she replied. "First, you need to ask my father."

Bo pulled the car to the curb and stopped. He turned and looked at her with wide eyes. "Excuse me? What are you, fourteen? What do you mean, I gotta ask your father?"

Samantha turned from the window and smiled sweetly at him. "My daddy and I have an agreement. Any man who wants to take me out has to talk to my father first. You do that and we can have dinner. And for the record, I was absolutely not dating at fourteen."

"You have *got* to be kidding!" Bo was incredulous.

"Nope. Not kidding."

"You're old enough to be a police detective. You have your own place, I assume, your own car, your own life."

"Daddy first, dinner second." Samantha Jane Hernandez had spoken and was not going to be moved.

Bo pulled back into traffic and continued toward the hospital in rare silence. They parked on Forest Park Avenue and walked two blocks to the north entrance of Barnes Hospital. When they got to the door, Bo finally spoke. "All right, Samantha Jane. I'll talk to your daddy." *I'll just call your little bluff there, honey!*

Samantha stopped at the door and swallowed. She took a deep breath. "All right. That'll earn you a medal for bravery. I'll see when he's available."

Bo opened the door and they went in. "We need to get to the Queeny Towers elevator. Michael Grant and Robert Shoemaker are on the same floor, just a couple of doors down from each other. We can stop by to check on Elizabeth Wise, but she's still critical and unconscious, as far as I know." They walked the long corridors to Queeny Towers. "So, what's he like?"

"Who?"

"Your father."

"I'm his only daughter. For that matter, I'm his only child."

They continued walking. "So how many guys have talked to him?"

"Two."

"Two? In your whole life? *Two?*"

"Yep."

"So how'd that work out?"

"Not so good."

"Uh-huh." Bo furrowed his eyebrows and ran his tongue along the inside of his cheek. They walked a few more steps, then he pointed to a sign ahead. "Turn left at this corridor. There's the elevators."

"I can read, you know."

9:36 a.m.

Sam Hernandez drove to Carson Hollister's apartment and circled the block. He noted a car directly across the street with two men in it. One had binoculars and was watching Carson's building. Sam recognized a hit team when he saw it, so he parked on the block behind Carson's, and walked through the alley to the back of the building. No one was watching that side. He climbed the steps of the fire escape to Carson's back door, and peered inside. He saw the wire running along the floor next to the baseboard. "These guys sure like to blow up stuff," he mumbled under his breath.

Sam hurried down the steps, back through the alley to his car and dialed 911. "You're gonna need the bomb squad. Back entrance. If you hurry, you can catch the guys who planted it parked in front of the building, across the street. Gray Chrysler. Leave off the lights and sirens and you won't scare them off." He gave the address, mentioned the missing plates, and hung up without providing any additional information. *So Jordan was smart enough to check the back door before he entered. I wonder what tipped him off?*

Sam drove to Kenton Farraday's home and updated him on the search for his son. Vivienne left for the grocery store, leaving the two men alone in the mansion.

"So you believe he's alive, then, right?" Kenton asked, after they were seated.

"There's no indication he's not, Mr. Farraday. I would think the first place he would've gone after his car blew up, would be home. Something was off—maybe he saw a strange car watching the building, like I did, and he got suspicious and went the back way, like I did. His kitchen window had been opened. There were paint chips on the ledge, and I know what the makings of an explosive device are when I see a wire like that. Jordan may not have been suspicious under normal circumstances, but after going through that kind of an ordeal, he was undoubtedly on high alert. I'd bet the rent he saw that wire and high-tailed it outta there. Smart kid."

Kenton smiled. "Takes after his father."

"The question is, where would he go where he would feel safe? He was only working at MSR a few months. He's got student loans and no car, and I'm guessing, not much money in the bank. So he can't have gone far."

Kenton chuckled. "Well, you're wrong about that, Sam. I instructed Martina to deposit a hundred thousand dollars into his account the day before the incident."

Sam went white and his eyes widened. "You *what?*"

Kenton sobered. "Why? What's wrong? I wanted my son to have a little something. So he wouldn't struggle."

Sam stroked his mustache and stared straight ahead, thinking. He was quiet a few moments, and then looked up. "I realize you acted with the best intentions. And, of course, we had no idea an attack was on the horizon. But that's going to make him a suspect with the police. They'll leave no stone unturned in their investigation, and a sudden windfall like that is, well, it puts him in an unfavorable light. I wish you'd waited until I brought him to you. We haven't even confirmed he's your son."

Kenton looked down. His shoulders slumped. "I didn't think...Oh, no. I was just so excited to have him alive, and now— I've made everything worse."

Sam stood. "Don't worry, sir. He's out there, and for now, I think he's safe. I'll find him. And you can shower him with all the money you like then, okay?"

Kenton hung his head and attempted to smile. "Okay, Sam." He struggled to stand, and walked Sam to the door. "What's next for you?"

"I need to start interviewing his co-workers, see who he was close to, who he might trust. There's a young lady at Barnes. She's in critical condition from the attack. I'm going to the hospital to check and see if she's conscious and knows anything that may shed a little light. She's the receptionist and would've been the first person to see the gunmen. Maybe they said something to her. Carson's got a couple of other co-workers at the same hospital who might know something. Then I'll go over to SLU and see if anybody there knows anything."

Kenton nodded. "Oh, and Sam. One more thing. That young man *is* my son. I *know* it."

Sam shook Kenton's hand. "It's more likely than not. But I *will* insist on a DNA test to confirm. Too much at stake."

"That's fair."

"Do you want me to stay until Vivienne gets back?"

"Oh, no. That's not necessary. She'll be home soon. I'd much rather you find Jordan. I'll be fine for a little while."

"Okay," Sam answered. "You're the boss. Your lawyer is Aaron Berman, right? And he knows what's going on?"

Kenton nodded.

"If the police find Jordan first, he'll need Mr. Berman right away, understand?"

"Only the best for my son. Aaron will be there. I'll call to give him an update."

"I'll be in touch, sir."

10:11 a.m.

Pamela Farraday closed the door to her office, lowered the blinds, and dug the burner phone out of her Hermés purse. The man answered on the second ring.

"I want my money today. The threat was removed, lady. Just like I told you."

"You're beginning to tire me," Pamela replied. "You've given me no proof of that. Just your word, and for some reason, that's not quite enough for me. I'll pay you when you deliver."

"You'll pay me today, or things'll get very difficult for you. Have I made myself clear?"

"Don't you *dare* threaten me! I hired you to do a job and all I can see is that you botched it completely! I've got a lot on the line, mister. When can I expect you to hold up your end of the deal?"

The other end of the line was quiet for a few seconds. "Noon Monday. I get my money by noon Monday, honey, or I'm coming after you. I don't make idle threats. I'll be at the same picnic table in Shaw Park day after tomorrow at noon. Be there. With my money. Or make sure your insurance is paid up."

The man hung up on her.

Pamela was furious. She pressed her lips together into a thin line and glared at the phone before she slammed it down on her desk. *I'll fix him. Nobody talks to me like that and gets away with it.*

She flipped on the news and changed channels until she found a station reporting on the MSR attack. She turned up the volume.

"Police are still following leads on the attack at Medical Staffing Remedies. If anyone has information, please call the tip hotline." The phone number flashed across the bottom of the screen, while the reporter repeated it three times. Pamela wrote the number down, leaned back in her chair and smirked to herself.

Her burner phone rang, and she jumped.

"Yes?" she hissed into the phone.

"Just a friendly reminder, lady. Unmarked bills. Twenties."

"Oh, I'll have it all ready for you. By the way, what did you use to blow up the car?"

"Now, why would you wanna worry your pretty little head about that?"

"I may have another job and I'd rather do my research off-line. What did you use?"

"C4."

"Do you have any left?"

"Plenty more where that came from."

"Good. I want you to bring me some. I want to see what was used. I want to see how it works."

"Look here. You can't just go blowin' off C4 in the middle of a park. What are you, nuts?"

"Okay, then. Bring me a little sample. I want to see how it does when I take it home. It's the only way I'll be convinced."

"You gotta be crazy. You're no explosives expert."

"I just want a little. To satisfy myself that he could not have escaped the blast."

The man sighed. "All right, lady. It's your funeral. As long as I get paid first. And the sample of C4 ain't free. Tack on another ten percent."

"Monday at noon."

They hung up. Pamela glanced at her watch. She looked over a couple of reports on her desk, and locked the door. She picked up her office phone and put it on hold, so no calls could be put through. Then she called the tip line from the burner phone.

"If you want to catch the guy responsible for the explosion in the Central West End, he'll be at a picnic table in Shaw Park day after tomorrow at noon. Southwest corner under a big oak tree. No, I don't want to leave my name. This may be the only chance you have to catch him." She hung up.

Her office door rattled and Pamela looked up, startled. She tiptoed to the glass panel and peered out through the blinds. Breathing a sigh of relief, she opened the door to her brother.

"Richard! You scared me half to death! What's the matter with you?"

Richard entered and closed the door behind him. "What's with you? Since when do you come undone when I walk in? Sheesh, Pam, you're white as a ghost! What's going on?" Richard took a seat and stared at his sister.

"This—hit man I found," she started. "He's threatening me. He wants his money now. I told him I'd have it in two days, anyway."

"So pay him!" Richard rose from his seat and locked the door. "We have the money. Pay him and get rid of him."

Pamela crossed her arms in front of her chest. "We've no proof. If I pay him without knowing our nephew is dead, then we lose even more."

Richard wrung his hands. "I knew this was a bad idea. What you should've done, instead of hiring some goon to kill this kid, is to have him find Jordan and see if we could buy him off. Sign a release or something. Now, this guy is *threatening* you? Your brilliant plan is spiraling out of control."

Pamela smiled and looked at Richard through narrowed

eyes. She reminded Richard of their mother, Sylvia—cold, manipulative, and evil.

"What?" Richard asked, exasperated. He began to pace. "I called the tip hotline and told them where to find this guy." She smoothed her long blonde hair. "I'll fix him. He thinks I'm bringing him the money and a little extra to buy C4. But he'll be arrested and charged."

Richard stopped pacing and walked toward Pamela, towering over her. "Are you out of your mind?" He clenched his fists and unclenched them, grabbing the edge of her desk. "What were you thinking?"

"He doesn't know my name or phone number. Everything's been a cash transaction. I'm not giving up everything that's within our grasp. We're so close. I'll find someone else to take care of Jordan."

"This is gonna backfire, Pam." Richard started for the door and turned. "We're gonna lose everything." He left her office, slamming the door behind him.

10:14 a.m.

Felix Santos and three of his men from the Bomb and Arson squad parked on the block behind Carson Hollister's street, not far from where Sam's car had been parked less than an hour earlier. Two squad cars approached Carson's apartment, one from the north end of the block, the other from the south. As they closed in on the gray Chrysler, the car began to pull away from the curb, but the police cars sped up to block it in. The men inside got out and gave chase, running in opposite directions. The police exited their cars, one calling for back-up, and ran after them, dodging down alleys and in between apartment buildings. A third car pulled up in the alley and Kate Marlin and Boris got out. She ordered Boris to stop the runner and hold him, and within seconds, one of the suspects had been apprehended by the large German Shepherd.

The cop chasing the second suspect cornered and cuffed him. Kate returned her suspect to the second officer and turned to her dog. "Would somebody like a steak dinner? Let's go, boy!" She turned the man over to the original responding officers and left with Boris wagging his tail by her side, tugging on his special ball, his reward for a job well done.

Felix Santos and his men stood at the back door of Carson's apartment studying the wire. "Can we locate the person who lives here?" one of them asked.

"I wish. It's the guy whose car was blown up in the Central West End. Somebody really has it in for him." Felix answered. "So far, nobody can find him."

"Anyone sure he didn't do it himself?"

"Doubt it. No evidence of that. Doesn't make any difference right now. We need to get this taken care of."

The apartment held six units on three floors. The first floor units were occupied. Young marrieds with their first babies in both units. An elderly man was Carson's next door neighbor, and he, too, was home. The people renting the units on the third floor were at work, the man told Felix.

"Any pets?" Felix asked him.

"No, sir," the neighbor answered. "The third-floor tenants work all the time. They don't have time for pets. I think Carson, next door, has the only pet. He found an alley cat and adopted her. Or she adopted him, one way or t'other."

Felix and his men assisted the elderly man and the two young mothers with their babies out of the apartment building. A uniformed police officer was summoned to take them to the police station until the building was deemed safe.

The team remotely entered the apartment, and three hours later, the explosive device was disarmed. A bomb sniffing dog was called in to see if any additional explosives remained in the apartment, but none were found. A sweep of the entire building was conducted, but nothing suspicious was discovered, and the tenants were brought back into their apartments. Adam Trent arrived and spoke to each of them, but learned nothing new.

Day 4

8:00 a.m.

Adam and his team gathered in front of the television set in Adam's office. "This is the footage from the ATM, showing Carson removing the four hundred plus in his account, but leaving a hundred thousand in there."

"That's just weird," Connor said. "I mean, if yous are gonna run, then take *all* the money, and *run!* Or at least, get the maximum amount you can withdraw each day. This don't make no sense."

"But look," Samantha said, pointing at Carson. "He doesn't even check his receipt. He just shoves it in his pocket. I don't think he knows it's in there. He looks like he's in a big hurry to empty his account and get outta there."

"What did you and Bo learn when you went to the bank?" Adam asked.

Samantha crossed her arms in front of her. "Interesting trip," she answered.

"How so?" Adam asked.

Bo spoke. "First, this money was hand-delivered to the Ladue branch of the bank, in *cash.*" He sat back in his chair, letting his words sink in. "I mean *cash!* Who in their right mind goes around with a hundred grand in *cash?*"

"They can't do that, Bo," Adam said. "The Patriot Act won't allow more than a few thousand dollars in cash to go into a bank account, unless you fill out all kinds of paperwork. It's to prevent money laundering and funneling money into terrorist organizations and such."

"Yep. I'm aware. We were able to figure out that it was the comptroller herself who oversaw the deposit and altered the books, but of course, that ain't gonna fly if someone shows up to investigate, which we did."

"What did the comptroller say?" Connor asked.

"Funny thing, about that," Samantha uncrossed her arms and pointed her finger in the air. "Right after that money hit Carson's account, the comptroller decided it was a good time to go on vacation. She seems to have disappeared without a trace."

"Oh, for heaven's sake!" Adam said. He rubbed his temples.

"Which branch did Carson get the money from?" Connor asked. "Where are we lookin'?"

"Southwest City. It's a long walk from Carson's apartment, but it's a short drive from Jalisa Moore's place," Bo answered.

"But Jalisa was only a couple days out of surgery when this took place," Samantha said. "She was still in quite a bit of pain when we interviewed her."

"Yous think maybe Carson's holdin' her against her will, makin' her take him places, or takin' her car?"

Bo shook his head. "I don't know what to think."

"I've got plenty more news for you and Samantha to follow up on," Adam said. "While you were out yesterday, 911 got an interesting call. Report of a bomb. Make that an anonymous report of a bomb. With specific instructions to go to the back door, and that the suspects would be in a gray Chrysler parked across the street in front of the building. Guess where?"

Adam's team looked at him with blank stares. "Carson Hollister's apartment. What do you make of that?"

"I'm thinkin' it makes this Hollister guy look more and more guiltier. I'm thinkin' he's lookin' more and more like a perpetrator and he rigged his place to blow up, so's that he can destroy evidence and set back any efforts to find him," Connor said.

"But why not clean out *all* of your bank account? Or go back the next day for a bank check?" Samantha asked. "I mean, if you're gonna run away, how far do you think you're gonna get with no car and four hundred twenty dollars? I know criminals tend to be pretty stupid, but Carson Hollister is bright. He doesn't fit the type."

Adam stood and faced the group. "There's a lot here that makes no sense. But it is looking like Hollister is involved. We just don't know how or why. The two suspects were in the gray Chrysler, just like the caller said. Kate and Boris got one of them and the other officers got the second guy. They're in holding and all they can say is, No speak English. But nobody believes that." Adam began to pace. "Like I said, when you all were out chasing down your leads and conducting interviews, it was a busy day here as well."

The team leaned forward in their seats as Adam continued. "The tip hotline got a call on the bombing. I've notified Felix and he'll have his team look into that tip as well. They responded to the anonymous tip at Carson's apartment and it was legit."

"What was the second tip?" Bo asked.

Adam snickered. "Said the person responsible would be at a table in Shaw Park." He shook his head. "Dumb, I know, but we gotta follow up every lead. Sounds like a waste of time to me, but Felix will handle it."

"Sounds like your day was pretty full, Adam," Bo said.

"One more thing." Adam held up a finger. "I told you I had lots of news. I want you and Samantha to run this one first today. I got a call from the hospital on Elizabeth Wise. When the nurse went into her room yesterday late morning, shortly after shift change, she found a teddy bear tucked in with her. I grilled the officer guarding the door. He swears the door was always covered and the only people going in or out were doctors and nurses. He said he never left his post and nothing unusual happened during his watch. Only people who worked at the hospital went in that room." Adam looked back and forth between Bo and Samantha. "I want the surveillance tapes from that hallway. The hospital should already have a copy ready and waiting for you at the nurses' station. That young lady needs to be kept safe. Now, get going. See you tomorrow morning. I want some good reports here."

"Weird stuff, huh?" Samantha asked Bo as they headed to the hospital in Bo's cruiser. "I should've asked Adam to have the recordings from the 911 call and the hotline tip call so we could listen to them tomorrow."

Bo smiled at her. "There's already a team assigned to those calls. We don't have the man power to double up on the same jobs. We can grab a bite of lunch after we get the tape. There's some great eats in the Central West End. Oasis Coffee has Middle Eastern food and the best gyros in town. Tortillaria has delicious authentic Mexican. Say, did you talk to your daddy? When do I get to meet him?" He shot a sideways glance at her.

"Oh. Almost forgot. He wants you to come to Sunday dinner this weekend."

"Sunday dinner? Y'all are really kind of old fashioned, aren't you? So it'll be your parents, you, and me?" Bo squirmed in his seat.

Samantha laughed out loud. "Uh…yeah. And my Aunt Su Li and Uncle David, and four of their five children, on account of Hannah's away at college. Unless she comes home for the weekend. Daddy wants to talk to you before everyone gets there."

"And then what? I gotta pass the aunt, uncle, and cousin test?"

She ignored the question and said, "We're out of church at eleven forty-five, and home by twelve fifteen. I suggest you come at twelve twenty, because everyone else will be there at one. That way, if you decide not to stay, you can leave before they get there."

"Church, huh?"

Samantha nodded. "Yeah. And if that scares you more than talking to my father, then you got a bigger problem than I thought."

"Church don't scare me. I was raised in church. Just haven't gone for a while, that's all."

"We're here. I hate being down here so close to lunch time. No place to park. Oh, look," she said, pointing ahead. "They're pulling out. Let's park up there. It's a pretty day. We can walk."

"Samantha Jane," Bo said, as if talking to a child. "We're in a cop car. I say let's park in front of the restaurants and walk across the street to the hospital. Think we'll get a ticket?" His eyes twinkled as he teased her, and he parked the car in the no-parking zone on Euclid, in front of a long row of restaurants.

"I might give you one."

They walked into the hospital and rode the elevator to the nurse's station outside of Elizabeth Wise's room. The guard was sitting by the door, reading a magazine. He looked up when Bo and Samantha approached. "I just came on duty," he told them. "Parker, he was pretty upset. Says he has no idea how that teddy bear showed up in her room. He even asked a nurse to spot him when he took a short bathroom break. But I'm gonna be extra careful."

"Good to know," Bo replied.

They spoke briefly to the nurse who had nothing to add, then picked up the video tape and left the hospital.

"I'm hungry," Bo announced as they walked out the door.

"Stop the presses," Samantha replied. "Hey, isn't there a Vietnamese place down here?"

Bo nodded as they crossed the street. "Yep. Little Saigon. You want that?"

"Yeah. That sounds good. My Aunt Su Li is Vietnamese and I grew up with her cooking. She's a great cook, and can cook foods from all over the world, but she hasn't made Vietnamese food for our Sunday dinners in quite a while. Let's try that."

"You got it. It's just a little further down. It's early in the lunch hour, so we should be able to get a good seat."

"We oughtta move the car, Bo. If nobody else can park here, then we shouldn't, either."

"It's fine. Quit worrying." They walked toward the squad car. "Let's drop the tape in the car on our way."

An angry voice pierced the late-morning calm. "Pig shoot!" The sound of bullets whizzed by Samantha's ears. She and Bo hit the pavement and crouched behind a car, unholstering their nine millimeter Glocks. People on the sidewalks screamed and ran into the businesses that lined the street.

"It's an ambush!" Bo shouted. He leaned into his radio. "Shots fired Euclid north of Forest Park Parkway. Officers under fire. Request immediate back-up. Request immediate back-up!"

"There's three of them," Samantha whispered. She popped up and returned fire, hitting one of the gunmen in the chest. He fell to the ground and she ducked back behind the car.

"Nice shot!"

"Yeah, thanks. There's one at two o'clock. Bo jumped up and shot, but missed.

Samantha shot again and missed. The gunman continued firing at them. Bo crept around toward the front of the car and shot again and hit the man. He fell forward and lay still.

"Where's the other one?" Samantha asked, looking around.

Bo couldn't see him. They both stood slowly, guns drawn, searching for the last of the gunmen. Bo saw him first. The gunman was aiming straight for Samantha.

"*Down!*"

He shot at the gunman while he leapt on top of Samantha, knocking her to the ground. He hit the gunman, but not until the man fired first, hitting Bo.

Samantha felt blood trickle onto her hand as she lay on the sidewalk where Bo had knocked her down and landed on her. She looked up at Bo as he lay on top of her, bleeding. "Bo! Bo! Oh, God! Oh, no! You've been hit!" She grabbed her radio and shouted into it. "Officer down! We need an ambulance! *Now!* Officer down! Euclid, north of Forest Park!" She turned back to Bo. His shirt was staining in a widening pool of blood. The wail of sirens grew closer, but Bo was bleeding out. "Stay with me, Bo! Help is coming!"

The ambulance screeched to a stop while several squad cars surrounded the area. Bo was quickly loaded. Samantha followed, numb from shock, urging him to stay with her. Two paramedics worked feverishly on Bo, as he drifted in and out of consciousness. Samantha heard one of them talking to the ER, less than four blocks away. "Gunshot wound to left lateral chest. I see an entrance wound, but no exit wound. Bullet still in chest." She watched in stunned silence as a large bandage was taped over the hole in the side of her partner's chest. An oxygen mask was placed on Bo's face and an IV started. She heard the paramedic tell the hospital to set up the operating room and have a portable CT scanner available to detect the precise location of the bullet. By the time the paramedic stopped talking, Bo was being taken from the ambulance into the emergency room. A doctor immediately inserted a chest tube and barked orders for several units of blood.

Seconds later, Bo was whisked away on a gurney into a room at the back of the emergency room. The ER doctor explained to Samantha what was going on, that with the bullet still lodged in Bo's chest, the situation was grave. He told her the surgeon would be down soon to talk briefly and then scrub for surgery. Bo was being prepped while they spoke. The ER doctor asked about Bo's family.

"His mother lives in Tennessee. It'll be hours before she can get here. His team is his family, too. Can I see him?"

The surgeon appeared, walking and talking quickly. "No. There's no time. I will perform a thoracotomy—a long incision below the fifth rib to remove the intrathoracic foreign object and insert a chest tube. Once the object is removed, we'll have to explore to determine the extent of any other damage. His ribs will be separated, and he'll be in surgery several hours."

"We'll need the bullet," Samantha said, choking on her words.

The surgeon turned and called over his shoulder, "Not my first rodeo." He left as quickly as he had arrived. Through tear-filled eyes, Samantha saw a team of green-gowned people wheeling Bo away through a set of double doors.

A nurse approached Samantha. "I know it's scary, but your partner is in good hands." The nurse's voice was kind and reassuring. She spoke slowly, as though her words could counteract the whirlwind in which Samantha was caught. "Let me show you to the waiting room. "You'll be updated periodically. When his family arrives, we'll show them where you are. Follow me."

Samantha waited in the surgical waiting room, pacing, sitting, pacing some more, looking out the window, and pacing again. Within minutes, Adam and Connor joined her. Adam informed her that Kate and Boris had stayed in the office to monitor the phone, but would be calling in.

"Dat's a lotta blood," Connor pointed to Samantha's sleeve. He noted the scrapes on her hands where she'd been knocked down, and a bruise forming on her cheek. "Yous wasn't hurt, was you?"

"No. Bo jumped in front of me and caught the bullet meant for me. He saved my life. They gotta save his!" She choked back tears.

Adam took her hand. "Samantha, they're doing all they can for Bo. We're all in this together. Bo's in good hands. How are *you?*"

Samantha took a box of tissues from the table. She dried her tears and blew her nose. She took a deep breath and released a long, measured exhale. "I'm fine," she replied, but her voice was unsteady. "Just worried. Trying to pray, but the worry keeps taking over. They came out of nowhere. It happened so fast. You know why they shot at us, Adam? Wanna know why?"

"Because they saw you get out of a police car. By the time you got back from the hospital, they had time to set up an ambush. Could've been a gang initiation, or someone who thinks the police should have a target on their backs because they're police—and for no other reason."

She nodded and swallowed, staring straight ahead. "Yeah. That's exactly what it was."

"Samantha, I know you're new to my team, new to Homicide, and this is the first time you've discharged your weapon in the line of duty." Adam kept his voice gentle, but a solemn undercurrent could be detected. "Protocol was for you to wait at the scene to give your statement, not go in the ambulance. I know you were upset and shaken, but you can't allow that to cloud your judgment. I've tried to smooth things over with Internal Affairs. It'll just depend on who they assign to this investigation."

Samantha covered her face with her hands and leaned back into the wall. She groaned. "You're right. I wasn't thinking. I—I'm sorry."

Adam nodded and squeezed her shoulder. "I think it'll be okay, given the circumstances. But I did want to give you fair warning."

She nodded.

"I need to call Captain Peterson. He's got two more days of vacation. But he'll shoot *me* if I don't tell him about Bo." Adam sighed and dialed the number. He rose, and dialing his cell phone, left the room.

Samantha sat on the nearest chair, leaning back into her seat, and closed her eyes. Connor stood and walked to the far side of the room to retrieve three coffees for them. It was going to be a long day.

11:14 a.m.

Carson circled the hospital in Jalisa's car. He saw more squad cars than he could count crawling all over the Central West End. "What's going on *now?*" he mumbled under his breath. Paranoid by the recent events in his own life, he parked Jalisa's car close to the MetroLink station one stop past the hospital complex and took the MetroLink back toward Barnes. A slight inconvenience, he told himself, but he didn't want to get bogged down amid a sea of police cars—especially when they were looking for him. But as a moth flies toward a flame, Carson had to see Lizzie.

He got off the train at the hospital and followed the same procedure as he had the last time, ducking into the Staff Only door and grabbing a white coat, double-checking that the name was not that of a female doctor. He passed the gift shop on his way to the elevators, doubled back when he saw the perfect gift, and entered. Carson knew that Lizzie was an animal lover. He saw a stuffed, fluffy white puppy with a red and white heart collar on it. Little red hearts were sewn onto the toy's chest with puppy love get-well messages on them. He paid for his purchase and tucked the gift under the lab coat, which today belonged to Jonathan Gatesworth, M.D. As he exited the elevator, he saw the uniformed officer still guarding the door to Lizzie's room. He dug out his cell phone and, walking toward her room, once again pretended to be having an important conversation, as he nodded to the guard and closed the door behind him.

He pulled a chair next to Lizzie's bed. Carson's heart sank as he noted no change at all in her condition. He didn't see the little bear he'd left a couple days earlier. He touched her arm and rubbed it lightly. "Lizzie, I don't know how much longer I can get away with this. Please wake up. Please get better." Fighting back tears, Carson rose and brushed his lips against her forehead. Lizzie did not move. "Please come back, Lizzie." He tucked the stuffed puppy next to her, straightened the covers, and left.

As Carson rounded the corner toward the elevator, he got a creepy feeling that he was being watched. The hair on the back of his neck stood up. Staring straight ahead, Carson quickened his pace and heard footsteps coming up fast behind him. He broke into a run, passed the elevators and started down the stairwell.

Sam Hernandez ran after him. "Jor—Carson, wait! Please don't run!"

But Carson Hollister was flying down the stairs as fast as he could, jumping over the last several steps, shedding the lab coat mid-air and leaving it where it lay. Once he was outside of the building, he broke into a full-speed run. Only when he'd gotten halfway back to the MetroLink station, did he dare to look back. He saw a well-groomed man wearing a suit, with salt and pepper hair, looking around. Carson hurried to the platform. He could hear the train coming. His eyes met Sam's over the crowd, and Sam ran toward the platform. The doors of the MetroLink train opened and Carson, running as fast as he could, jumped in as the doors started to close. He looked out the window as Sam, winded from running, reached the platform as the train pulled away.

"Sir, there'll be another train in about seven, eight minutes. You okay, sir?"

Sam, out of breath, looked behind him. A MetroLink guard was approaching him.

"Yeah, yeah. I'm fine," Sam answered, trying to slow his breathing. "Can you tell me where that train is going?"

"That one's goin' east to Shiloh, Illinois," the guard answered.

"Thanks," Sam said. He turned to climb the steps and hurried to his car.

"Next train'll be along real soon," the guard called out after him, but Sam didn't turn around to acknowledge him.

Once he reached his car, Sam turned on the engine. Having no idea which of the many stops between the Central West End and Shiloh, Illinois was Carson's, he shut off the engine, and walked back to the hospital, frustrated. He had come to interview as many of the MSR victims as he could find. Seeing Jordan there, wearing a hospital lab coat, of all things, was a clue Sam felt certain his adversary didn't have.

Carson got off the train at the first stop past the hospital and scanned the area, breathing hard. The man who had chased him was not there. Most of the people milling about the train stop appeared to be students, laden with back packs and wearing headphones. Being extra cautious, Carson walked to where he'd parked Jalisa's car. He popped the hood and looked for signs of explosives. He crawled as far under the car as he could to see if anything looked amiss, then checked under the seat. Satisfied the car showed no signs of tampering, Carson got in and raced off. Not seeing the man in the suit, he slowed the car. *No sense in getting a ticket. Just blend in.*

He stopped at an ATM to check his bank balance. The hundred thousand dollars was still in his account. *It's got to be a trap! I'm not biting. Unless I can figure out an exit strategy. But I can't leave Lizzie.*

Carson drove toward the offices of MSR and parked a block away. His heart was still pounding from the chase, but he felt confident he'd gotten away. *This time.*

The Central West End was buzzing with workers hurrying back to their offices after lunch, dog walkers, sometimes with five or six dogs hooked to a leash, and a handful of students out of class. He approached the office of Medical Staffing Remedies. The yellow police tape had been removed. A piece of plywood covered the front door, but the walls of windows had already been replaced. Carson could see inside, and slowed his pace. New drywall had replaced the bullet-riddled walls, as the mudding cured in anticipation of fresh paint. Repairs to the reception desk were completed. The floor, however, had not yet been replaced. Carson saw dark stains by Lizzie's desk. He remembered that Heavens to Murgatroid had stood close to Lizzie. He didn't know whose blood had left the sickening marks, but he supposed it was a mixture of Miriam's and Lizzie's. Carson felt as though a knife had stabbed him. He turned away and walked back to the car.

2:08 p.m.

"How's Lizzie?" Jalisa asked Carson as she opened the door of her apartment.

Carson plodded to the sofa and sat down with a thud. "No change." His voice was flat.

"No change means she's not worse, Carson," Jalisa offered in encouragement. "At least she's still fighting."

Carson tried to smile. "A man was there. At the hospital. He chased me. I barely got away."

Jalisa's eyes widened. "Was he a cop?"

Carson shrugged. "I don't know. I don't think so. He didn't say he was a cop. He knew my name."

"He didn't have a gun, did he? Did he try to hurt you?"

Carson shook his head. "No. He was actually polite. He asked me not to run. Even said please. Older guy, wore a suit."

He stood and trotted to the kitchen, returning with two glasses of water. Handing one to Jalisa, Carson sat on the sofa.

"I stopped by the office. It's still a mess, but you can see a lot of progress has already been made. New drywall up. It'll likely be painted tomorrow. Door's still boarded up, but the new windows are in. Looked like a pretty big crew working in there. The carpet and hardwood floors were taken up, so all you see is sub-floor." Carson looked toward the window. "There's dark stains on the sub-floor in front of Lizzie's desk." He looked at his lap and mumbled, "I'm sure it's blood."

Jalisa patted Carson on his shoulder and eased herself into her reclining chair. "The partners sure aren't wasting any time getting the office back together."

Carson shrugged again. "They've got an insurance policy that says in the event of an emergency, the employees still get paid." He snorted a half-laugh. "I guess if they're paying us, then they want us back to work as soon as possible, right? It's my guess that policy was in the event of a tornado, flood, or fire—something along those lines. Nobody could've ever predicted an attack like this." He took a long drink of water. "By the way, all that money is still in my account, can you believe it?"

Jalisa's eyes bugged and she shook her head. "I don't get it at all! Carson, is there something you haven't told me? How many people are after you, anyway? No. Never mind. You probably don't even know how many. You *must've* done *somethin'*. All these people, all of a sudden, after you! What are you hiding?"

"Jalisa! *Nothing!* I swear to you! I don't know. I can't answer your questions. You think the police aren't going to ask me that and more? Like how does a hundred grand miraculously appear in my bank account? What do you think—I don't *wanna* talk to the cops? I can't answer anything they'll ask! Yet, I'd really appreciate a little protection—but I don't even know from whom!" Carson stood and paced.

Jalisa was silent for a few seconds. "Know what I'd do?"

Carson looked at her with one eyebrow raised, and sat back down. Miss Buttons jumped into his lap and pressed herself against his chest. He stroked her soft fur and she calmed his spirit. "What?"

"I'd wait until the bank closes, and I'd go and empty out that account from the ATM, even if you had to go to several ATMs, and get outta Dodge! You can go pretty far with that much cash. Maybe go where no one could ever find you."

"Brilliant, Jalisa. Abandon Lizzie? Abandon my mother? Run away from—who even *knows* who I'm running away from! Besides, what do you wanna bet that money was planted there, and as soon as I withdraw it, some kind of alert goes out and next thing, I'm dead. Or accused of stealing something that isn't mine. I have no idea where that money came from. At first, I thought it was a banking error. But there's been more than enough time to discover a mistake like that." Carson sank back into the sofa cushions and closed his eyes.

"Did you ask the bank?"

Carson kept his eyes closed as he shook his head. "No. I'm too afraid that if I say anything, there'll be trouble. I can't figure this out. I don't know what to do."

Jalisa stood and changed the subject. "Aunt Mae brought a casserole. It's really good. Want some?"

"Yeah, I'm hungry. And that's another thing. How long can I keep staying with you? I bet the office opens in a couple more weeks. What then?"

Carson stood and followed Jalisa into the kitchen. She reheated a chicken and vegetable casserole, and they sat to eat. "Then, I guess, you'll either have to eat my cooking, or cook something yourself," Jalisa answered him, trying to lighten the mood. "I told Aunt Mae she didn't need to bring anything else, as I'm feelin' quite a bit better and gettin' around without pain. I haven't even taken a pain pill today, yet."

Carson smiled. "That's great. Jalisa, I appreciate all you've done for me. I don't know where I could have gone."

Jalisa waved her hand in the air. "No worries. You're no problem, and it's been helpful having you here." She took a bite of casserole. "Mmm. Not too sure what'll happen when Malcolm comes home for Thanksgiving. *If* he comes home, anyway. You been able to check on your mom?"

Carson sighed. "I drove by the home where she's living. A cop car was right in front. So I turned around and left." He shook his head. "I should call." He shoveled a large forkful of casserole into his mouth. "Your Aunt Mae is really a good cook!"

Jalisa swallowed her last bite and wiped her mouth with a napkin. "You should see Thanksgiving! Stay here much longer, and you just might!"

Carson leaned back in his chair and closed his eyes. "Mmm. Thanksgiving. This is the first holiday season without my dad, and since my mom got…you know…Alzheimer's. She made the best everything—sweet potatoes, mashed potatoes, stuffing, turkey, homemade cranberry sauce, green beans, and pies—lots of pies. We'd eat the leftovers nearly 'til Christmas!"

"What were you gonna do this year?" Jalisa asked.

Carson shrugged. "Cloverlawn has a Thanksgiving meal they put on for the residents and their families. It won't be anything like home, but we can eat together. Assuming I'm still alive by then."

"I'd invite you to Aunt Mae's. She cooks enough for a small country, you know. But she'd have a lot of questions. And I do mean *a lot!*" Jalisa stood and cleared the table. "But I can bring home all kinds of leftovers, if you want. She'll probably dish them up and send them with me, anyway."

Carson tried to smile. He stood to help clean up. "Sounds good. But I'm hoping that this mess will be resolved by then."

5:49 p.m.

The sun began its timeless descent, casting a soft orange glow through the waiting room at the hospital, warming the chill of Autumn. The door opened and a short, frail looking woman with white hair pulled into a loose bun, entered, leaning on a cane. A younger woman in her late forties followed her and helped her to a seat.

Adam stood and walked to the women. His voice was soft and kind as he pulled a chair toward her and sat facing them. "Mrs. Whitney, I don't know if you remember me, but…"

The older woman looked at Adam with tears in her eyes. She spoke with a soft Southern voice. "Of course I know who you are, Adam Trent. We met when Bowman got his promotion to detective. Bo talks about you all the time." Tears spilled onto the woman's cheeks. Her daughter placed her arm around her mother's shoulders and gently squeezed.

"He's still in surgery, ma'am, but Bo's a fighter. We've had a nurse come in twice to give us an update, and he's still fighting." Adam patted the woman's hand. He turned to Connor and Samantha, and motioned for them to come over.

"Mrs. Whitney, this is the rest of Bo's team. This is Connor and Samantha. Samantha was with him when he was shot. This is Bo's mother, Annabelle Whitney, and his sister, JoBeth."

Annabelle's face lit up. "So *you're* Samantha Jane? Bo's told me so much about you." She reached for Samantha's hand and held it. "Bo was right, honey. You are beautiful."

Samantha swallowed hard, embarrassed. "Nice to meet you," she said. "I'm sorry it's under such terrible circumstances."

"Do you want to stay at Bo's apartment?" Adam asked Annabelle. "I've got a key."

JoBeth answered for her mother. "No, thank you. There's a hotel right next to the hospital. That'd be preferable. We don't know our way around the big city, and this way we can walk to any place we need and still be close to Bo." JoBeth's voice was quiet. Adam thought she looked tired, and figured she had driven the whole trip.

Adam nodded and handed her his card. "I understand. If you need anything, anything at all while you're here, you call my cell phone anytime, day or night, understand?"

"That's mighty kind of you," Annabelle said. "We just need to know Bo's gonna be okay. He's my baby, you know. One of those surprise blessings. Quite an age difference between him and JoBeth." She paused and sighed. "I've already buried three of my children." Annabelle looked away and brushed a tear from her cheek. "I can't lose another." Her hand shook as she took a tissue from her purse.

"Mama. We haven't lost Bo. He's in good hands and Adam just told us he's fighting," JoBeth said, rubbing her mother's shoulders. "And we all know that Bo ain't one to lose a fight, now, is he?"

Annabelle looked up at her daughter and smiled through her tears. She patted her daughter's hand and shook her head.

Connor left and re-appeared with coffee for the group. "If yous are hungry, I can show yous lots of good places to eat," he offered.

"Thank you kindly, but I believe we'll likely stay here and eat at the hospital," Annabelle answered.

The group sat in silence. A team from the crime lab had taken the bullet once it was retrieved from Bo's chest, along with his bloody clothing, and placed them in an evidence bag. Several other officers and detectives from the Clark Street headquarters stopped by to check on Bo, but there was no news. Samantha gave her statement more than once, but could not remember to whom. She was verbally reprimanded for breaking protocol at the scene, but the investigator from IA appeared to have a modicum of sympathy, and she was left with a warning and reprimand, but no additional consequence for her breach. The warning and reprimand would remain in her personnel file for three years and if there were no additional incidents, it would be expunged.

The group gathered in the surgical waiting room repeatedly glanced at the clock, counting the hours Bo was in surgery, hanging on to any shred of hope they could muster. The wait seemed interminable.

Finally, the door opened, and the group looked up expectantly as the tall surgeon Samantha met hours earlier strode toward them. He appeared tired, as he pulled a chair close and faced Bo's team and family. They all sat forward in their seats.

"I'm Dr. Brock," the surgeon began. "I met you in the ER," he nodded to Samantha. Turning to Annabelle and JoBeth, he said, "Are you Mr. Whitney's family?" They nodded. "Is it all right to speak in front of his co-workers?"

Annabelle smiled sweetly. "They're his family, too. We all love Bo." She winked at Samantha Jane. "How is my son?"

If he pulls through, I just may kill him myself, Samantha thought to herself.

Dr. Brock took a breath and cleared his throat. "Mr. Whitney is in recovery now. He's serious, but stable. It was no small miracle that no additional organs were involved, other than his lung. A larger caliber bullet would have killed him. Of that, I'm certain. Most bullet wounds that land in the chest go into the heart. Mr. Whitney was *very* lucky. Four units of blood were needed. Once he's stable enough to leave the recovery room, he'll be moved to the Intensive Care Unit. He'll be sedated, intubated and on a ventilator with two chest tubes. One will drain the blood from his lung and the other will treat his pneumothorax."

"What's dat mean?" Connor asked.

"Collapsed lung," Dr. Brock answered.

"Bo keeps himself in excellent condition." Adam said. "Won't that help him to recover?"

"He'll probably recover a little faster than most, but his recovery will be quite a bit more painful than most. Mr. Whitney has a great deal of muscle mass, meaning there was a lot more muscle we had to cut through and separate during the surgery. That's going to make his recovery very painful." Dr. Brock looked from one worried face to another. "That's what morphine's for. We're going to keep him as comfortable as possible."

"Is he gonna make a complete recovery? I mean, be able to come back to work?" Samantha asked.

Dr. Brock nodded. "He's going to be our guest here for about ten days. Then he'll gradually increase his activity. We'll encourage him to walk and to do some limited weight lifting on his left side. I'll be monitoring his progress. Then he'll go to physical therapy for about four weeks. He can have light duty at six weeks, and he should be back to full duty in three months." He looked over the rapt audience. "Any questions?"

"When can we see him?" JoBeth asked.

"He'll be in recovery about two more hours, then up to ICU. He can have visitors in the morning, but only two at a time, and no more than fifteen minutes each visit, tops. The nurses *will* enforce that. This was a very serious injury. Any other questions?" The group shook their heads. Dr. Brock stood to leave. "You folks take care and get some rest. Mr. Whitney is lucky. He has you all to care for him, and he had an angel watching over him." He grinned. "He also had a really great surgeon." He turned and left.

Annabelle and JoBeth stood. The others followed suit. "It was a long drive to St. Louis," Annabelle said. Her voice sounded weak and she seemed unsteady on her feet. Her cane wobbled beneath her hand. "The doctor said we can't see Bowman until tomorrow, so I think I'd like a little soup and some rest. I'm so thankful he's going to be all right." She wiped her face with a tissue, dabbing at her eyes.

JoBeth supported her mother and gave Samantha, Adam, and Connor a small, tired smile. "Mama's right. We need to get some rest. It was a hard trip. Most important thing is, he made it through the surgery okay. Knowing that much sure brings a little peace."

Connor took a wheelchair from the corner of the waiting room and brought it for Annabelle. "I'll stay right with yous until yous are settled in your hotel." He looked up at Adam. "I'll take care of the ladies, Adam. See yous in the morning." He settled Annabelle into the wheelchair, arranging her sweater and coat around her.

"Thanks, Connor. Don't come in early. Get some rest and I'll see you whenever you get in. Goodnight, Mrs. Whitney, Miss Whitney."

"Oh, Adam! We're just Annabelle and JoBeth. We're all family here. We're so relieved that our Bo will be all right." She turned to Samantha and smiled. "Samantha Jane, it was lovely meeting you. And Connor, you're just sweeter than pie, takin' such good care of us. Goodnight." Annabelle waved, and JoBeth mouthed, "Thank you," and followed Connor as he pushed the wheelchair.

Adam turned to Samantha. "I talked to Cap earlier. You've had enough stress for the day. Go home, grab a bite of dinner and you're off work for two days, got it?"

Samantha produced a weak smile. "Thanks, Adam. See ya."

Samantha left the waiting room and stopped at the restroom before leaving the hospital. She straightened her uniform and tried to scrub Bo's blood from her shirt sleeve, but only made a bigger mess. Splashing water on her face, she looked at herself in the mirror. The large scrape on her cheek was puffing and discoloring, working its way into a huge shiner. Smaller scrapes decorated her other cheek, chin, and hands, with a large cut on her right hand. *Not exactly my best look.* She smoothed her hair and shrugged. *Not exactly my worst look, either.* She reloaded her firearm and gasped. Her gun was empty after the shootout; a dangerous fact she hadn't realized.

Samantha stopped again in the main floor lobby and called her father, but a recording answered, saying the number had been disconnected. "That's weird," she mumbled. "What gives?" She called her mother's cell phone and Su Li answered. "Hi, Samantha. Your father got a new phone, and your mom's out taking Wolfgang for a walk," Su Li said and gave her Sam's number. Samantha thought it odd, but didn't ask any questions. Weariness settled over her, and she dialed again. Her father answered.

"Dad?" she asked, fighting back tears, as the events of the day fell hard on her.

"Honey, what's wrong? Are you okay?" Sam's voice was comforting, and Samantha started to cry.

"Where are you?" her father asked.

"Can I come home for dinner? Grilled cheese is fine. I don't really care. I just wanna talk to you."

"Your mom is spending a few nights at Su Li's. I'll explain later. Let's meet. You've always loved La Bonne Bouchee. I can be there in twenty minutes. How's that sound?"

Samantha pulled herself together. La Bonne Bouchee sounded wonderful—the height of comfort food. "On my way, Dad. See you soon."

Samantha walked the short few blocks toward where the cruiser was parked. She had no choice but to drive it. Her own car was in the lot on Clark Street, behind headquarters. As she drew near, she surveyed the area, listening. The yellow crime tape had been removed. Aside from broken glass littering the street and sidewalk, there was no sign of the ambush and shootout that had occurred hours earlier. The Central West End nightlife was awakening, its music, noises, and traffic growing louder. Rich aromas of pizza, burgers, and spicy foods from around the world wafted through the neighborhood, inviting anyone breathing to come and partake. The sudden sound of a case of wine dropping on a floor nearby made Samantha jump. She froze and held her breath, her eyes darting left and right. She heard cursing and yelling over the dropped wine and swallowed with relief. Exhaling, Samantha walked up and down both sides of the street before approaching the police car. Nothing seemed suspicious or out of the ordinary. She was grateful the police tow truck had not yet removed the car, or she would have had to find transportation.

She walked toward the driver's side, noting bullet holes in the front fender. The back driver's side window had been shot out and shattered glass lay in the back seat of the car and along the street. She checked the tires and was relieved they had not been flattened. Samantha got in the car, sped away toward Highway 40 and drove westbound. She took 270 northbound and exited at Olive, turning left to travel the short distance to the restaurant. She hoped it would still be open and serving dinner.

The parking lot was nearly empty. She didn't see her father's car, but she saw her father standing in front of the door of La Bonne Bouchee. *I ought to give him a speeding ticket. There's no way he could have legally beat me here.*

Sam stood in front of the restaurant, his eyes scanning the parking lot, searching for his daughter's car. He saw the squad car pull in and noted the damage. With a lump in his throat, he ran to her while she parked, reaching the driver's side door as Samantha got out of the car.

"What. Happened." It was more a statement than a question. Sam hugged Samantha close to his chest and she sobbed. "Are they still open? I'm hungry," she told him.

Sam half-laughed and put his arm around her. "I paid the staff extra to stay. I told them it was an emergency."

"And that worked?" She looked at her father in disbelief.

Sam shrugged. "Looks like it."

The famous Sam Hernandez charm. Works every time, she thought.

They went inside and took their seats. Sam ordered the Vol-au-Vent with a cup of French Onion soup and Samantha ordered the soup and salad combo. In the light of the restaurant, Sam noted his daughter's scraped hands and the bruise on her cheek. "So, what's the other guy look like?"

"Daddy!"

Sam's smile faded. She hadn't called him Daddy since the ninth grade. Sam grew serious and lowered his voice. "All right, honey, I'm listening."

She told him about the ambush and about Bo saving her life and being in the ICU after a long, risky surgery.

"That's some partner, Samantha. He's very brave."

She grinned at her father. "Oh, he's braver than that, Dad."

Sam raised his eyebrows. "Meaning?"

"He agreed to talk to you."

"So? I talk to Adam, and to Gavin—Captain Peterson. Pretty sure I've talked to Bo and Connor as well, at some point."

Samantha shook her head. "Not that kind of talk. *The* talk." She paused and moved her napkin to her lap. "He wants to ask me out. I told him he had to ask you first. It took him a little while to agree, but then he told me to go ahead and set it up, so I set it up for Sunday, before our dinner. That's braver than being shot."

Sam sat back in his chair and assumed a poker face. "I see."

The waitress brought their meal and set it before them.

"Just what kind of guy *is* Bo? Besides brave." Sam took a bite of dinner.

"Southern. Very Southern. Drawls and says, y'all, stuff like that. Stuck on himself. Big time. Thinks he's God's gift to women. Flirts with anything in a skirt. Incorrigible, I suppose. Arrogant—but in a funny sort of way. Great sense of humor and bugs Connor to no end." She gulped down her water and shrugged at her father. "But we all work well together. He's a good cop."

Sam set down his fork and crossed his arms in front of his chest. He furrowed his brow and stroked his mustache. "And you wanna go out with him, *why?*"

"He's *really* kind and sweet to animals."

Sam rubbed his face with his hands and sighed. "You and your mother," he mumbled, looking suddenly tired.

Samantha giggled in spite of her pain, and Sam shook his head.

"It's funny you were at Barnes today. I was, too. Working on my case. Sounds like we might have just missed each other. I guess I must've left before the excitement." Sam took another bite. "How's your dinner?"

Samantha picked at her food. "I guess I'm not as hungry as I thought. I just wanted to talk to you. It's been a pretty horrible day, and I'm worried about Bo." She nibbled at her salad. "So is this that big case you've been so excited about? The missing heir?"

"Yeah. I've been gathering information. Nothing too exciting, although getting this guy is proving a little more difficult than I thought." He looked his daughter over. "Do your hands hurt?"

Samantha nodded. "They sting a little bit. I'll put something on them when I get home. I'm just kind of sore all over. Bo saw the third gunman first and jumped on top of me to cover me. He knocked me down on the pavement. But like I said, his quick thinking and quicker action saved me." She began to pick the cheese off the side of the soup cup. "We're also looking for someone who's been pretty hard to find. Criminal matter." She shrugged and waved her hand. "Goes with the territory, I guess. And now that Bo's out of commission, we're short a detective."

Her throat swelled as she choked back tears, and she swallowed some soup to soothe it.

"I'm just grateful you weren't hurt worse. I've been shot twice. It's no picnic. Your mother will have a fit when I tell her, you know."

"So you have to tell Mom?"

"Honey, what do *you* think? She'll find out one way or another, at any rate, and she'll be hurt when she learns I kept something like this from her. I'm afraid this is non-negotiable. I'll try to downplay it."

Samantha nodded and took another bite of soup, digging for the cheese at the bottom of the cup more than the broth. "Yeah, I suppose. I just don't want her to worry."

Sam smiled at her. "That goes with the territory. It's called parenthood. What were you and Bo doing at the hospital?"

"Checking on witnesses, picking up evidence."

"Are you okay to drive home? You wanna come back to the house with me?"

"I'm fine. I'm really tired and need some rest." She looked down at her lap and sighed. "What if Bo doesn't get better?"

"Then he'll be spared from having to talk to me."

"Funny. Hey, why is Mom staying at Su Li's?" She took a bite of salad.

Sam leaned back in his chair. "My case has gotten too dangerous for her to be at the house. I won't worry about her if she's at Su Li's. Wolfgang's with her."

Samantha snorted. "Big help, there. Goofy dog. Adam's got a friend in the K-9 unit, Kate Marlin. Now *she's* got a dog! Big German Shepherd named Boris. He's as big as Fred was, but has more black in his face and ears. Pretty boy. Not as pretty as Fred, though. That was one great dog." She pushed her half-eaten food away and stood. "Thanks for talking, Dad. Sorry I dragged you all the way out here, especially when you're working on such a sensitive case."

Sam stood, nodded to their server, and left a large amount of money on the table, a thank-you for keeping the kitchen open late. He put his arm around Samantha. "Honey, I'm never too busy for you. Not for you and not for your mother. Not ever. You be careful going home. For that matter, give me a call when you get to your place. I wanna know you're safe. Promise?"

She reached up and kissed her father on his cheek and hugged him. "I promise, Daddy. Thanks for dinner. Goodnight."

Sam walked her to the car and watched as she left the parking lot and drove east on Olive toward the city. He felt a sharp pain in his chest as he walked to his car. He tried to steady his breathing while he held on to the door handle. He opened the car door and sat down. The pain in his chest remained. *This is not a heart attack. Not yet, anyway. I could have lost her today and there was nothing I could do to protect her.*

Sam took a few deep breaths, leaned back and closed his eyes. *Chest pain. I should go to the ER. This is nothing more than stress. I don't have time for this.* He rubbed his temples. *Julie was right. We should have made her practice more. She should have gone to Juilliard.*

9:14 p.m.

Samantha drove toward her apartment in the city, but abruptly changed her mind, passed her exit and continued toward the hospital. She parked in the covered garage, as close to the entrance door as she could, next to the handicapped spots. She was tired and her body ached, but she knew she could never rest until she was confident her partner was out of danger.

She pressed the elevator button to one of the ICU floors, walked to the nurses' station and, not seeing protection outside the patient doors, asked where Bo's room was. He had to have been out of the recovery room by now. It was nearly ten o'clock. The nurse eyed Samantha with suspicion, frowning over her glasses, and peppered her with questions, then informed her it was past visiting hours, and reminded her that she was not family. Samantha flashed her badge—and her temper. "*This* says I *am* family. He's got a cop outside his door. You can either tell me where his room is, or I'll walk around until I find it myself." She stared at the nurse like a hungry tiger about to pounce on its meal.

"Down this hallway, make a right and go to the end of the hall. There's a second ICU that's set up like this one. You'll see the room," came the nurse's curt reply. She turned her back on Samantha and flipped through a medical chart.

Samantha followed the nurse's directions and saw a uniformed cop sitting outside the door of Bo's room, at the second nursing station, which, like the first, was set in a circular pattern with the nurses in the middle and the rooms around the perimeter. She hurried around the circle and spoke to the officer. "Bo's my partner," she said, showing her badge.

The officer nodded. "Far as I know, he's still sleeping. Detective Trent is in there. Go ahead."

She opened the door and peeked in. Dr. Brock had prepared Bo's family and team as to what they should expect, but it was still hard for Samantha to see her partner lying still, with tubes and an IV. A nurse was standing beside the far side of the bed typing information into the computer. Adam sat in a chair near the other side of the bed.

"How is he?" Samantha asked in a voice just above a whisper.

The nurse turned around and smiled at her. "He's holding his own. He's been through a lot, but he's resting comfortably. He'll wake up when he's ready, but the longer he sleeps, the faster he'll recover. He'll be in a lot of pain once he's conscious. We're going to try and avoid that as much as possible. If he wakes while you're here, you'll have fifteen minutes to visit, and then you'll need to leave."

The nurse finished tending to Bo and left the room. Samantha pulled a chair beside Adam. "He just got back from the recovery room about twenty minutes ago. I thought you were going home to bed?"

Samantha shook her head. "Go home and do what? Sleep? Don't think so." She pointed to a basket sitting on a table. "What's that?"

Adam reached for the basket, and handed it to Samantha. "Jenna—my wife, believes that two things make every problem more bearable. Food and prayer, but not necessarily in that order. She packed some nice sandwiches, cookies, and a thermos of coffee in the event I, and a third world country to be named later, faced starvation at the biggest hospital complex in the state." He offered the basket to Samantha.

Samantha shook her head. "Just ate. I needed to talk to my dad. But coffee sounds good." She reached for the thermos and Adam handed her a cup.

"Jenna, Amy, and Blue are home saying prayers."

"Who's Blue?" she asked, sipping the coffee. "Mmm. She ought to make this down at the station. Much better than the sludge we get!"

Adam smiled. He looked tired. His eyelids were heavy and his eyes were red from strain. Faded frown lines etched his face, and stubble covered his cheeks. "Blue's the family dog. Amy's dog, really. They're inseparable. She's a pit bull of some kind. Been with us forever."

"Yeah, I'm a dog person. Grew up with anything that followed us home. We had a German Shepherd, cats, and even a little fox who was orphaned and found her way to our back porch. Mom fed her and nursed her back to health. Released her into the woods, but she showed up every day for years, waiting for food. We even got her a little ball to play with. It was cute." Samantha looked at Bo and swallowed, pressing her lips together. "Is he gonna make it?" She leaned back into her chair and squeezed her eyes shut, forcing her tears to retreat.

"My crystal ball's in the shop, but his numbers are good, and the doctor sounded positive," Adam said. He looked at Bo lying still and silent as machines beeped and hummed. "One thing I know about Bo. He's a fighter. And he's tough. He can be a bit of a jerk sometimes, especially around attractive women, but he's a good man. When he's not being a jerk, that is."

Samantha raised an eyebrow and sat back in her chair. "Sounds like you know more than *one* thing about Bo."

"I had a few reservations about putting you two together on this case. But Connor's computer skills are superior to, well, everybody's, so I couldn't afford to take him away from where he shines the brightest. Kate's availability is fleeting. She's not homicide, she's K-9, but she pops in to help sometimes, if she's available." He chuckled. "There's another dog person for you."

"Yeah," Samantha relaxed. Adam was easy to talk to. At least in a crisis. "Bo and me—we're fine, Adam. No problem. No worries." She felt tears welling in her eyes again. "He took a bullet for me, you know. That should be me lying there, or maybe even in a casket. I'm a lot smaller than Bo. He saved my life." She looked away as a tear escaped, running down her cheek and landing in her lap. "Ah!" she shrugged. "That might be worth dinner and a movie." She smiled at Adam. "As long as he pays." Samantha was quiet for a few moments. "At least we got those guys. Small comfort, but it's something. They really got off a lot of shots." She looked at her hands in her lap.

Adam studied his new detective. "You got three of them, Samantha," he said.

She jerked her head up. "What do you mean?"

"Three of your attackers were killed in the shoot-out. Two more took off after their buddies dropped. Cowards always run. But we caught them."

"We never saw the other two." She leaned her head back and covered her face with her hands.

"St. Louis is in a season of violence," Adam said. Samantha straightened up in her chair and reached for more coffee as she listened to Adam. "Our country is in a season of violence. It's open season on cops. If that's not bad enough, we're more and more limited in how we can respond, even if it's to save our own lives, or that of our partners…or innocent civilians. The media has an anti-cop feeding frenzy every time there's an officer-involved shooting, and in their typical sensation-seeking m.o., they report whatever sells. They don't even bother to fact-check, or *try* to ascertain any truth. It's all about the ratings, or their own agenda, and that comes at the expense of truth." Adam shook his head. "We've got good cops leaving the minute they've earned their retirement. Recruitment is down, and some of our younger men and women are leaving the force for other types of jobs altogether. Who are people gonna call when they need help? If something doesn't change, we're eventually gonna descend into total anarchy."

"I've never heard you sound so disillusioned, Adam," Samantha said.

"You haven't been a cop nearly as long as I have," he answered. "Captain Peterson is one of the reasons our team has lasted as long as it has and been as happy as we are. Cap always has our back. He'll go to the wall to defend us. He fights for us, and when we're outta line, he's the one who'll bust our chops—so nobody else has to. You'll see soon enough. He's on his way back here. I hated to tell him about Bo because Captain Peterson hasn't had a vacation in years, but this," he pointed to Bo, "This couldn't wait." Adam shook his head. "We're all afraid Cap's gonna retire soon. What happens after that, nobody wants to find out."

The nurse entered Bo's room. "Sorry to interrupt, but there's a Gavin Peterson outside. I realize my patient is unconscious, but I still have to abide by ICU policy. No more than two visitors at a time in a room."

Adam and Samantha stood. "We understand. We'll both go out to see him," Adam said. The nurse nodded and left. Adam chuckled and put his hand on Samantha's shoulder. "Right on cue, huh?" They stepped into the hall.

"Cap." Adam shook his hand. "Samantha Hernandez has already started on her first big case and is doing a fine job. She was an excellent choice."

Samantha and Captain Gavin Peterson shook hands. "Good to see you, Detective Hernandez. I would've been here sooner, but Melanie wanted to go home first and prepare some food for the team while we wait on Bo."

Adam put his hands in the air. "Jenna beat her to it. I've got enough food here, even if the entire precinct shows up."

"Great," Captain Peterson said. "Let me text her so she can go to bed. Of course, she won't, you know."

Adam nodded. "Cop wives."

Captain Peterson looked up from his phone. "How is he?"

Adam filled him in while the two of them stepped into the room to see Bo. Samantha waited outside in the hall, fidgeting. The men emerged several minutes later.

"I'll stay the night if you want to go home," Samantha told Adam. "Oh!" she said and snapped her fingers. "Bo has a cat. She'll need to be fed, watered, and have her litter box cleaned."

"Let's see if we can't find a key for his place," Captain Peterson answered. "I'll take the cat home and Mel and I can look after it until Bo's able. That'd make more sense than having someone go over there every day. Melanie's home most of the time. She'll enjoy the company."

"Her name's Penelope," Samantha added.

Adam turned to Samantha. "I've got a key. Cap and I will take care of the kitty, if you want to stay a while. Call me if anything happens."

The men left. Samantha returned to Bo's bedside and sat in the chair Adam had vacated earlier. She stared at the tubes and medical paraphernalia and listened to the machines, their rhythmic beeping, the numbers flashing, lines flickering in patterns foreign to her. She looked at Bo, lying helpless, and prayed for him to recover. Samantha also felt helpless and shook her hands at the unfamiliar emotion. "If you weren't such a jerk about parking the squad car illegally, we might have still been arguing over talking to my father, you know," she began. "And we'd have got lunch. The car's all shot up and I haven't even reported it yet." She paused. The machines continued humming and beeping. "Captain Peterson's got Penelope. I'll call that vet and find out about the puppy you—we—rescued." She stood and paced. "You're costing me my beauty sleep." Samantha sighed and looked around the room. Sterile. Barren, save for necessities only. Fresh flowers weren't allowed in the ICU rooms. She turned her gaze back to Bo. "I met your mom and your sister. They're worried sick." She slumped into a chair and stared at the monitors.

Day 5

6:47 a.m.

The sun rose, and blazing yellow shone through the small parting of the curtains in Bo's room. Samantha hadn't realized she'd been up all night. She stretched and paced. The clock on the far wall indicated it was almost seven a.m. Tired and achy, Samantha sat back in the chair beside Bo's bed. "And what the heck have you been telling your mother about me? You really are an arrogant jerk, you know?" her voice caught and she looked down at her lap, fighting back tears. She rose and walked to the window, peering out the curtains at the parking lot below.

"I love you, too, Samantha Jane," a weak, raspy voice whispered from the bed.

Samantha turned and faced Bo. He looked like he was still asleep. "Bo?"

Bo opened one eye. His throat hurt from the intubation, which he had removed by himself. "I'd say you're beautiful when you're mad, but the truth is, you look like hell, honey."

I am so *gonna kill him when he's better!*

"You don't look so good yourself," she replied.

"What time is it?" he asked.

"Almost seven in the morning."

Bo seemed confused, as he processed Samantha's answer. "You been here all night?"

"Uh-huh." She nodded.

"So you *do* care. I knew it." Post-surgical pain notwithstanding, Bo still managed to smirk.

Samantha considered smothering him with a pillow when a light tap sounded on the door and Sam entered, stopping beside his daughter. He placed his arm around her shoulders and looked Bo over.

"So you're the guy who wants to take my daughter out?" he asked.

Bo winced in pain. Samantha handed the morphine button to him and he pumped it. "Yes, sir."

Sam stood unmoving. "And why would that be?"

"What?" Bo was heading full speed into a drug-induced blur.

"Samantha, honey, why don't you give us a moment?" Sam said in a low voice.

Samantha stepped out of the room without a word, taking Jenna's coffee thermos with her.

Sam stood beside the bed. "I asked *why* you want to take my daughter out?"

Bo's head was swimming. "Well, sir, I *like* her. She's smart, sweet, purty, real nice. I'd like to get to know her better."

"Uh-huh. What I hear, is you like *a lot* of women. Right?"

"Umm."

"Samantha is my only daughter. She's my only child. She'll always be my little girl. Do you hear what I'm saying?" Sam crossed his arms in front of his chest.

"Yes, sir," Bo whispered.

"Nobody hurts my little girl."

"No, sir."

"Samantha was raised to be a lady, and she deserves to be respected as such. Am I clear?"

"Yes, sir." Bo struggled to keep up with the conversation, as the morphine dripped nirvana through his veins.

Sam relaxed. He hadn't intended to interrogate Bo quite to the extent that he did. He looked at the man in the bed who took the bullet intended for his daughter. His eyes started to tear. He wanted to thank Bo with every fiber of his being for saving Samantha. But Sam Hernandez was a father first, and had to be sure Bo was right for his daughter. *Time to let up on the boy from Tennessee.* He spoke to Bo in a soft voice, blinking back tears. "You saved my daughter's life. I guess that gets us off to a pretty good start."

"Yes, sir."

"Don't blow it," Sam warned.

"Yes, sir. I mean no, sir. I won't blow it."

"I'd really hate to have to put you back in that bed."

7:57 a.m.

"Carson! Wake up!" Jalisa shook Carson until he woke, startled. "You were havin' that dream again, weren't you?"

Carson rubbed his eyes and ran his hands through his hair, tugging at it. He sat up in bed. "Yeah." He looked up at Jalisa's worried face. "Same dream. Did I wake you? In the next room?" He swung his feet over the side of the bed.

"Boy, you were makin' enough noise to be heard in the next zip code. Keep it up and *everyone* who's after you will be able to find your sorry self!"

Carson sighed. "Sorry, Jalisa. That dream is so vivid. It's like I'm right there. I'm terrified, but can't do anything. I can't explain it. I'm sorry I woke you."

Jalisa started for the door. She turned before she left. "Maybe you're afraid of having children, and since you're so gaga over Lizzie, you're afraid she might want a lot of kids and that scares you."

"Don't quit your day job, Jalisa. Somehow, I don't think you're much cut out for arm-chair psychiatry. I've had this nightmare ever since I can remember. Since I was a little kid. My parents used to come running into my room at least a couple nights a week."

"Did they ever try to get you professional help? Sounds like a life-long problem to me. And I don't need no psychiatry degree to see that." She leaned against the door jamb.

Carson remained seated on the edge of the bed. "No. Something like that would have been beyond their means. Dad worked hard for everything we had. Our home was modest. Our lifestyle was modest. They had a college fund for me, but it didn't go very far. We could afford what we needed, but there sure wasn't much for extras. If there had been, you think I'd have put my mom in a place like Cloverlawn? As it is, she'll eventually need a Medicaid bed. I'm going through her money like crazy just to pay her rent and medication. It makes me sick."

Jalisa's eyes softened as she looked at Carson. "You were really close to your parents, weren't you? I think that's sweet."

"Oh, Jalisa, my parents were great. I miss my dad every day." He looked at the floor. "I miss my mom, too. She's there, but she's not. It's hard. More and more, she doesn't have any idea who I am, and then, all of a sudden, I'll show up, and for a few minutes, I've got my mom back." He sighed. "And then, she's gone again."

"You can at least be grateful you had what you had for as long as you had it. My dad walked out on us when I was little. Mom was an addict—died with a needle still in her arm. Malcolm was determined to protect me from a destructive future. I don't know where I'd be without my brother."

"And Aunt Mae, don't forget!" Carson grinned at her.

Jalisa laughed out loud. "And Aunt Mae. I'll let you get up and dressed. We're getting low on cereal for breakfast."

"I'll do some shopping for you. It's the least I can do. Make a list and I'll take care of it. What time is it, anyway?" Carson asked.

"Eight, sleepyhead."

8:46 a.m.

The team meeting in Adam's office that morning was somber. Bo's absence from the group hung over them like a black cloud, palpable and heavy. "It's just the three of us today," Adam announced.

Kate and Boris sat across from Adam's desk. Connor sat next to Kate.

"Any news?" she asked.

"Bo was still unconscious when Cap and I left. Cap'll be in later today. He and Melanie drove all night to get back, and he and I left the hospital just before midnight. He's gonna need to sleep. Samantha was there when we left. I told her to take two days off. She's pretty rattled."

"Of course, she is," Connor said. "She's young, dis is her first big case as a detective, and they're shot at on their way to have lunch? Dat's pretty lousy, if yous ask me."

"She'll be okay," Kate added. "She's made of good stuff, I can tell. She just needs a day or two to work through it." She scratched Boris behind his ears.

"Speak of the devil?" Adam glanced at his doorway. Kate and Connor turned to look.

"Samantha!" Kate said. "You're lookin' like somethin' the cat dragged in. What are you doin' here?"

"I came straight from the hospital. Been there all night. I need to return the squad car and fill out a report. I also need my own car. It's still out in the lot. But I've got news on Bo." The bruise on her cheek had developed bright colors, framing the scrape on her face in a large, uneven circle. Her hands had scabbed over, but still stung, and her rumpled clothes hung on her small frame like rags on a scarecrow. Samantha had refused medical attention and failed to bandage her cheek or her hands. Her bright eyes were puffy and dull and her posture slumped.

"I was just asking how Bo was doing, when you walked in," Kate said.

"He woke up."

"That's great!" the others answered together. They began to deluge Samantha with questions.

Adam spoke over the group, "Hey, hey, hey! Let's let Detective Hernandez have the floor! For such a small crowd, we sure can make a lot of noise."

Samantha tried to smile. She was dizzy from lack of sleep, and felt off-balance. Tottering where she stood, she reached to steady herself against the wall.

Connor jumped up and grabbed a chair for her. She took it gratefully and sat down.

"Yous ain't lookin' so good, there, Samantha," Connor said.

"I haven't slept. I think I'll go home and sleep. I'll be back tomorrow, but I wanted to update you on Bo." She stifled a yawn. "He woke up a little before seven this morning. Like the doctor predicted, he's in a lot of pain, but they're doing their best to manage it. His nurse is very attentive. I think he's getting good care. I stayed until the doctors made their rounds. Everyone seems happy with Bo's progress, but it's a slow-go until he's back here."

"Did he say anything? Was he able to talk?" Adam asked.

"He's a little delusional about my feelings for him, so apparently, his brain got whatever oxygen he needed to remain obnoxious."

Kate threw her hands up. "He never gives up! That man never gives up!" She laughed. "Feel free to ignore him. It's not like it'll make him go away. It's more for your own sanity!"

"Bo don't mean no harm. He's just annoying. Like a gnat that won't leave yous alone. He's good people, Samantha."

"I know," Samantha waved her hand. "I'm just letting you all know he woke up nuts as usual, so he'll be fine. You don't need to worry about me. I'm not made of porcelain. I can handle Bo. Good grief, he's been annoying since we had the case at Mansford Mansion where I got to sit in and watch your team work." She yawned and was unable to stifle it this time.

Adam pressed his lips together. "You're a good sport, Samantha. Bo never means any harm. He's just—"

"Impossible? Incorrigible? Hopeless?" Kate interrupted. "Take your pick."

"Right. We're all on the same page, and we're all happy he's gonna recover," Adam said. He pointed at Samantha. "Samantha, you look like you're about to fall over. One of us will drive your car home and one of us will follow. You're not fit to drive."

"I'm fine, Adam, quit worrying," Samantha answered.

"It's not a request, Samantha. It's an order."

"Yes, sir," she said in a soft voice. Samantha looked down at her hands.

"Short-handed or not, I want to get this briefing over with. Connor, why don't you follow and I'll drive her when we're finished?"

It was another order, politely stated, as was Adam's style. Connor flashed the thumbs up sign. Adam smiled. Samantha was young and new to his team. She'd learn in time.

"Adam, I'll stay and watch phones while you're all gone, but I need to tell you, there's a lot of chatter about the I-44 drug run this week. Boris and I may get called out for some drug sniffing fun. If so, you want the calls forwarded to your cell, or should I tell the desk to put them in your voicemail?"

"Voicemail will be fine, Kate. We won't be gone long. I appreciate you and Boris pitching in for whatever time you can," Adam replied.

Boris cocked his head with his ears forward each time he heard his name. His tail wagged as he looked up to Kate for instructions, but no commands were given, so he stared at the table where the donuts had previously been. Sadly, no goodies were set out, and his nose told him none were in the room.

Adam gathered his notebook and addressed the group. "Let's start with yesterday's incident before we move on to the MSR investigation. Bo's room will be guarded 'round the clock by a uniformed officer. He's gonna be in the ICU for a while. They only allow two visitors at a time and for fifteen minutes, tops. S'posed to be just family, but we can see him. You'll have to show your ID first."

Adam looked at Samantha. "Now, Samantha, let me know if I leave something out. There were five gunmen that ambushed Bo and Samantha. They took down three. We've got the other two locked up pending arraignment. We need to be very, very careful out there. It's open season on law enforcement. Bo and Samantha were on their way to lunch. They weren't chasing any-one. They had finished interviewing some of the MSR victims over at Barnes, and were shot at only because these thugs saw them getting out of a police cruiser and set an ambush for them. It's dangerous out there. The bullet that lodged in Bo's chest skimmed right over the armhole in his vest. If it weren't for the grace of God, we'd be writing his eulogy. If you feel safer driving your own personal vehicle for work, keep your mileage logs, and I'll sign your requisition forms for reimbursement. Questions?"

"When can Bo return to full duty?" Kate asked.

"The doc said at least three months," Adam answered. He scanned the group, but no one had additional questions. He consulted his notebook and flipped a page. "Okay, next up. Elizabeth Wise had another stuffed animal left in her bed. When I told the hospital about the shootout when Bo and Samantha picked up the first security tape yesterday, they agreed to courier this latest tape to us. It should be here before noon today."

"Oh, yeah. That reminds me," Samantha said, raising her hand. Her speech was slurred. "Here's the tape we picked up. Might as well compare. Sorry. Forgot I had it." She produced an envelope and handed it to Adam with a yawn.

"She's about to drop where she sits, Adam," Kate said. She cast a concerned glance toward Samantha.

"Going as fast as I can," he said, as he watched Samantha force herself to stay awake and alert. Adam cleared his throat. "Speaking of noon today, Felix, from our fair City's Bomb and Arson Squad, is teaming up with County Bomb and Arson to run down the lead we got concerning possible activity in Shaw Park, which, as you know, is in County's jurisdiction. They'll have bomb sniffing dogs. We don't expect this is legit, but as you know, every lead must be followed. I'll keep you posted." He looked at Connor. "Connor, what've you got for us?"

Connor stood and read from his notes. "Armand Teller, the IT guy at MSR. At first glance, he's clean as a whistle. Phone, laptop, desk computer, all good. A little too good for a thirty-somethin' single male. But digging deeper, I found a little dirt. Mr. Teller likes to gamble, plays on-line poker while at work, and looks at dirty pictures—all on his bosses' dime. Knows how to hide things so's nobody finds out," he paused and smirked. "'Cept me, of course. Nuttin' keeps me from findin' out what alls everybody's lookin' at. Anyways, 'cept for doin' some non-work during work time, and bein' shall we say, not so upstandin', I couldn't find nothin' to say Armand Teller either coulda or woulda been behind the attack or involved in any way." Connor turned his palms upward. "So while he ain't no boy scout or nothin', I'm confident he ain't connected to the crime at issue here, neither."

Adam erased Armand Teller's name from the board. "Find out anything on Danita Jefferson?"

Samantha spoke. "We were gonna look into her after lunch yesterday. Along with a second interview with Jalisa Moore, since she should be doing better after um...um..."

"Surgery?" Adam finished her sentence.

"Yuh-huh."

"I'll take Danita Jefferson," Kate offered. "Didn't she claim she took a half day off for a doctor appointment? That oughtta be easy enough to check."

"Do we know anything about the hundred grand in Hollister's account?"

Connor cleared his throat. "Nuttin' we didn't already know. The comptroller who handled the deposit, is still on vacation at an undisclosed location. Her cell phone's turned off and she ain't logged into her computer. My guess is she ain't coming back to work. But without her overriding the bank's policy, the mystery donor never coulda deposited a hundred gran' into that account."

"Why can't something like that ever happen to me?" Kate asked out loud.

"We can talk about our theories 'til the cows come home, but without any evidence, we can't go forward on this. I last checked that account, and the money, every dime of it, is still in there," Connor added.

Adam closed his notes. "All right, everyone. We're short-handed right now. I'm not looking for a lot of progress today. Let's get sleeping beauty home, and meet again tomorrow. Looks like we're in for a rainy day today anyway. How 'bout we stay in and catch up on paperwork?"

Connor moaned.

Kate's cell phone rang. "Marlin. Yeah, right, right. Okay. On my way." She looked up at Adam. "Possible drug bust on 44, just like we were looking for." She beamed. "Big one. Have nose will travel. Shouldn't take too long, Adam. I'll be back as soon as I can. Let's go, Boris." Boris shot to attention and left with Kate, his tail waving high in the air.

9:10 a.m.

Sam Hernandez rolled toward the center of his bed and reached to Julie's side to stroke her hair, as he did every morning. When his hand felt only an empty pillow, his eyes flew open and he sat up. "Oh, yeah," he mumbled, realizing Julie was at Su Li's house. He ran his hand over the pillow and put it to his nose to inhale the scent of Julie's shampoo. Even though she wasn't far, Sam still missed his wife. He'd gone back home after talking to Bo to review his notes, and ended up falling into bed for a short power nap. Refreshed, but chiding himself for the nap, Sam picked up his new cell phone and called Su Li.

"Morning, Su Li. I'm assuming that with three kids to get to school, you're up already."

"Morning, Sam!" Su Li's voice sounded chipper for so early in the morning. He could hear her banging pots and pans, and pictured her multi-tasking in the kitchen while they talked. "David takes Becky in and Matthew and Levi ride together. Your pampered princess has not graced us with her presence this morning, but I've no doubt she'll be down soon. Should I have her call you, or should I wake her?"

"Don't wake her. I was going to be rude and invite myself over for breakfast, unless you have plans."

Su Li's voice was light. "No problem. Once the house is quiet, Julie and I were planning a leisurely breakfast, so feel free to join us."

"Thanks. See ya soon."

Sam showered, shaved, and dressed. He reviewed his notes for the day's work and took them with him as he walked to the Jernigan's home on the far side of their property. He believed he was untraceable at this point, but would not be separated from his notes. He slept with them on the bedside table, ate with them next to him, and never left them in the car. He'd come so close to touching Jordan yesterday! *Poor kid was scared to death. Where is he staying, and why was he at the hospital? There must be somebody there he cares about enough to risk going to see. I'll start there.*

Su Li opened the door and ushered Sam in. "The shower turned off upstairs about ten minutes ago. Julie should be down any minute. Bacon, eggs, and French toast okay with you?"

"Mmm," Sam said. "Julie's favorite, and mine. You know if you keep spoiling her like this, she'll never want to come home."

"*I* spoil her? *I* spoil the great Julie Hernandez? *Look who's talking!*"

"Hey! I'm not spoiled! Not in the least! I'm quite happy and content to settle for the best of everything." Julie entered the room in jeans, a pink pullover sweater, and bare feet. Her damp red curls hung loosely down her back. Sam stood and held her as she reached up for a kiss. "If I'd known you were here, I would've put on some make-up."

Sam squeezed her gently. "You've never needed it, and you still don't."

"Liar."

"Getting sick over here, you two," Su Li chimed in. "Sit down and I'll serve you breakfast." She brought a bowl of scrambled eggs and a platter laden with French toast and bacon. "Bon appetite."

"Mommy feed Noah," a small voice broke in. Noah stood in the middle of the kitchen, clutching his worn, faded blue blanket. Wolfgang stood beside him.

"Let's get you a plate. Look, Uncle Sam is here, sweetie." Su Li scooped up her young son and carried him to his seat.

"Are they going to live with us?" Noah asked. "And Wolfgang?"

"They're just visiting for a little while, honey. Then they'll go back to their own house and we'll have Sunday dinners there again. Here's your breakfast. Let's eat."

Sam and Julie enjoyed their privacy in the breakfast nook while Su Li attended to Noah at the kitchen island.

"Happy to have you here for breakfast. I figured you'd be out the door before I was out of bed," Julie said. She put a forkful of eggs into her mouth.

"I do have to get going soon." Sam paused. He looked down and remained silent.

"All right," Julie said, staring at him. She reached her hand out to his. "What's going on, Sam?"

Sam took a deep breath. "Remember when Samantha was seventeen and we agreed to let her go downtown with her friends for a Cardinals game? And about ten-thirty that night the phone rang, and the first thing she said was 'nobody got hurt?'"

"My first gray hair. I remember it well. It was just a fender bender, but heart-stopping nonetheless." Julie withdrew her hand and squeezed the napkin on her lap. "I don't think I like where this is going."

Sam cut Julie off before she could work herself into a panic. "There was an incident yesterday. Samantha's fine, honey, so please resume breathing. She's got small scrapes on her hands, but she's unharmed."

"What happened?"

"She and Bo were working a case. They were on their way to have lunch and were caught in an ambush."

"Oh, *no!*" Julie paled and her eyes filled with tears.

Sam got out of his chair and went to her. He put his arm around her. "Honey, honey, she's okay. But Bo, her partner, was shot. It's bad, but he should recover. Samantha is very shaken up. But she'll be fine. She *is* fine."

"I need to call her," Julie said, and started to rise.

"No, baby. She needs to rest." Sam gently pushed her back into her seat. "She stayed the entire night with him and didn't go home until he woke up from surgery. She's really tired and needs to sleep. Promise me you won't disturb her?"

"Why didn't she call me?"

"She did. Su Li answered and gave her my number. I saw her. Trust me, Julie, our daughter is fine. She actually may be a little more than fine." Sam covered his wife's hands with his and smiled.

"Meaning?" Julie's tears receded and she cocked her head at Sam.

"Meaning Bo, who *is* going to recover, would like to be something more than Samantha's partner. I met her at the hospital and while we were there, he regained consciousness." Sam omitted details he thought best not to mention.

Julie looked at him, puzzled. "So this young man comes out of anesthesia after surgery from being shot, and he's already asking our daughter for a date? Was it a head injury?"

Sam laughed. "You'd think, right?"

"How does Samantha feel about him?"

Sam's laugh grew to a guffaw. "She says one thing, but feels another. Claims since he took a bullet for her, she's willing to go to dinner and a movie with him, as long as he pays. Tries to sound condescending and disinterested. But every other thing about her—tone of voice, eyes, body language," he chuckled. "She likes him, Julie. I think he drives her a little crazy, but she really likes him. She's just not admitting it."

"Are you telling me that Bo saved her life?"

Sam took Julie's hands in his and kissed them. He became serious. "Yeah, sweetheart. Bo saved her life." His eyes misted and his voice softened. "Even if this relationship thing, or whatever you want to call it, doesn't work out—we'll be forever in his debt."

Julie sat up straight. "We should've made her practice more, should've *insisted* on a career in music. We should've—"

Sam interrupted her. "We should've let her make up her own mind as to what she wanted to do with her life. We *did* that, Julie. She *chose* law enforcement. And she's happy with her choice. Yeah, she's a little rattled right now, but a good night's rest and a hot soak will do wonders. Samantha's strong. She's our daughter, and if our daughter ever decides on her own, *without any help*, that she wants to walk another path, then we'll also support *that* choice."

"Choices have consequences," Julie reminded him. "Taking chances has consequences."

"Yes, that's all true, honey, but if you never take any chances, if you always choose the safest path, you'll never know what would have happened, what *could* have happened, if you had gone ahead and followed your dream, taken that chance. Choices can also lead to great rewards and fulfillment. You chose music. Then you chose me." He squeezed her hand. "Our little bird wants to fly. We can't clip her wings."

"But she could get hurt. She could be killed," Julie protested with fresh tears.

"Has she ever been out of God's hands?" he asked her, brushing her curls behind her ears.

Julie shook her head.

"Then let's leave her there, babe. His hands are far more capable than ours."

Julie leaned back in her seat. She smiled at her husband. "I really hate it when you're right."

Sam returned to his seat and finished his breakfast. *So much easier said than done.*

He stood. "I gotta go. Can't wait until you can come back home. The sooner I close this case, the sooner we get our lives back to normal. I don't like waking up alone."

Julie walked him to the door. They embraced and shared a long kiss. She leaned on his chest while he held her. "Please be careful, Sam."

"Careful is my middle name, ma'am," he said, tipping his imaginary hat.

"Yeah, yeah, I know. Just doin' your job, I get it." She shoved him playfully out the door and shut it behind him.

Su Li came into the foyer bearing chocolate. "I heard."

10:47 a.m.

Sam walked home, brushed his teeth, and left in the car Bull loaned him with his notes on the seat beside him. Having known that Jordan had been at the hospital the day before, gave him hope. Someone there was so important to him, that the young man considered it worth the risk of being seen. He stopped at a drive-through and ordered a large coffee. Su Li only served tea, and he didn't want to take time to make it at home.

After nearly an hour in the car, Sam pulled off at the Kingshighway exit, and weaved through interminable traffic to Barnes. He had a list of the employees who had been taken to Barnes and a second list of those taken to SLU Hospital.

Sam parked in the garage and headed to Callie McKnight's room. Callie had required surgery after breaking her ankle when she jumped out of the window. Sam guessed she would be leaving the hospital soon. He knocked on her door and entered after a female voice said, "Come in."

"Ms. McKnight?"

The young woman sitting on the side of the bed was dressed in black yoga pants and a loose-fitting orange sweater. Her long, blonde hair was pulled through an elastic band, forming a ponytail high on the side of her head. Sam could see fading streaks of magenta and turquoise running through her hair. She was holding her cell phone, and appeared to be texting. A plastic hospital bag filled with personal belongings sat on a cart overflowing with flowers, balloons, and get-well cards. Sam surmised that Callie McKnight enjoyed a busy social life.

"Are those my discharge papers?" she asked Sam, nodding to his notes.

"No, sorry," his voice was soft, compassionate. "I know that can take a while. My name is Sam Hernandez," he said, handing her a card. "I'm glad you get to go home. You've been through quite a difficult ordeal."

"You can say that again!"

"Ms. McKnight, do you feel up to answering a few questions for me? I promise it won't take long."

Callie chuckled and shrugged her shoulders. She looked past the open door toward the hallway and set her phone by her side. "It doesn't look like I'm going anywhere anytime soon. Shoot. Oh! Bad choice of words! Sorry!"

Sam grinned. *Cute kid.* "We believe Carson Hollister may have been injured that afternoon, and may be confused and in need of help. Have you, by any chance seen him?"

"Carson? Gosh, no." Callie answered. "Everyone was running and screaming. It was terrible. We were all so scared. I—I don't remember seeing Carson that afternoon at all."

"I see." Sam nodded. "Was he close to anyone in particular at the office? Any good friends, girlfriend, anything?"

Callie laughed. "Ask anyone—he was head over heels about Lizzie Wise, our receptionist." She leaned forward and lowered her voice, even though they were the only two people in the room. "But believe me, that was a one-way street."

"So Lizzie didn't like him?"

"Lizzie's nice to everyone. She's quiet, but seems real sweet. She tolerated Carson, but as far as I know, she doesn't have a boyfriend. Funny, because she's so pretty."

"Well, sometimes, the right chemistry just isn't there," Sam said. Callie was chatty and happy enough to talk. Sam attributed that to her youth and being stuck in the hospital for a few days. "Was there anyone he was particularly close to, hung out with, friendly with?"

"Hmm." Callie frowned and pressed her lips together. "You know, Carson was kinda new to the company. I know that when Jalisa had a sudden appendicitis attack, Carson personally rushed her to the hospital. When she got out, he took her home and checked on her, but I don't know much more than that. Jalisa and I talk a lot. We're both secretaries, so I called to see how she was doin', ya know. Plus, MSR is a small office. Everyone knows everybody else's business. Jalisa was real grateful and all that, but I think most of her friends are at her church. You really think Carson's hurt? That'd be a shame. He seems like a real nice guy. Good worker. Sorry I can't be more helpful. I hope you find him."

"Thanks, Ms. McKnight. I hope your ankle heals soon."

Callie looked up at him hopefully. "Yeah. I got some physical therapy scheduled. I wish they'd get here before the pain meds wear off. I'm ready to go home. Not that the food here wasn't scrumptious!"

"You take care, ma'am. Thanks for the help."

Sam left her room and headed for the elevator. Robert Shoemaker was still in the hospital, as well as Lizzie Wise, who was in the ICU, but in a different section than Bo. He arrived at Mr. Shoemaker's room. The door was open and Sam tapped on it as he entered.

Robert Shoemaker was propped up in the bed, watching TV. An IV tube was connected to the inside of his forearm. He looked at Sam.

"Hello?"

"Good morning, Mr. Shoemaker?" Sam introduced himself and gave the man his card. "I'm trying to locate Carson Hollister, and I was wondering if you might be able to answer a few questions for me. That is, if you feel up to it. I won't stay long."

"The police were already here asking about Carson. I don't think I was very helpful to them and I doubt if I can be helpful to you. I'm a recruiter for MSR, so I don't have much interaction with the accounting department, where Carson worked. Seemed like a good kid."

"Was he close to anyone in particular? Drinking buddies, girlfriends, anything like that?"

"That kid was sweet on Lizzie Wise, our receptionist. Lord was he smitten! I heard she's still critical. Poor kid. Nice girl, but she wasn't interested in Carson. I don't think he had anyone else in particular. The accounting section is way at the back. It's just Carson and Ed Carmody, the senior partner. Murgatroid had her finger in that pie as well."

"Murgatroid?" Sam asked.

"Sorry. Miriam Murgan. They told me she was killed. Sorry to say no one will miss her. She really had it in for Carson."

"Why's that?"

"About a week ago, I guess—I don't know, the time's got me all messed up around here! Anyway, one of the secretaries, Jalisa Moore, had a sudden attack of appendicitis. Carson saw her double over and rushed her to the hospital in his own car. According to Miriam, company policy says we call for an ambulance, but to be truthful, if Jalisa had waited for an ambulance,

she probably would have either died or had a much longer recovery. Carson's quick thinking saved her."

"Were they friendly before that?"

"It's a friendly office. Upbeat, happy atmosphere. Very
low turnover. Except for Murgan, we all got along well. But if
you're asking if they were friends, then I'd have to tell you, not
to my knowledge." Robert reached for his morphine pump and
pressed the button.

"Mr. Shoemaker, I'll not take up any more of your time.
Thanks for your help. I hope you feel better soon."

Sam left Robert Shoemaker's room and walked toward the
elevators to leave. He stopped short, and realized that Bo was on
this floor. He turned and headed toward the ICU. A uniformed police officer guarded Bo's door and looked up when Sam approached.

"Good morning. Would you ask Bo if he'd like to see Sam
Hernandez?" he asked the cop.

A nurse was summoned. She entered Bo's room and
when she came out, nodded permission for Sam to visit.

"How're you feeling, Bo?" Sam asked.

"Is Samantha Jane all right?" Bo asked instead. His voice
was still weak and raspy.

Sam suppressed a smile. "She's just fine. Rattled, of
course, and she'll be sore. Not as sore as you are. I'm gonna call
her soon. I was here at the hospital on a case and thought I'd
stop in to see how you were doing. Any message for my daughter?"

"Did'ja know there's no phones in ICU?" Bo asked. "Just
tell her I said, hey, and I got permission to take her out." Bo attempted a grin, but it turned into a grimace.

"You're in an awful lot of pain," Sam said. "Do you need
some pain medication?"

"Just had some about a half hour ago. Whatever they're
giving me isn't strong enough, that's for sure."

Sam shook his head. "Just wait until they get you up to
walk. You don't get pain meds for that."

"Yippee. Can't wait. You been shot before?"

"Twice. The most important part is living to tell about it."

"When are you gonna call Samantha Jane?"

Sam had planned on calling her later in the day, but reconsidered after Bo's question. "Why don't I call her right now, and you can talk to her?"

Bo tried to smile.

"Hey, honey, how are you feeling?" Sam spoke into his phone.

"Better, Dad. I'm sore. Soaked in Epsom salts when I got home earlier this morning, and I was just getting ready to do it again now. I didn't think I'd sleep well, but turns out, I slept like the dead. Not long, but deep."

"Good. You needed it. Listen, I'm at Barnes on that big case I've been working. Needed to talk to some folks here, but I stopped in to see Bo."

"Really? How is he?"

"He needs a shave. But you can ask him yourself." Sam handed the phone to Bo.

"Hey there, Samantha Jane!" Bo said. He tried to make his voice sound stronger.

"Hi. How are ya feeling?"

"Like I got shot and had surgery. You know, I asked your dad and I got permission to take you out."

"Yeah? How'd that go?"

"Lemme put it this way. It's easy to see why you didn't have many boyfriends."

Samantha ignored the remark. "Adam gave me the day off. I slept in some, but I feel okay to go back into work. I was gonna stop by and see you before heading down to the station."

"You ought to take advantage of that time off. Doesn't happen often. There's no phones in the ICU rooms. I'm on your daddy's cell."

"Okay. See ya later. Let me talk to my dad again."

Bo handed the phone back to Sam. "Thank you," he whispered.

"You take care, Bo. I'm leaving so you can get some rest." Sam turned to leave and finished his conversation with Samantha on his way out.

Back in his car, Sam took out his notepad and jotted a message. He drove to Farraday Enterprises in Clayton and found Martina at her desk working on a stack of papers.

She stood to greet him. "Mr. Hernandez! Can I get you coffee?"

"No, thanks. I'm just gonna be here a minute." He handed Martina a sealed envelope. "Are you going to see Kenton today?"

Martina nodded. "I plan to go late this afternoon, unless he calls me to come sooner. You want me to give this to him?" she asked, taking the envelope. "You didn't want to see him yourself?"

"If I go over there, we'll get to talking, and it'll take time from what I need to do today. He'll understand. Do you mind?"

"Oh no, it's fine. I'll be sure Mr. Farraday gets it. Is there anything else you need?" Martina opened her purse and put the envelope inside a zippered pocket.

"Not at this time. Thanks, Martina."

Sam left and drove to Shaw Park, a couple of blocks from Farraday Enterprises, and found a quiet parking spot. He removed the anti-bugging device from the trunk and, satisfied the car was clean and his phone had not been paired again, set up his laptop. Bull had taught him some new tricks during their last visit. It took him several minutes, but Sam finally hacked into the bank tapes and watched Carson withdrawing money. He located the ATM on the map and consulted his notes. The ATM was not far from Jalisa's apartment. Sam shut off his laptop and looked around to see if anyone was watching him. There were not many cars in the lot with the cold November drizzle blanketing the park. The predicted rain was petering out, leaving a damp, gray, uncomfortable mist. Sam headed toward Jalisa's place, checking often to ensure he was not being followed.

11:28 a.m.

Felix Santos, dressed in dark slacks and overcoat, looked like any number of dog walkers who used their lunch hour to take their dogs for a stroll through Shaw Park. A brief rain shower earlier that morning left the park with a dank gray mist, as the temperatures began to drop. The cold breeze dried up any remnants of moisture. Two other explosives experts also ambled leisurely, their canine companions sniffing and watering the trees and bushes. Another Bomb and Arson Squad detective from Felix's team casually read a newspaper on a bench. The youngest member sat at a picnic table closest to the table at which the tip hotline caller indicated the bombing suspect would be found. Dressed in jeans and a gray Washington University sweatshirt with Wash U in large letters on the front, he removed books from his backpack and pretended to study. None of the dogs, two German Shepherds and a Doberman, had been given their commands to sniff for the dozens of chemicals for which they had been trained, so they walked with their tails held high, enjoying the brisk November day. The picnic tables were empty, save for one at the far side of the park, where a couple relaxed with wine and cheese. Felix's team wore earwigs so they could communicate with each other.

"Anything, anybody?" Felix asked, as he petted his dog, Dyno.

"Nope," said the pretend student. He put on a headset and took out a pen.

"Negatory," replied the other two dog walkers.

The detective behind the newspaper answered, "There's an old guy in a gray sweat suit and running shoes. Looks like he's carrying lunch in a paper bag. Nobody else at my end, save for the couple playing hooky from work with wine and cheese."

"Doesn't sound too promising," Felix said. "I hate following leads you know aren't gonna pan out."

"Not the couple, anyway. Too much baggage. Old guy's heading your way, Lyle. I wouldn't get my hopes up, though. Timing stinks on this. It won't be long before the park is full of office workers coming out to enjoy lunch before the weather turns too cold."

Felix glanced toward the parking lot. A handful of cars were turning in; the early lunch crowd. The last thing Felix wanted was an incident with a lot of civilians around.

"I see him," Lyle replied.

"This is starting to look like another bad tip. How much longer you wanna stay here?"

The man in the sweat suit passed Lyle and his dog, and continued on his walk. His gray jogging outfit blended in with the overcast November sky.

"Keep your eye on the guy in the gray," Lyle interrupted.

"Why?" Felix asked. "What did you see?"

"I saw a guy that isn't as old as he looks from a distance, for one. But Major growled as he approached. Major doesn't like him, and if Major doesn't like someone, the problem is with them, not the dog."

"So your dog growled and sweat pants is now a prime suspect?" said the man behind the newspaper. "Major sniffs for explosives, not attitudes."

Lyle was unmoved. "I'm tellin' you, Major can multitask. He's the smartest dog that ever lived. He doesn't like this guy. And that means somethin'. He's got intuition when it comes to people's character. I've seen it time and time again. That guy passed me and Major stiffened and growled low and soft. That's his warning that this guy's givin' off bad vibes. I trust my dog." Lyle began to walk toward the man in a slow casual manner.

"I've got eyes on him," came the third dog walker. He turned and walked from the opposite direction toward the man in the sweat suit. "We're closing in. Major's intuition is good enough for me. I'm giving Rambo his sniff command." He bent toward his dog. "Rambo, Ka-blewey!" Rambo took off like lightening, just as the man sat at the appointed picnic table. The Bomb and Arson Squad detectives from both City and County converged, surrounding the man. Rambo, an enormous Doberman, stopped inches from the man, lay down, and stared at him as though the dog hadn't eaten in a week and the suspect was a sirloin steak.

Surrounded on all sides by the teams with weapons drawn, and three large dogs who looked hungry, the man put his hands up.

Rambo, Dyno, and Major stared at the paper bag. Rambo's handler peeked inside. "Well, well. What did we bring for lunch? Good boy, Rambo!" He reached into his coat pocket and brought out a treat and a ball. The other handlers followed suit. "Good boy!"

11:53 a.m.

Connor sat at his desk catching up on paperwork, while Adam did the same in his office. Kate and Boris walked in.

"Back from the big drug bust already? Was it everything yous hoped for?" Connor asked.

Kate gave a thumbs up with a broad smile. "Boris earned his pay, that's for sure!" She looked at Adam through the glass partition in his office and waved.

Adam came out and approached Connor's desk. "Hey, Kate, didn't think I'd see you so soon. All good?" He scratched Boris behind the ears.

"Yep," she answered. Before Kate could continue, Samantha walked in.

"Were you not told to go home and sleep?" Adam asked her.

"Yes, sir," Samantha replied. "I did that. I soaked in two hot Epsom salt baths and slept like the dead. Adam, I feel great. I'm ready to get to work. I'm barely sore at all and rarin' to go. I give you my word, I'm fine. I saw Bo on the way in, but I won't tell you anything else, unless you let me come back to work." She grinned at her superior and crossed her arms in front of her.

Adam rolled his eyes. "Blackmail? Really?" He sighed. "Okay, your leave is over. But if I see signs of fatigue or anything else that says you're not ready, I'll send you home on sick leave and it'll count against your sick days. Understand?"

"Yes, sir!"

Kate chimed in. "You look a whole lot better than you did this morning."

"Thanks, Kate. I feel brand new. I didn't sleep long, but I slept hard."

"So, don't keep us waiting. How's Bo?" Adam asked.

"Obnoxious."

"That's it? Obnoxious?"

"Yeah, pretty much. He's really in a lot of pain, so I didn't stay long."

A messenger arrived, carrying a large brown envelope and a clipboard. "Is Detective Adam Trent here?" he asked.

"That must be the tape from the hospital. Better late than never, I guess," Adam said. "I'm Detective Trent."

Adam signed for the envelope and the team went into his office to review the tape.

"We'll look at Samantha's tape first. That'll show the first day a stuffed animal showed up. Then we'll review this one—see if there are any similarities."

The team, with Kate, gathered around the TV while Adam started the tape, and fast-forwarded to the time frames in question. When it had finished playing, the three shrugged.

"Didn't see nothin' unusual, Adam," Connor said. "Are yous sure we're lookin' at the right date and time?"

"Yeah. All I saw were doctors, nurses and a few techs. Everyone had a name tag, and nobody looked suspicious." Adam sighed. "All right, let's view the new tape. Maybe something will stand out."

Adam inserted the new disk and they watched again.

"Doesn't really look much different," Samantha said, and they all agreed.

"Let's watch them both again. We're obviously missing something," Kate said.

"Still nothing unusual," Samantha said, after the second viewing. "Adam, is there any way we can view the tapes side by side? Borrow another TV, maybe?"

"I was just thinking the same thing. Back in a sec." Adam left and returned a few minutes later with a second TV and set it up. "Got this from Robbery across the hall."

"Can we slow down the speed?" Samantha asked.

"Sure," Adam said. "I'm also going to zoom in a bit." He adjusted the remote controls, while the group perched on the edge of their seats with their eyes glued to the screens.

"There! Right there!" Samantha shouted, pointing. "Can you zoom in some more and freeze it—the one on the left?"

"Okay." Adam did so.

"Now, slowly advance the tape on the right," Samantha said.

Adam complied. "You must be seeing something we're all missing, Samantha."

"Maybe," she answered, her eyes never leaving the screen. "There! There! Zoom in and stop!"

"Same doctor. Talking on the phone, just nods to the guard."

"That don't look too unusual to me," Connor said, shrugging. "Can you read his name?"

"Zoom in some more!" Samantha's voice pitched higher with excitement. "Look! Do you see it? That's the same doctor, but his coat has a different name. Who *is* that?"

Kate gasped. She dug a photograph out of her set of notes and set it down hard on Adam's desk. "Carson Hollister!"

Connor breathed a sigh of relief. "At least it's nobody leaving a subtle threat, and at least we know Hollister is alive and well and still in St. Louis. I gotta tell yous, I been worried 'bout that girl, ever since those stuffed animals was showin' up. We still ain't been able to track her family, and I'm startin' to think that Elizabeth Wise maybe ain't her real name, anyways."

"And Hollister wouldn't be threatening her. He was pretty sweet on her, from what we've learned," Samantha said. She paused and then laughed. "He's got a lotta nerve stealing doctors' coats and walking past a cop to see her. Gotta give him that. Why don't we have one of us sitting guard outside her door? He wouldn't get away with it a third time."

"This kid's smart," Adam said. "He may not show up a third time, after seeing that his first gift disappeared. He probably realized there'd be security tapes and his actions raised a red flag."

"The hospital got a call shortly after the attack, asking about Ms. Wise," Kate said. "They claimed they were family, remember? Can we listen to that recording?"

Adam rose and pulled a tape from his file cabinet. He turned the volume up as they listened.

"The voice is definitely female, and sounds black," Samantha said.

"Where was dat ATM he got dat money outta?" Connor asked.

Adam showed a map with a red circle marking the last known sighting of Carson prior to the hospital tapes.

"Jalisa Moore!" Samantha exclaimed. "I think we need to re-visit Ms. Moore. Why didn't she just leave her own name? Why claim to be family? She calls, and that same night, Carson withdraws money from an ATM close to her apartment? Carson would've known she'd be home on sick leave. This is a little too much coincidence for me."

"Maybe Carson was threatening her," Connor offered.

Samantha shook her head. "I doubt it. He's obviously been away from her place twice that we know of. She had plenty of time to call the police. My guess is she's hiding him out of gratitude because he took her to the hospital, visited her, and brought her home." She shook her head again. "That doesn't sound like the actions a dangerous criminal would take. They weren't friends prior to her surgery, but who here isn't grateful for a kindness?"

"You're with me, Samantha," Adam said, pulling on his coat. "Kate, if you don't mind watching the phones? Connor, see what you can pull up on Jalisa Moore's activity since the attack. If you find anything important, call me."

"Adam, I been monitoring everyone every day. Ain't nothin' strange nowheres. Lemme come wit' yous."

"Okay. Let's go, you two."

Adam, Connor, and Samantha left. "I'll drive," Adam said as they descended the stairs.

They parked down the street from Jalisa's building to avoid being seen from her windows.

"Connor, you take the back of the building—just in case. It's six floors up. This guy is slippery. Samantha, you're with me." Adam pressed the elevator button and they listened as the motor whirred on its descent.

12:03 p.m.

"I got everything on your list and more," Carson called to

Jalisa as he entered the apartment. "I also picked up a new cell phone."

Jalisa walked to the kitchen to meet him. Miss Buttons was in her arms.

"I'm starting to like your cat, Carson," she said. "Looks like she likes me, too. Ooh, what'd ya get?"

Carson pulled groceries out of three bags he'd brought up in the elevator. "All kinds of stuff. Cookies, ice cream, donuts, cereal, and milk of course, eggs, bacon, frozen pizzas, bananas, and there was all kinds of Thanksgiving food on sale. Pumpkin pie…"

"Sheesh, Carson! How much did you spend? At this rate, you're gonna need that hundred grand, just to keep fed. Any vegetables or meat?"

"Uh."

"Right."

12:10 p.m.

Sam congratulated himself for climbing six flights of stairs and arriving at Jalisa's floor without being winded. He wasn't certain which door led to Jalisa's apartment. None of the doors were marked. He guessed and started at the far end of the hallway and knocked.

A tall woman with fried orange hair, dressed in a pink and red floral print caftan answered. She was holding a black cat. A gray-striped tabby was perched on her shoulder, and a calico wove between her legs.

"Sorry to bother you, ma'am. I'm looking for Jalisa Moore's apartment?"

Kitty Katz smiled at Sam, glad for any company. "Jalisa's door is the one right across from the elevator. Be sure and tell her to bring her friend's cat over to visit me when you see her. I miss that adorable cutie!"

"Does Jalisa have a friend staying with her?" Sam asked.

Kitty gasped with delight. "Oh, such a nice young man! He rescued the sweetest cat. Pretty little orange and white thing. I just love to smooch the kitties! Mew, mew!"

"I'll be sure to tell her. Thanks." Sam ran down the hall. When he was already halfway to Jalisa's door, he heard the elevator arrive, and unbuckled the latch on his holster. Kenton had been firm in his warning that Pamela and Richard would stop at nothing to get rid of Jordan. Sam drew his nine millimeter Glock and aimed as the elevator doors opened. Adam and Samantha got out.

"Samantha?"

"Dad!"

Then they all three said together, "What are you doing on *my* case?"

Sam re-holstered his gun before being ordered to do so. They looked from one to the other.

Samantha's eyes flashed at her father. "Are you following me? Are you so over-protective you'd actually interfere with my murder investigation? You're tracking a missing heir, Dad. We're working on the Central West End terrorist attack!"

Sam sighed and countered in a gentle voice. "I've been on this case since before the bombing. And, for the record, it was not a terrorist attack. Carson Hollister *is* my missing heir. I've been tracking him for days. What's *your* interest in *my* guy?"

"We can't discuss an ongoing investigation," Adam said.

"Oh, *please!*" Sam argued. "If you think Carson Hollister had anything to do with that attack, you're chasing the wind. Carson Hollister's real name, the name his birth parents gave him, is Jordan. Jordan Farraday, as in the heir to Farraday Enterprises. He was kidnapped as an infant and left in an orphanage in Romania. His father, Kenton Farraday, was told his son had died while he was out of town on a business trip. Turns out, Mr. Farraday is terminally ill with little time left. The woman who stole the baby finally, after twenty-five years, confessed to him what she'd done. Mr. Farraday hired me, and I discovered that Carson Hollister is the missing child. All I need is his DNA for my final proof. Then I'll see him safely to his father's home. The people *you* want are Kenton Farraday's sister and brother, Pamela and Richard. *They're* behind the attack. If they can get rid of Jordan Farraday before Kenton dies, they inherit *all* of Farraday Enterprises. Jordan is the rightful heir."

"Look, Sam," Adam began. "We have to take him in for questioning. There's evidence that doesn't add up and we need to talk to him."

"The hundred grand was deposited into the kid's bank account by his father, or more accurately, his father's personal assistant, if that's what you want to know," Sam said. "Kenton Farraday thought he was helping. He's desperate to see his son. He's been grieving his death for twenty-five years. That money was withdrawn from Kenton's bank account the day before the attack and deposited into Jordan—or Carson's account the same day, so he would have immediate access. If Kenton had known the lengths to which Pamela and Richard were willing to go, he'd have waited."

"That would explain why Carson hasn't touched it," Samantha added. "He doesn't realize it's actually his money."

"We still have to take him in. We can't just take your word for it." Adam's tone softened.

"Fine," Sam answered. "But I'm going with you."

"You can follow in your own car. We can't let you ride with us. I know you already know that."

"I do." Sam turned to his daughter. "May I have a word before we proceed?"

Adam nodded his assent and took a couple of steps back.

"Samantha, I have never interfered with your career. I respect you as a person and as a police detective. Overprotective of my only daughter, my only child? Well, yeah, maybe a little. But you should remember how long ago I got this case. There was no way at that time that I could've had any idea our paths would cross. Not even when we were both at Barnes Hospital. It's so huge, I didn't even suspect. *Neither did you.*" Sam's tone was firm, but still retained the gentleness that made him an expert interrogator, and an even better father.

Samantha looked down for a moment, then back at her father. "I'm sorry, Dad."

Sam hugged her. "Okay. We're good. Now, let's see if we can both do our jobs with some mutual respect and cooperation without stepping on each other's toes."

Adam's radio cackled and Connor's voice came through. "Everything okay there? I haven't heard anything from yous."

"We're ready to proceed, Connor. What's it look like from your view?"

"All quiet. No funny business."

"Roger. Keep your eyes open," Adam returned. He motioned to Samantha. "Your show. I'd prefer a female voice—less threatening."

Samantha nodded and knocked on the door. "Jalisa Moore. It's Detective Hernandez. Would you please open the door?"

Inside the apartment, Carson finished putting away the groceries. He froze.

"Out the back door," Jalisa whispered. "Hurry!"

"What about you?" Carson whispered back.

"Just go! I'll think of something."

Carson started and stopped at the sight of Connor, who stood six foot four inches, blocking the landing at the back door. He slumped. "I'm trapped, Jalisa. I'm sorry I got you into this."

Jalisa looked at the floor. Her eyes welled with tears. "I don't want to go to jail." She smiled through her tears. "But I'll tell you this. It's actually been kinda fun. I'm glad it's the police, though, and not those other guys."

"I'm not gonna let you go to jail."

Samantha knocked again. "Jalisa, please open the door. We don't want to force this."

"Stay here," Carson told Jalisa. He walked to the front door and opened it, defeated. "I believe you're looking for me," he said, resigned. "Jalisa's got nothing to do with this. I forced her to hide me. She didn't want to, but I knew she was weak from her operation, and I made her do everything."

Adam rolled his eyes and sighed. "No, you didn't." He raised his voice toward the inside of the apartment. "Jalisa, you're not in trouble. We just want to talk to Carson."

Jalisa came to the door, holding Miss Buttons against her chest. Her cheeks were streaked with tears. "Carson didn't make me do anything. He doesn't know anything, but he does need protection." She looked at Carson. "I'll take good care of Miss Buttons for you."

Carson nodded and Adam and Samantha led him toward the elevator. He spoke to Sam. "You were chasing me at the hospital. Are you a cop?"

"Not for a while, son," Sam replied. "You don't know me, Carson, but I know a lot more about you than you even know about yourself. Now, listen to me, and listen carefully. I'm going to follow the detectives to the station and talk to you for a few minutes. Do not say a word to anyone until you've spoken to me, is that understood?"

Carson didn't understand, but he agreed. "Yes, sir."

"Not one word." Sam warned again.

"He heard you the first time." Adam shot a dirty look toward Sam.

The elevator doors opened and the four of them stepped out. "We need to be very careful leaving the building and going to our cars. The gunmen who attacked at MSR still have orders to kill Carson. If we found him at Jalisa's, then they may as well."

Carson stopped in his tracks as they entered the lobby. "We can't let Jalisa be in danger. They'll kill her!"

Adam spoke into his radio. "Connor, go around to the front door. See if you can convince Jalisa to let you take her to a safe place. I want a protection detail on her until this case is over. If she refuses to leave, then I want you to stay with her. She may be in danger. If she lets you stay with her, then call for some back-up. You may be seeing some action, and you'll be out-gunned."

"On it," Connor answered.

Sam stepped out of the apartment building first and scanned the surrounding area. Seeing no one, he motioned for Adam and Samantha to follow. He walked quickly to his car and popped the hood. Nothing funny. He checked the undercarriage and the trunk. When Adam saw the precautions Sam took, he asked Samantha, "Is he always this paranoid?"

"Did you see the parking lot at Medical Staffing Remedies?" she countered. Samantha trotted out to Adam's car and popped the hood of his vehicle as well. "All clear," she called out after she mimicked her father's car check.

Carson was placed in the back seat and Sam followed as they proceeded to the Clark Street station.

Sam picked up his phone and called Kenton. "Hello, Vivienne? Can Kenton talk? No, don't wake him if you don't have to. Do you have the number for his attorney? Good. Call him and tell him to high-tail it to the Clark Street police station. We have Jordan."

When they reached the police station, the group pulled into the parking lot, and Adam and Samantha escorted Carson in, while Sam followed on their heels. "May I have the courtesy of ten minutes with him before you get started?" Sam asked.

"That's not normal procedure," Adam responded.

"Look, I got there first and if I'd knocked on the correct door on my first try, we would've been out of there before you got off the elevator."

Adam sighed and Samantha remained quiet. "Ten minutes, but we listen on the other side."

"Agreed."

Samantha poured her father a cup of coffee. "Dad, did you get another car?"

"Long story. Thanks for the coffee."

Carson kept his word to Sam and remained silent for the duration of the trip. Adam escorted Carson into an interrogation room and seated him at a metal table. Sam took the chair opposite him. Adam left and joined Samantha in an adjoining room, where they could see and hear Sam and Carson.

Carson found his voice. "Who are you, if you're not a cop and you're not trying to kill me?"

Sam smiled at the young man. "My name is Sam Hernandez. I'm a private investigator."

"Just so you know, I've got a lot more questions than I've got answers."

"I'm sure you do." Sam sat back in his chair.

"I don't know who's trying to kill me or why. I don't know why my office was attacked. I've got all that money in the bank and I don't know where it came from. I don't know anything!" Carson's voice broke and he put his head in his hands.

"I'd like to tell you a story, okay?" Sam's voice was soft, comforting.

The young man looked up. "Sure."

"There was a very wealthy and powerful man who ran… well, I guess you could say, he owned an empire. He had businesses all over the world. While he and his wife were in another country, they had a baby. His family had a trust agreement under which the first-born child would inherit all of the business when the father died. That trust agreement had been in force for generations. The man's name was Kenton Farraday. I'm sure you've heard of Farraday Enterprises."

Carson looked at Sam, his face scrunched in confusion. "Um, yeah?"

Sam smiled again at Carson. "Stay with me here, son. Kenton Farraday's wife died only a few weeks after giving birth. Shortly after her funeral, Kenton left the baby with his trusted staff while he went on a short business trip. Unfortunately, not all of his staff was as trustworthy as he thought. A scheme was devised and while Mr. Farraday was away, the baby was stolen and left at an orphanage. Kenton Farraday was told that his son had gotten sick and died. He grieved the loss of his wife and son for twenty-five years."

Carson stared at Sam with a perplexed look on his face. "Okay?"

"The Farraday infant was stolen twenty-five years ago. Now, Mr. Farraday is dying. He has a rare lung disease and without a lung transplant, his days are numbered. With no heir to succeed him, the reins of the Farraday empire will pass to his younger brother and sister, who are twins. They will inherit a multi-billion-dollar empire, and now that their brother is terminal, they are counting the days until it all comes under their control."

Sam sipped his coffee and continued. "However, the nurse who had stolen the baby was consumed with guilt until she couldn't bear it any longer, and twenty-five years after her crime, she came to Kenton Farraday and confessed to her part of the plot. She told him his son had not died after all, but had been left at an orphanage. At that point, Mr. Farraday hired me to find his son, the *rightful* heir to Farraday Enterprises. I found him and was on my way to pick him up and bring him to his father, when the office he worked at came under attack. I was only a few minutes too late to complete my mission, but those few minutes had deadly results. Carson, I realize this is a lot to take in right now, especially after all that has happened, but your real name is Jordan Robert Farraday. The reason these hit men were trying to kill you is that the Farraday twins don't want to lose the vast amount of money and power they've been waiting twenty-five years to grab. The Farraday empire will soon be yours. My mission was to transport you safely to Kenton Farraday. Your father is very anxious to meet you."

Carson shook his head, stunned. "No. There's been some mistake. My dad died less than a year ago. My mom is in a nursing home. You're wrong. You've got the wrong person, and all those people died for nothing. And Lizzie…" Carson's voice broke.

Sam pulled a folder from his briefcase and laid out several documents in front of Carson. "This is a copy of your adoption papers. Those are Eldon and Mary Rose Hollister's' signatures." He showed Carson the age-progressed photo. "This is an age progression of your last photograph. Usually, an age-progressed photo needs to be of a three-year old child or older, but this was the last photo taken of you when you were only a few weeks old. The likeness is amazing. Wouldn't you agree?"

Carson stared as he held the papers in his shaking hands. Tears streamed down his face.

"I take it your parents never told you about your adoption. The Romanian orphanages were sad, horrible places. Eldon and Mary Rose Hollister rescued you from a lifetime of poverty, and possibly even early death. All I need to confirm your true identity is a DNA test. Will you agree to one?"

Sam removed a swab and Carson opened his mouth willingly.

The door opened and Aaron Berman walked in. "Don't say a word, Jordan. I'm your attorney. I'll have you out of here in just a few minutes."

"I don't have an attorney," Carson replied.

Aaron laughed. "You're Kenton Farraday's son. Believe me, you have an attorney. Several, for that matter, but I don't represent the business side of Farraday Enterprises, only the personal side as Kenton's lawyer and friend."

Sam stood and offered his hand. "Mr. Berman, I'm Sam Hernandez, the private investigator Kenton hired to find Jordan. I'm on his side, for the record." He gave Aaron his business card.

Aaron Berman shook Sam's hand. "I see. Kenton never gave me your name. Pleased to meet you. If you'd be so kind as to update Kenton, I'll stay in here while the police ask my client a question or two. I'll have him out of here in no time. Then, you can take him and introduce father and son."

Sam stood and left Aaron with Carson, who, according to Kenton, would be called Jordan, his birth name. Samantha and Adam were waiting outside the door. "Told ya so," Sam grinned at them.

"I can have the lab rush that DNA test for you," Adam offered.

Sam handed the sealed swab from Jordan's cheek to Adam, and Adam gave it to an officer with instructions to rush the results.

The two police detectives entered the room and sat down. "We'll just be a minute or two," they assured Aaron.

Outside the room, Sam called Kenton Farraday.

"Give me some good news, Sam," Kenton said.

"Aaron is with Jordan now, sir. We're all down at police headquarters. Jordan is safe. I anticipate you'll meet him within the hour."

Sam heard Kenton's voice choke with tears. "Thank you. Thank you. Thank you."

A few minutes later, Jordan and Aaron emerged from the interrogation room with Adam and Samantha behind them. Adam's phone rang. "It's Felix Santos. Will you please excuse me?"

Adam strode to his office. Samantha addressed her former suspect. "We appreciate your cooperation. No charges will be filed. You're free to go."

"What about the people trying to kill me? What about Jalisa's safety?" Jordan asked.

"We have a security detail at Jalisa's apartment, remember? We're going to have warrants issued for Richard and Pamela Farraday. I can request security for you, if you like."

"I don't think that'll be necessary, Samantha," Sam said. "It's my job to keep Jordan safe. Like we agreed earlier. You do your job and I'll do mine."

A lab tech appeared and handed Samantha a piece of paper. "Detective Trent is still on the phone. I assume you want this?" the tech said.

"Thanks, Ashton." Samantha looked at the paper. Sam looked over her shoulder and broke into a wide smile when he saw the paper. "You have a 99.83 percent chance of being Kenton Farraday's child," he said to Jordan. "Are you ready to meet your father?"

Jordan swallowed and took a deep breath.

"You've had a big shock, Carson. That's not even your real name. You have a lot to process, and you have a very different life ahead of you, starting with a whole new name."

Jordan nodded, but still hadn't found his voice.

"We can wait a few minutes if you want to gather your thoughts. But I suggest you get used to using your real name. The Farraday group has always referred to you as Jordan." Sam put his hand on the young man's shoulder.

"What's he like...my...father?"

"He's a very sick man. As I told you, he's dying. He uses a walker and he's on oxygen twenty-four/seven. But when he learned you might be alive, that hope breathed new life into him. He's very excited to see you and is hopeful that you would like to cultivate a relationship with him."

Aaron Berman added, "Your father and I have been best friends since college. He loved your mother and has been grieving ever since his return from Romania."

"So I was born in Romania?"

"Carson, er, Jordan, it's not that we don't want to tell you what we know," Sam began. "But there are things you need to hear from your father, not from us."

Adam approached the group. "I just got off the phone with Felix, from Bomb and Arson. He was the lead investigator on the explosive device that blew up your car," he shrugged. "They followed a lead that nobody put much stock into, quite frankly, but

it panned out, to everyone's happy surprise. The hit man behind
the attack and the attempts on your life has been apprehended.
He's singing like a canary, hoping to cut a deal. He said he was
hired by a woman, but didn't know her as anything more than Mrs.
Smith. He and this Mrs. Smith maintained contact through a couple of burner phones, and she paid him in cash—a lot of cash. Felix
showed him photos of six different women. As soon as we heard
Sam's story, we sent out photos of Pamela and Richard. He picked
out Pamela Farraday without hesitation."

Adam turned to Samantha and Kate. "Samantha, I want
you and Kate to pick up Pamela and Richard Farraday. Here are
your warrants." He handed Samantha two packets of paperwork
and turned to Sam. "It looks like your charge, there, is safe. You're
all free to go." Adam shook hands with Sam, and then returned to
his office.

"You ready, son?" Sam asked Jordan.

"Yes, sir."

Sam glanced over at Jordan who stared silently out the window as they drove to the Farraday home. *Poor kid. Been through so
much in such a short time. I can't imagine what he's thinking.* "It's
just up ahead, here," he said to Jordan, pointing.

"Gates?" Jordan asked.

"Gates to the subdivision, and more at your father's house."
Sam entered the code and drove slowly toward Kenton's home,
passing the sprawling mansions of Kenton's neighbors. Jordan
watched wide-eyed. "Here we are," Sam said. The gates to the Farraday home stood open, and Sam turned and drove up the long,
circular driveway.

The door to Kenton Farraday's home opened wide and Vivienne Simonet welcomed Jordan and Sam into the spacious foyer.
The aroma of homemade chocolate chip cookies enveloped them
and Jordan inhaled deeply.

"That wonderful smell is my famous cookies. Your father
asked that I make them fresh for your homecoming," Vivienne
explained. "Please follow me. He's waiting for you." She ushered
them into the spacious family room where Jordan saw a man sitting
in a wing chair with a walker in front of him. A long tube ran from
his nose to a portable oxygen unit at the side of the chair, and Jordan immediately thought of Lizzie.

Kenton's eyes welled with tears as soon as he saw his son. He struggled to stand and Jordan walked to him to assist him. Kenton grabbed his son and held on to him, pressing the young man into his chest, sobbing. "You're alive! You're alive! Thank God, you're alive!" He held Jordan out in front of him and studied him, unable to take his eyes off of him. "Let me look at you, Jordan. Oh, my! I can see your beautiful mother in your eyes, your cheekbones!" Kenton choked back more tears.

Sam cleared his throat. "Mr. Farraday, here are the final DNA results. There's no question. This is your son, Jordan Robert Farraday." He set the papers on the table next to Kenton's chair. "As we speak, warrants are being served. It won't be long before your brother and sister are arrested."

Kenton turned to Sam. "I can never thank you enough." He wiped his eyes with the back of his hands. "Vivienne!" he called out in a strong voice.

Vivienne hurried into the room.

Kenton spoke to her. "Vivienne, there's an envelope for Sam. Please give it to him." He turned back to Sam and shook his hand. "You'll find a little extra something in there. Thank you. From the bottom of my heart, thank you." Kenton leaned into his walker and motioned for Jordan to follow him. He took the photographs from the mantelpiece and sank into the sofa, patting the cushion next to him. Jordan sat obediently.

Sam turned to go.

"Mr. Hernandez?" Jordan finally spoke.

Sam turned to face him. "Yes?"

"I—I'll need a ride, sir," Jordan stuttered.

Sam chuckled. "No, Jordan. I don't think you will." He waved and left.

Kenton put his arm around Jordan's shoulder and patted him. "I've already purchased a car for you, son. If you don't like it, you can change it for whatever you want. I'm sure you have a lot of questions. And we have a lot to talk about. What would you like to drink with those nice warm cookies Vivienne just baked?"

"Um...do you have sweet tea, maybe?" he asked.

"Of course we do, Jordan," Vivienne answered. "I'll be back in a jiffy!"

Vivienne hurried to the kitchen. She was gone less than a minute and returned with a pitcher of sweet tea and a large platter of fresh-baked cookies. "Here you go. I'm going to leave you two to get acquainted. Colette will be by in a couple of hours with dinner." Vivienne disappeared, leaving Kenton and Jordan alone in the family room.

"I realize you've gone by another name, but here, we've always called you Jordan. I hope you can get used to it. It is, after all, what you were christened. You must have a lot of questions." Kenton coughed, paused, and took a drink of water.

"I do," Jordan answered. "I'm still a little in shock, I guess. I—I just want to know everything."

Kenton cleared his throat. "I was devastated when they told me you died. I had buried your mother only days earlier." Kenton wiped his eyes. Jordan squirmed in his seat.

"Jordan, I know this is all new for you. I also know that the couple who raised you loved you very much. For what it's worth, I believe that your real parents are the people who read bedtime stories to you, stay up with you when you're sick, applaud your first steps and take you to school on your first day. Your real parents heal your first broken heart, give you curfews and are there for you during the important times, as well as the everyday times. I get that, I do. I missed all of that. You were stolen from me, and we lost all those years. But I hope that you will come to understand how deeply you were loved by your mother and me."

Kenton paused again, took a drink of water, and continued. "Her dying wish was that you grew up knowing how much she loved you." Kenton began to weep again.

Jordan felt uncomfortable. He leaned forward and rubbed his hands together. His entire world had been turned upside down in the space of a single afternoon. He hadn't even known his real name. His head was swimming. He longed to know more, but was unsure what to ask.

"I want to know everything, my story, my family, my mother? I guess you probably have some questions for me as well."

Kenton nodded. "Were the Hollisters good to you? Was your childhood happy?"

"They were great. My parents loved me very much. They were older—a lot older than my friends' parents. I was told I was a miracle baby. I guess they were afraid to tell me I was adopted. Maybe they thought I would look for my parents and I wouldn't love them. I don't know. Dad died several months ago, and Mom—well, Mom's in a nursing home. She has Alzheimer's. So I can't ask either one of them."

"My father, too, is suffering from Alzheimer's. He's at Heather Hills Memory Care."

"I wish I could afford a nice place like that for my mom."

Kenton smiled and his eyes misted again. "Consider it done, son. I don't think you quite realize how much you can afford." Kenton called for Vivienne, who appeared with fresh cookies and a second pitcher of sweet tea. "What's her full name, Jordan, and where is she currently living?"

"Mary Rose Hollister. She's at Cloverlawn."

"Not after today. Vivienne, I want you to arrange for Mary Rose Hollister to be transferred to a private room at Heather Hills. I want the best for the woman who raised my son."

Vivienne set the platter and pitcher on the end table. "Right away, Mr. Farraday." She left the room.

Jordan looked up at his father. It was all so new. "Thank you. She was a great mom. Sometimes when I see her, she doesn't have any idea who I am, but other times, it's like nothing's wrong at all."

"That's the nature of this wretched disease. My father, your grandfather, hasn't known anybody for over two years. He's failing and will soon be gone. It's very hard to watch. His name is Robert. We have a tradition in our family that the first-born takes the grandparent's first name as his or her middle name. So you were named Jordan Robert. I hope you don't mind if we all call you Jordan."

Jordan shrugged. "I guess that's okay. It'll take some getting used to." He was quiet for a few moments. "What was my mother like? Is that her picture?" he pointed to the photographs Kenton had taken from the mantel.

"Yes," Kenton said. He gave Jordan the photos. "Her name was Tatiana. She was the most beautiful woman I'd ever seen. Long, lush brown hair, dark eyes that sparkled with joy, and the sweetest smile. She loved you, Jordan. She fought hard to get better so she could raise you, but she was overcome with infection. Look at her face. You can see yourself, can't you?"

Jordan nodded. He felt a connection to the photograph he could not explain. "There was no medical help for her?"

"We weren't in the United States when you were born. Tatiana was Romanian. Farraday Enterprises, the company you will soon be running, had expanded into Romania after the fall of Communism. We were part of a massive re-building effort in a country that had been oppressed for decades. Our family moved into a rental home in Bucharest from which my father oversaw the operations. My siblings and I were sent to different areas of the country. I met your mother in Dumbrava, the tiny, remote village where she lived. We fell in love and were married. Romania was third world back then. There were shortages of food, hot water, medicine, syringes, you name it, there was a shortage of it. The nurse who delivered you called several times for the doctor, but it wasn't until she left and personally insisted that he come, that he actually did arrive. But by then, hope of saving my beautiful Tatiana was fading. We were holding hands when she died. The last words she ever spoke were, 'You will take good care of Jordan. You will tell him I loved him.'"

Jordan took in everything Kenton told him, trying to process the onslaught of information. "How did I end up in the orphanage? Mr. Hernandez told me I was stolen." He saw Kenton's jaw clench, and a flash of anger crossed his face. He imagined this powerful man had a powerful temper before his illness drained him of strength.

Kenton took a deep breath before he spoke, and Jordan watched as the anger dissipated. "Your mother and I were thrilled at your birth. Your grandfather was proud of you. Colette Dubois, our French chef, who you will meet later, was elated to have a baby in the house." Kenton paused and Jordan saw a brief return of the anger come and go. "But your grandmother and my siblings, Richard and Pamela, were not happy at all."

"Why not?"

Kenton struggled for control before answering his son. "Tatiana was very poor. Mother was a social climber who fed my sister a steady diet of materialism and class superiority. They considered

Tatiana beneath them because of her impoverished background. She spoke English with an accent. They scorned her as ignorant, but her accent was delightful." Kenton smiled and Jordan saw a far-away look on his father's face, as if he had transported back in time.

"She spoke English well?" Jordan asked.

Kenton returned to the conversation and nodded. He took another sip of water and became serious once more. "Tatiana was pregnant when we got married. Mother, Pamela, and Richard accused her of trapping me so she could nab a rich American husband. But I tell you, Jordan, nothing was further from the truth. Mother and Pam, and Richard, to a lesser extent, were fueled by greed, avarice, and an insatiable lust for power. You see, Farraday Enterprises is governed by the Farraday Family Trust, and has been for generations. The trust dictates that the first-born child inherits control of the company once the existing President and CEO steps down or dies. My dad was the first-born, then I was, then you were. It really frosted my mother that the child of a peasant farmer would one day run one of the largest businesses on the planet."

Kenton coughed and poured himself a glass of tea. Jordan shoved two cookies into his mouth and washed them down with tea. Kenton continued. "We had a Romanian housekeeper who was also a nurse, Ana Popescu. Your mother was terrified of her." Kenton hung his head. "I ridiculed her, but I later did see that Ana was, indeed, a frightening and domineering woman. And, Ana could be bribed to do anything. After Tatiana's funeral, my mother paid a large bribe to Ana to kill you."

Jordan gasped. "My own grandmother hated me so much she wanted me dead?" He shivered.

"Ana ordered our chauffeur to drive her deep into the woods, many miles from Bucharest. My father and I had left on a business trip. We were getting ready to return to the United States, and I had to finalize our transactions in Cluj and Baia Mare, the two cities to which I'd been assigned. Pam and Richard did the same in their areas. You were left in the care of my mother, Ana, and Colette. Colette was given a drug which made her sleep for hours, and that's when Ana took you and put you in the back seat of the limo. But when she got to the woods, she didn't have it in her heart to kill an innocent baby. So she left you at an orphanage, and the Hollisters adopted you a few months later and raised you as their own child."

Kenton stared ahead at nothing in particular. A tear escaped and rolled down his cheek. "I was told you had died, and that everyone else in the house, Colette, Ana, Mother, and Alexandru, the driver, had gotten very sick. Ana and Mother were faking, of course, but Colette had been so heavily drugged, she didn't know anything, and Alexandru was fired from his employment and threatened with complicity if he said anything. He was younger than you are now, and terrified of Ana, just like Tatiana was. We had already scheduled our return flight, and with nobody the wiser, we left Romania shortly after your funeral."

"I see." Jordan frowned and cocked his head sideways. "So this nurse, and your mother—they were the only ones who knew the truth?"

"Ana told Mother she had killed you, as Mother had instructed her to do. Alexandru didn't know what had happened to you. He ran into the woods and tried to find you. He pleaded with Ana to tell him. He was a good kid, but out of his league. To answer your question, only Ana knew the whole truth. If Mother had known you'd been left at an orphanage, she might have tried again to kill you."

Kenton's jaw clenched and Jordan watched his father's face redden in anger. "My mother was a selfish, petty, wicked woman. She married my dad for his money and the prestige and perks that came with marrying into the Farraday family. She passed her deceitful, manipulative traits on to Pamela. Pamela and Richard saw Mr. Hernandez helping Ana into his car last week and they somehow figured out you were alive and posed the only threat to their inheriting everything when I'm gone."

"So what you're telling me is that I really am the reason behind all the deaths and injuries to my co-workers—I'm the cause for the suffering."

"No, Jordan, not at all!" Kenton's face softened from anger to concern. He took Jordan's hands in his and squeezed them. "You mustn't think such a thing! Pamela and Richard are responsible for their own actions. Nobody can force you to do something terrible. What they did—hiring those thugs—all the death and suffering—was a result of their own greed and power lust. They made a choice—a very bad and dangerous choice, to do the wrong thing. The responsibility for their crimes is squarely on their shoulders, not yours. You're a victim as much as anyone!"

Jordan remained silent as he tried to process all his father was telling him. He looked up as Kenton cleared his throat and released the weak grip he had on Jordan's hands. "Where did you go after the attack? Even Sam couldn't find you for days. And he's good!"

Jordan took a deep breath and released it as he gathered his thoughts. "First, I went home. I took the bus, but I don't even remember how I got on the bus. I was banged up pretty bad, but anyway, I made it home. But when I got close to my building, I saw some guys parked in front of my apartment looking at my windows with binoculars, so I got suspicious and went around to the back. My kitchen window had been opened and I saw a wire along the baseboards. I got scared and left—just started walking. I learned from Detective Trent that my apartment had been wired to blow, just like my car. Fortunately, when they opened the window, my cat, Miss Buttons, jumped out and she found me. We ended up at my friend, Jalisa's apartment and Jalisa hid me until today. She still has Miss Buttons."

"I see," Kenton said. "It sounds like we need to let your friend Jalisa know how much she is appreciated. I'll work on that."

"She still has the police protecting her apartment, until all the arrests are made. But you're right. I do want to do something nice for her." Carson looked at the photographs of Tatiana, a younger Kenton, and himself as a baby. "Do I have any relatives in Romania? Did my mom have family in Dumbrava? Do they know about me?"

Kenton was silent for a long time. He hung his head and rubbed his face. When he finally looked up, Jordan thought his father had again transported to another time and another place. When Kenton spoke, he sounded far away. "Son, I've done some terrible, terrible things. Things that cannot be undone or made right. Since Tatiana's funeral, your funeral, and my recent diagnosis, I've felt as though I'm getting what I deserve. My sins have found me out and I'm paying for them. What I'm about to tell you isn't easy for me. It involves the worst kind of confession for deeds I can never be sorry enough. When I saw you today, standing here in my home…I thought maybe, for an instant, I had been forgiven. Nobody knows what I'm about to tell you, but I think you have a right to know. Just know this, Jordan—that I am a changed man, and I am deeply ashamed and full of regret for my actions."

Jordan shifted uncomfortably.

Kenton took a sip of iced tea and continued. "My family has always had money and power. We're used to being in control and getting our way. I've struggled my whole life with a violent temper. When your mother told me she was pregnant, she also told me that her father was furious and was going to force her to have an abortion. I was enraged. He was going to kill my child." Kenton coughed, took a drink of water and paused a few moments before continuing. "You see, a few years before I met Tatiana, I got my girlfriend pregnant. Because I was a selfish college student, I didn't want to deal with anything like that, so I forced her to abort the baby, something she didn't want to do. The results were disastrous. She felt so guilty, she committed suicide. It was awful. I couldn't allow a repeat, and decided that this time I would be responsible and do the right thing. I told Tatiana I would marry her and we would raise our child together in America."

"Did you love her?"

Kenton's eyes welled again with tears. "Oh, yes. I loved her very much. We had obstacles, of course, differences in culture, experience, things like that. A sweeter person never lived. I told Tatiana I would talk to her father. Her mother died when she was just a toddler, so it was only her and her father. I went to see him. He'd gone outside to plant and was ranting and raving at the sky, swearing that she would have the abortion immediately."

Kenton began to stumble over his words. He looked sideways at Jordan and his voice raised in pitch, as he rubbed his nose.

"You're tired," Jordan said. "We can continue tomorrow, if you want." Jordan refreshed Kenton's tea glass.

"No, no, son," Kenton insisted. "I don't have a lot of time left, and I want you to know the truth." He scratched his nose again. "Tatiana's father, Ovidiu, was angry, as she'd told me. But I gave him money and told him I would care for her and the baby, that we would get married and once we were settled in America, I'd bring him here to live. He was a peasant farmer and happy to accept money and the offer of a better life."

"Oh?"

"I took Tatiana to Bucharest where she could receive better nutrition and care until you were born. Then we would live in the States as a married couple with a child."

"So my grandfather didn't come to Bucharest?" Jordan asked, raising his eyebrows.

"Oh, no. He needed to sell his place, wrap things up in the village, say his goodbyes, all of that. But I told her that her father agreed we could be married and that he would come to live with us when we were settled. She was happy to hear he'd had a change of heart." Kenton coughed, cleared his throat and rubbed his nose. "Unfortunately, when we tried to contact him to come to the wedding, he didn't respond, and later, to announce that he had a grandson, he said he changed his mind, and he was again disowning his daughter. Tatiana was hurt, but I told her to let it go, that she tried, but he would never change."

Kenton, unwilling to paint himself in an unfavorable light with Jordan, altered the truth. The bitter pill of confessing he had murdered Ovidiu, hidden his body in the woods, and lied to Tatiana about it, was too unpalatable to swallow, especially when a convenient lie would never be discovered.

"And when you brought her to your family's home in Bucharest, nobody liked her?"

"My father accepted her. He didn't like the situation, but he was a kind, compassionate man, and determined to make the best of it. Colette loved her. But then, Colette loves everybody. Mother was nothing short of a hateful shrew, as was Pamela, and Richard, well, Richard has always been spineless. He's a follower, not a leader."

"But my mother was happy with you, right? So she was okay?"

Kenton, unprepared for Jordan's question, hung his head and sobbed. "I'm sorry. I'm so, so sorry." His body shook as tears flowed. He composed himself and continued. "I was not as good to her as I should have been. I wanted her to fit in with my family. I wanted her to do everything I said, but she missed her father and her friends in Dumbrava. I was out of my mind. I had an insatiable appetite for control. I was often mean to her. She didn't deserve the treatment she suffered at the hands of my family or of me. I flew off the handle at the littlest things. I don't know what was wrong with me. I begged her to forgive me. I promised to be better. Before she died, she told me she forgave me. I was too stupid to see how wonderful our lives could have been if I'd just been decent to her. I have no idea what came over me, but I'll tell you one thing. The day you were born, it was a new beginning. The dark cloud that hung over my soul vanished at the sight of you. All I needed was one more chance to make everything right, and we would be a happy family. But I never got that chance. Tatiana developed an infection, which turned to pneumonia, and we couldn't save her." Kenton wept into his hands.

Jordan put his arm around his father. "I'm sorry."

Kenton raised his head. "At least I had you. I had my son, and as long as you were with me, I had a part of Tatiana with me. And then, you were gone."

"I'm here now." Jordan couldn't bring himself to call Kenton Dad, but he was moved by his father's life of regret and guilt. "I'm here for as long as you need me."

Vivienne entered the room, walking with soft steps. "Excuse me, Kenton, Jordan. Mary Rose will be moved to Heather Hills at nine o'clock tomorrow morning. All has been arranged. Jordan, you will have some papers to sign, as her power of attorney, but they'll be drawn up and ready for you when you arrive." She brought Kenton his medication, set it beside his glass of tea, and left the room.

"I need to go and see her," Jordan said. "Although she will probably not remember, I want to try to prepare her for the move." He stood.

Kenton took his hand and pulled gently. "Stay just a little longer. Colette will be here soon with dinner. Can you wait until after dinner? We still have much to discuss."

Jordan sat back down next to his father. "Of course."

"Jordan, when I die, all of this will be yours." Kenton swept his hand in a broad arc. "But I don't want to wait until then. Everything I have is yours now. We have a lot of lost time to make up for. Would you consider moving in here, to this house, to live with me? You would have plenty of privacy. Vivienne's quarters are on the main floor. My bedroom is upstairs in the east wing of the house. You could have the entire west wing all to yourself. What do you say?" Kenton took Jordan's hands in his.

"I mentioned I have a cat. I love Miss Buttons. Is it okay if she comes, too?"

Kenton patted Jordan's knee. "Of course. As long as you take care of her. Vivienne has her hands full taking care of me and this house."

"Promise. Thanks." Jordan smiled at his father.

Kenton melted at Jordan's smile. It had been twenty-five years since he'd seen his son's smile. It was still a little crooked, resurrecting the memory of his son as a baby when he last held the happy, cooing child. He patted Jordan's knee.

"Mr. Hernandez told me you were an accountant."

"Yes, sir, a junior accountant." Jordan brightened. Discussing work was more comfortable than processing his family history.

"Would you say you have pretty good business acumen?"

"I think so. I have a good knack for numbers. I can do a lot of math in my head."

"Farraday Enterprises will soon fall under your control. I'd like to discuss what that entails and ask if you're up to it."

Jordan swallowed, finishing his tea in one gulp before answering. "My strength is definitely math...and a good work ethic. My parents instilled that in me. I took several business courses in college and did well, but running something as enormous as Farraday Enterprises...I'll have to admit, it's pretty daunting."

Kenton nodded with approval, and patted Jordan on the back. "I think we can start tomorrow. But first, there are a couple of things I'd like to go over with you. My executive admin, Martina, is sharp, capable, and dedicated to the company. As the head of Farraday, you can hire or fire at will, but you'll have a hard time finding someone as good as Martina. She knows the company inside and out. You'll find she's a loyal and trustworthy employee. I would suggest you keep her on, but again, that choice is yours."

"I'm sure I'll keep her, then, sir." Jordan struggled with what to call his biological father.

"That would be a wise choice. You'll like her. You've met Vivienne. She was originally hired as a nurse for my father, but she also did light housekeeping. When Dad required more intensive round-the-clock care, Vivienne stayed on with me as housekeeper, and now she serves as my nurse as well. This house will pass to you, but if you don't want it, then it goes to Vivienne. The terms are in my Last Will and Testament, and you've met Aaron Berman, my attorney. I'm hopeful that you will also keep Vivienne on, and allow her to continue living here. She has no family. Now that my brother and sister will be spending time in prison, my only family is Colette, Martina, and Vivienne. And, of course, you." Kenton beamed with pride. "I know this is a lot for you to take in, but I hope you will come to value these people as I have. They'll serve you well."

"I'm sure you're right."

"I haven't even asked you—is there somebody special in your life?"

Jordan blushed and squirmed in his seat.

Kenton grinned. "What's her name?"

Jordan squirmed again. "She's more special to me than I am to her, I'm afraid. Her name's Lizzie."

"Well, if Lizzie doesn't see how wonderful you are, then she can't be too bright! Can I meet her?"

Jordan looked away. "She's in a coma. She was shot during the attack. They don't know if she's ever going to wake up."

Kenton hugged his son. "I'm sorry, Jordan. I truly am. I don't know what to say. I can arrange for the best specialists see her, if you like."

Jordan nodded. "That'd be nice. Mr. Hernandez said you put all that money into my account, is that right?"

"Yes. I thought I was doing a good thing. I certainly never intended for it to cause all the problems it did. I only wanted to help you out. I was so excited to learn you were alive. I just couldn't help myself. But Jordan, anything you need—anything you want, you tell me."

"I'd like to pay my student loans, and get my mother some nice nightgowns and clothes. She likes lilac scented lotions and creams, that sort of stuff."

Kenton leaned back into the sofa cushions and looked at the ceiling. "The Hollisters raised you to be responsible and respectful. You turned out just fine, which is a relief, to say the least. I'm proud of you. Just sad that I didn't contribute to the fine young man you've become."

The doorbell rang. Vivienne ushered Colette into the kitchen where she set her packages on the counter before coming to check on Kenton.

"Kenton. I didn't realize you had company," Colette said, looking at Jordan. Her voice was gentle and sad, but still carried the lilt of her French accent. "You're looking well. Better than I've seen you in some time."

"Colette, do you know who this young man is?" Kenton asked her. His voice shook with excitement.

Jordan stood and held out his hand to her.

Colette shook his hand, but addressed her answer to Kenton. "No, I don't believe I've seen him." She studied Jordan, but shook her head.

"Look carefully at his face. Twenty-five years ago, we thought he died."

Colette's eyes widened and her hand flew to her open mouth. "*Mon Dieu!*" she cried. "Can it be?" She stepped to Jordan and touched his face, staring into his eyes and seeing her friend Tatiana in the face of the young man who stood before her. She wept as she hugged Jordan, clinging to him. "Jordan! You are alive! I cannot believe it! I cannot believe it! We must celebrate! This is incredible!" She turned to Kenton, wagging her finger to scold him. "You should have told me, Kenton Farraday. Such a momentous occasion, and I would have changed the menu! Shame on you. Your old chef has nearly had the heart attack!" She became serious. "What have Pamela and Richard to say about this?"

"Colette, you better sit down," Kenton warned. "We'll fill you in over dinner."

12:44 p.m.

Samantha and Kate exited the Farraday Penthouse elevator and walked past Martina's desk to Pamela's office. They did not knock, nor did they ask Pamela's secretary to announce them. Pamela looked up sharply at the intruders. "You can't just barge in here unannounced," she sneered at them.

"Pamela Farraday, we have a warrant for your arrest," Samantha said, handing the paperwork to her.

Pamela sputtered and spewed. "You can't do this! Do you know who I am?" she screamed at them. "I'll have your badges."

Kate ignored the empty threat, took Pamela's hands and handcuffed them behind her back.

Richard ran into Pamela's office, having heard the commotion from his office next to hers.

"What's going—oh, no!" His shoulders slumped. "I told you, you went too far!" he hissed at his sister. Richard covered his face and sunk into a chair.

"Shut up, Richard!" Pamela snapped at him.

"Richard Farraday," Samantha began.

Richard cut her off. Tears streamed down his cheeks as he looked up at her, pleading. "Please. Can I call my wife?"

Samantha looked to Kate, who shrugged and nodded.

"You can call her from here…while we're standing here."

"Thank you." He picked up the phone and called Alison, his wife. "I'm sorry, Alison. I've made a mess of everything and now I'm going to pay for it." He sobbed and told her he and Pamela were being arrested and taken downtown.

Richard stood and Kate handcuffed him while Samantha read the twins their rights. Then Kate and Samantha led the two out of Pamela's office, toward the elevators. As they passed Martina's office, Martina stood in the doorway, watching, along with the executives who'd come to their own office doors to watch the show. Pamela curled her upper lip and sneered at Martina. "Call my attorney now!" she ordered.

Martina answered in a sweet voice. "I work for Kenton—and Jordan. I don't work for *you*." She turned her back on the parade and returned to her desk.

7:20 p.m.

Jordan Farraday struggled to get used to his new name—his *real* name, as he drove to Cloverlawn Memory Care Center to see his mother. His head swam until it throbbed, as the upcoming changes to his life swirled through his thoughts like debris in a whirlpool. Kenton had purchased a brand new metallic blue Audi TT for Jordan. He could have a new car every year if he wanted one, or a different color for every day of the week. Conspicuous consumption at its most sickening, he thought. Jordan would be moving into his father's mansion in Ladue, where he would have a housekeeper and a French chef, a six-car garage, designer clothes, and anything else that money could buy. His mother would be moving to the posh Heather Hills Memory Care home where she would receive the most advanced treatments for Alzheimer's. His father would see to it that the country's top specialists would take over Lizzie's care. He was grateful, he admitted to himself. A lot of good things could be accomplished if money was no object. But his heart sank when he thought of Lizzie. She was the one person in the world that Jordan wanted, but her heart, he knew, couldn't be bought. And if he could buy her, he wouldn't want her. If Lizzie Wise's affections could be bought, then she wasn't the girl he thought she was. *I just won't tell her. That's it! I* know *she likes me.* For Jordan, a seedling of hope spawned a harvest of optimism, however ill-advised it might be.

As the reality of his new life began to sink in, Jordan considered the options his father had presented to him concerning the staff his father cared about. Jordan genuinely liked Vivienne, and would keep her on when his father was no longer with them. He thought Colette was wonderful. She made him feel loved as she told him stories about his mother, Tatiana, and the first few weeks of his life. Colette had announced at dinner that she would stay in her own condo, rather than move to the Farraday home, but she agreed to cook five times a week for Kenton and Jordan, since Pamela and Richard would be eating prison food. She had been saddened, but not surprised, when Kenton told her of his siblings' plot to kill Jordan.

Jordan had not yet met Martina, but felt confident he would like her as well and keep her on. Her expertise would be invaluable. There was little time to learn everything about running Farraday Enterprises. His father had laughed at him when he said he wanted to give Mr. Carmody two weeks' notice. Jordan resented Kenton's superior attitude—as though now that he was a Farraday, common courtesy would no longer be required. While he viewed Kenton with compassion, for his illness and his life of regret, he saw glimpses of the man who had confessed to treating Tatiana poorly. Mr. Carmody had taken Jordan under his wing, hired him when he had no experience, and paid him a decent wage. Jordan felt that two weeks' notice was in order, and he called Mr. Carmody from his new car as soon as he left the house. Edmond Carmody said he was sad to lose him, but he was happy for Jordan, and wished him well. He told Jordan that the office wouldn't even be open for another two weeks, due to the extent of damage the building sustained.

Kenton Farraday was a complicated man, Jordan decided. He saw a kind and generous captain of industry, a strong leader, smart and capable, but frustrated by his inability to overcome the illness that would eventually rob him of life. But he also saw a man capable of as much cruelty as love, with an arrogant streak and an inherent drive to control others. Yet, Vivienne, Colette, and he assumed, Martina, were unwavering in their devotion to him. And, Jordan had felt loved—deeply loved when Kenton threw his arms around him and hugged him, weeping.

Caught up in his thoughts, Jordan almost missed the exit to Cloverlawn. He braked hard, and the car responded like a dream. Slowing his speed, he took the ramp to the outer road that led to the facility in which his mother was living. He parked for the last time at Cloverlawn, walked through the double doors, and signed the visitors' book.

Odessa, the receptionist, grinned at him. "It's past visiting hours but I hear your mother's leaving us tomorrow for Heather Hills so I'll make an exception this time for you. Did you win the lottery or strike it rich at the casino?"

Jordan blushed and shook his head. "No. Let's just say my mom's got a guardian angel." While he believed Odessa was only being friendly, he was in no hurry to announce his new-found status, especially to those with whom he had a passing relationship, and Odessa's question made him uncomfortable.

Odessa leaned forward and whispered. "I'm happy for her. *I* sure wouldn't want to spend *my* life in a place like this. But I'll miss her." She leaned closer. "You do know the director was trying to reach you. Did she? About the excitement around here?"

"What are you talking about? My cell phone was…um… out of commission, and I only today replaced it. Is everything okay?"

Odessa sat back in her seat, willing and happy to talk. "There were a couple of men that just walked right in here last week! Didn't sign the registry, didn't stop at the desk, just barged right on in and went straight to your mother's room!"

"Is my mother okay?" Jordan was alarmed.

"She's fine. I called the police and then our security guard, Bud." Odessa chuckled. "Sorry. I know this isn't funny, but when they got to her room, she and her roommate were in their beds watching the television. A couple of other residents were in chairs watching TV with them. The men demanded to know which one of them was Mary Rose Hollister, but none of the women could remember their own names, much less anybody else's! Bud got there just as one of the men raised his hand to strike your mother, and he stopped the assault before he could hurt her. Then the police got here and they chased those men all over until they ran out the fire exit, which, of course, set off the alarm, which then brought the fire department, and everyone had to be evacuated! In November! And most of them wearing their nightgowns! Those alarms can wake the dead! It was scary, but also exciting. As you can imagine, this isn't the most thrilling place to work. Anyway, we tightened up security big time. Matter of fact, today's the first day I've been at the front desk by myself since it happened."

"But nobody was hurt, right? Just scared?" Jordan asked.

"Yeah. We didn't know what those men wanted. And this happened right on the heels of that attack in the Central West End. What is this world coming to?" Odessa straightened a stack of papers on her desk. "Well, anyway, by the next morning, nearly all our residents had forgotten about it. *Literally.* But the director, of course, had to notify the families. She asked me if I had another number for you, because she couldn't reach you on your work number or your cell. But your mama's fine—no worries. And good luck at the new place! I guess you want to see her now, right?"

"Thanks, Odessa. I assume she's in her room?"

"Oh, yeah. Dinner's been over more than an hour. Nothing much happens after dinner around here."

Jordan walked down the hallway to the room his mother shared with another woman. He wouldn't miss the smell of old urine and mold that seemed to ooze from the walls. He smoothed out his clothes and walked to her bedside, pulling a chair next to her so they could talk.

"Hi, Mom. It's me." He couldn't bring himself to say Carson. That's not who he was. "How are you feeling today?"

The woman in the bed turned and looked at him with a blank stare. The nurse had recently brushed his mother's silver and white hair, but it stood out from her head in several directions, accenting her pale skin and blue eyes. She was humming a tune he couldn't identify.

"Mom, there are going to be some changes I want to tell you about. In the morning, you're going to move to another place. It's very nice, and they're going to take real good care of you. You may not remember that we talked about it, but on the other hand, you might, so I'm just going to let you know now that you won't be living here after tonight."

Jordan fidgeted. He'd gone over this conversation in his mind a dozen times between Kenton's house—his new home, and Cloverlawn. But now that it was time to have the conversation, he felt awkward.

"Mom, there's something else. Something I just learned today." He paused and picked at a thread on his slacks. "I know that you and Dad adopted me. You rescued me out of an orphanage in Romania." He swallowed. "My real name isn't Carson, Mom. It's Jordan. I was stolen as a baby and left at the orphanage. I met my biological father today."

Jordan saw a spark of recognition light his mother's eyes. She began to cry. He took her hand in his. "Mom, I didn't mean to upset you. I just want you to know that I know. You don't have to keep it a secret anymore. You never really did. I'm not angry. I understand. You're always going to be my mother. Nothing is going to change."

Mary Rose Hollister straightened her posture and spoke. Her voice trembled with age, but her words rang with such clarity that Jordan felt his mother had returned to him. She smiled. "We loved you the minute we saw you. We ached to see you in that horrible, filthy place. We should have told you, but we never wanted you to feel unloved or unwanted, even for a second." Mary Rose stared into space and Jordan thought he'd lost her again. But she turned to him and her eyes came into focus. "When Eldon was transferred to St. Louis only three weeks after we brought you home, we thought it was a sign from heaven. We didn't know anyone in our new location, and so it was easy to say you were ours. Nobody would know any different. You were our miracle baby and we loved you." She looked at her hands resting in her lap. Jordan's heart soared. He had his mother back. "We were wrong to not tell you, but we didn't want you to be hurt." She patted his hand.

"I understand, Mom."

Kenton was right, Jordan reminded himself. Your real parents are the ones who stay up with you through the night when you're sick, when you have a bad dream, or when you need one more bedtime story to go with that extra drink of water. They sacrifice their sleep, their comfort and their last drop of blood if need be, to love, protect, and care for their children. Eldon and Mary Rose Hollister had been outstanding parents.

"I'll come and see you in your new place tomorrow, Mom. And I'm gonna bring you some nice new nightgowns, the soft, warm ones. You'll like that. Winter's right around the corner. Thanksgiving's almost here. You'll join me in my new place for a wonderful meal. Doesn't that sound good?"

Mary Rose Hollister looked at Jordan with a blank stare. She resumed humming the tune only she knew in her far-away world.

"Goodnight, Mom," Jordan said. He rose, kissed her on her forehead and left, wiping his eyes.

8:51 p.m.

Jalisa Moore walked toward her front door, unable to ignore the persistent knocking. Detective Connor Maguire and the security detail under him had left thirty minutes ago. His assurances that the perpetrators had been arrested and she was safe brought her a modicum of comfort, but she was still uneasy being alone in the apartment. She stifled a giggle when she saw the comical Miss Buttons rolling in front of the door. Jalisa tiptoed to the peephole and looked through before opening it.

"Carson! I thought you were in jail! Are you okay? It's getting late." She opened the door wider and when he came in, she hugged him. "Tell me what happened!"

"We better sit down, Jalisa. You are *not* gonna believe what I'm about to tell you!"

They took their seats and Miss Buttons jumped onto Jordan's lap, pressed her head into his chest and purred. He hugged and petted her. "First, tell me how you are. I thought you had the police guarding you. Where are they?"

"They left. They said I was safe because the bad guys had been arrested. I'm still a little rattled. You just missed Aunt Mae. This place has been like a revolving door today. The cops left, and five minutes later, Aunt Mae showed up. She just left, and now you're here. I almost had to invite you to Thanksgiving!" she teased. "I want to hear everything that's happened! Tell me!"

"I hardly know where to begin. But I do know why I keep having those bad dreams. I was in that place when I was a baby. Those dreams are my earliest memories, tucked away, that come out at night. And for the record, my name is not Carson Hollister."

Jordan told her all he had learned from Kenton Farraday, and that he'd talked to Edmond Carmody and was going to begin training to take over for his father.

"Shut up! You're not serious! Tell me what really happened."

Jordan winked at her and pulled out the keys to his Audi TT, jingling them in front of her. "Wanna take a little spin in my new wheels? Kenton Farraday—um—my dad bought it for me. C'mon!" He rose and started for the door.

"Get out! You're joking!" But Jalisa followed him anyway.

"Oh, wow, Carson!" she said when she saw the car. "It's really yours? Little step up from the Escort, huh? Plus, it's in one piece."

"That's not my name. It's Jordan. It really is. We need to get used to that." He opened the door for her. "Let's go for a ride."

Jalisa sank into the black leather seats and ran her hand along the shiny wood dashboard. "I can't believe this!" she said, as he drove away. "You're a rich boy? Snazzy new car and everything! Don't you go forgettin' who your friends are, now."

Jordan pulled the car to the curb and stopped. "Jalisa," he said, in his most serious tone. "I will never forget you. You saved my life."

"You saved mine first."

"Okay. Well, as long as we're even, then maybe I *can* forget you, since we're keeping score." He laughed, and pulled the car back onto the street. "Speaking of Thanksgiving, I was going to invite you over. My new French chef is amazing."

Jalisa answered in a high sing-song voice. "Oh, I'm so glad that your new French chef is so amazing. I make a delicious hot dog with a side of macaroni and cheese, if you must know. La-di-dah." She waved her hand in the air.

Jordan looked at her sideways and chuckled. "It's been a lot to swallow, and there's a lot to learn. I'll have my father, Colette, Vivienne, and Martina to help me along." He was quiet for a few moments. "Jalisa, all kidding aside, I do owe you. We both know it. I want to do something to say thanks. Your car isn't in much better shape than my old one. I was thinking, maybe you might like to pick a new one. Or is there something else?"

"Carso—Jordan. Wow. *That's* gonna take some getting used to! I don't want anything from you. It was a fun ride. And we ended up becoming friends. My life is pretty quiet. I go to work and to church. I have to keep things on the down low because of my brother. Getting something from you? It'd be too weird. I don't need anything."

"I don't feel right about it. What if I beg you? Jalisa, *please* let me buy you a new car? Will that work?"

"I'll think about it."

"Sheesh! You're a hard sell! I need to get you back home." Jordan turned the car around. "It's been a long day, full of surprises, and I'm exhausted." He parked in front of her complex, got out, and opened her door. "I'll walk you to your door. I need to pick up Miss Buttons and all her paraphernalia, anyway. Thanks for taking care of her."

"I've grown fond of her. I'd like to be able to come and visit her," Jalisa said.

"What, not me? You don't wanna visit me, just the cat?"

Jalisa shrugged. "I'll think about it."

They stepped into Jalisa's apartment. "Have a seat. I'll get the kitty's things. They're spread all over the place. I'm thirsty. Want a glass of water?"

"Sure, if you don't mind. Thanks." Jordan sat down on the sofa and leaned his head back into the soft cushions. He closed his eyes and began to doze.

A key turned in the front door and the next thing Jordan knew, a giant grabbed him by the front of his shirt, and twisting it, lifted him off the sofa, suspending him in mid-air.

"Who do you think you are and what are you doing in my house?"

Jordan made choking sounds and kicked his feet, to no avail.

"Malcolm! Put him down *now!*" Jalisa ordered. Malcolm set Jordan down and glared at him.

"And what is *that?*" he demanded, pointing at Miss Buttons.

Jalisa put her hands on her hips and stood between her brother and her friend. "Last I heard, they call it a cat. Welcome home, Malcolm, and what's with the attitude? Where are your manners?" She crossed her arms in front of her chest.

"I'm sorry, baby sister, but I come home after a dangerous assignment and see some guy asleep on the sofa, and then an animal in my house—"

"*Our* house, Malcolm. I live here, too."

"There better not be cat hair in my bedroom."

"Will you chill? Boy, getting shot at all the time is turning you into a real crab. This is Jordan. He's my friend."

"Is that all he is? 'Cuz it's awful late at night for a friend to be here all stretched out on the sofa like he lives here."

"That's all, Mr. Moore. We're just friends," Jordan answered, lifting his hands in surrender.

"Stay outta this, Jordan. He's *my* brother."

"Right, right. Sorry," Jordan said, moving away from both of them. His throat was sore from where Malcolm's hands had squeezed, and he rubbed it.

"Let's start this all over again, huh?" Jalisa said. "Jordan, this is my brother, Malcolm. He's a hero," she stated with pride. "Malcolm, this is my friend, Jordan. He saved my life, so he's also a hero. Now you two play nice and shake hands."

Malcolm still glared at Jordan as if he was a threat to national security, but he extended his hand anyway. Jordan took it and Malcolm delivered a bone-crushing handshake.

Jordan gulped as he forced back tears. "Pleased to meet you. I've heard all about you."

"I ain't heard nothin' about you." Malcolm turned to his sister. "So how'd this pipsqueak save your life, and why ain't I hearin' about it 'til now?"

"I—I didn't really."

"I said stay out of this, Jordan," Jalisa ordered.

"Yes, ma'am."

Jalisa turned to her brother. "I had an appendicitis attack at work. Jordan saw me in such terrible pain, he didn't want to wait for an ambulance. He stood up to Murgatroid and took me to the emergency room right away and they got it out just before it burst. Then he not only visited me in the hospital, he brought me home and got me groceries, made sure I was okay. I didn't tell you because I didn't want to worry you. Between Jordan, church, and Aunt Mae, I was okay."

Jalisa faced Jordan. Toning her voice down, she spoke to him in her usual calm manner. "Sometimes when Malcolm comes home, he needs a little time to decompress. His work is very stressful. He'll be much nicer in a day or two." She stepped back and looked at both men. "Now, are we good?"

"I apologize," Malcolm muttered. "Thank you for caring for my baby sister. Sorry if you need to change your underwear."

"No problem. Thank you for your service to our country." He gathered Miss Buttons and the bag full of her things and started for the door. "Good talk. Later, Jalisa."

Jordan resumed breathing once the elevator doors closed. He hugged Miss Buttons, who let him know in no uncertain terms that she was not a fan of elevators. "Now you be good in my new car, got it?"

It was late when Jordan returned to his father's home. Vivienne was waiting up for him.

"Your father's asleep. He tires easily and he talked more today than he usually does in a week. I hope you had a nice visit with your mother." She took the bag from Jordan and reached to scratch Miss Buttons' ears. "Oh, what a pretty girl! It'll be so nice to have a pet in the house. Can I help you get settled in?"

"No thanks, Vivienne. I saw a friend after visiting my mom. It went later than I expected. I'll get Miss Buttons set up in my bedroom."

"You have that entire wing of the house," Vivienne reminded him. "If there's nothing further you need, I'll turn in now."

"Goodnight, Vivienne. Thanks for everything."

Jordan set Miss Buttons down and she began to explore her new territory. He surveyed his new home. The kitchen alone was bigger than his entire apartment. Once again, Jordan felt overwhelmed by the sudden prosperity and accompanying responsibilities that had been thrust upon him. *My grandfather went halfway around the world and used his wealth and influence to help others. I can do the same.*

Jordan picked up the telephone and called the hospital to check on Lizzie.

"No, sir. There's been no change."

Day 6

7:46 a.m.

Adam arrived at the station with a box of donuts from Donut Drive-In, as was his habit when the team closed a big case. Samantha and Connor would be in soon. He wasn't sure about Kate and Boris. Kate would drop in when Adam got a case that interested her, but only if she wasn't knee-deep in her own work. She usually was, so he didn't expect her, but he got some of the iced French donuts she loved, just in case.

Captain Gavin Peterson knocked on the door jamb. "Got a minute?"

"Sure, Cap. What's up?"

"Let's talk in my office." Captain Peterson turned and walked to his office, while Adam followed. He shut the door. "Have a seat."

"Everything okay? Don't tell me the Farraday twins have gotten out already."

Captain Peterson shook his head. "No, no. Nothing like that. Bail was denied, over the protestations of their fancy-pants lawyers! I'm confident we've given the district attorney a great case, and the sister, at least, isn't gonna see daylight for the rest of her life. I think the brother was offered a reduced sentence for his cooperation, which he was happy to give. Still, he'll be doing quite a bit of time before he's out. What they did was unconscionable."

"Good to know. It doesn't always work that way when you're dealing with the very wealthy. The justice system only works if it applies equally to everyone, and some of these sleaze balls pay their way out of getting what they deserve. We had a lot of victims, and for what? More money, more power. Greed, greed, greed."

Cap nodded. "Look, Adam, I know you and your team are going to have your celebratory donuts this morning before delving into the next batch of cases. Go ahead. You all worked hard and you deserve it." He looked through the glass partitions of his office, but no one was near. "There's something else I want to discuss with you before your crew gets in this morning."

Adam raised his eyebrows.

"I'm taking early retirement. Melanie and I got our first vacation last week in years. We discovered we liked it." He picked at the corner of a notepad. "We cut it short when Bo was shot." Cap looked away and studied the wall clock with more fascination than it warranted. He sighed. "Look, Adam. We're not getting any younger. Mel's dad passed away last year and left us a little surprise. Not a lot, but enough for us to get away, do some traveling, and supplement our pensions. I've given the best part of my life to this job, and Melanie has stood by me, supported me, and never—or at least almost never—complained. I've done right by my men and by the people of the city I serve. Now, it's time to do right by the woman who has loved me and sacrificed for me. I'm letting you know now, but once your team has had their little party, I plan to tell them before you send them out on their new assignments. And, before word spreads, I want my people to hear it from me first."

"Wow, Cap. I wasn't expecting to hear this. Not now, anyway. Congratulations." Adam crossed and re-crossed his legs and bit his lower lip. "I can't imagine working for anyone else. You're leaving big shoes to fill."

"That brings me to the second topic I wanted to discuss. *I* know that *you* know that I don't get to choose my replacement. That job is in the hands of higher up honchos than I'll ever be. But they *have* asked me for recommendations, and they'll at least give my input some consideration. I'd like to put your name in for the promotion. You're my first and only choice for this position. What do you think?"

Adam took a deep breath and sighed, leaning back in his

chair. "That's quite an honor." He was silent for several moments, considering Captain Peterson's words. "You know," he added, "I've been trained by the best. If the position is offered to me, then I'll accept. Thanks for the recommendation."

Captain Peterson stood and held out his hand to Adam. Adam stood and shook his hand. "I was hoping you'd say that," Peterson smiled. "Good luck."

The men looked through the glass walls of the office and saw Connor and Samantha enter the squad room. "I better get going," Adam said. "You're welcome to join us for donuts. With Bo not here, there should be plenty to choose from."

Captain Peterson raised his eyebrows. "Yeah? Did ya get the raised donuts with the sugar sprinkled on the outside? Those are my favorites."

"Then you better join us!"

Adam walked out of Gavin Peterson's office and into his own. "Morning," he nodded to them, as he walked to his desk and sat down. He motioned for Connor and Samantha to follow and take their seats. "Samantha, we've got a custom in this office, that whenever we've closed a big case, I bring in donuts. So help yourselves. We can pat ourselves on the back and enjoy a few minutes to celebrate before we pull out our next assignments. Anybody see or talk to Bo? We'll have to thank him for not being here, so we have leftovers."

"I saw him this morning on the way in," Samantha said. "He's up and walking with a walker, and they expect to move him to a step-down room tomorrow. So good progress."

"Very good!" Adam said. "What are you doing for Thanksgiving, Samantha?" Adam shoved a chocolate glazed donut in his mouth and passed the box.

"My Aunt Su Li, Uncle David, and their five kiddos come to our house and we roast a turkey. Dad smokes a second turkey, so there's plenty of meat. The women cook while the men toss a football outside. Then, after we eat ourselves into a coma, the women put their feet up while the men do the cleanup. And then everyone watches the game. What are you doing, Adam?"

"We've always gone to my folks' farm out by Union, but this year, with my parents getting older, we're going to host. I'll go out and pick up my parents. Kate, Boris, and Robo will join us. We put Kate's dogs and our dog in the back yard and they get their own feast."

Connor grabbed a jelly donut. He bit into it and jelly gushed out and onto his shirt. Without missing a beat, Connor swiped his finger over his shirt and sucked the jelly off of it before wiping it on another section of his shirt. "We get up early and the older kids and I go serve at the homeless shelter downtown while Kathleen stays home and prepares a big dinner, but this year, we're shakin' things up and goin' to my sister's after the shelter. Time to give Kathleen a little break, but she's makin' pies and a couple of veggie dishes."

"Sounds good. You both requested off for the long weekend. With Bo in the hospital, there's no one to cover, so Samantha, you're low man on the totem pole. I'm going let you off with the understanding that if we get a call that can't wait, you're the detective on call, got it?"

Samantha looked down. "Yes, sir."

"Detective Hernandez?" Adam could tell by Samantha's tone that she was disappointed. "Trust me. I won't call you in unless it's a big case. Thanksgiving's important, but the nature of our job doesn't always agree with our preferred holiday schedule. Like the commercial says, crime doesn't take a holiday. But this unit deals with the bigger cases, so it's not too unusual for us to get a short break."

"Bo usually offers to work the holidays, since he's a single guy and his family's in Tennessee," Connor added. "But it's about fifty-fifty whether he's busy or not. He may be aggravatin' all right, but he's a good man to volunteer so's the rest of us can have the holidays with our families."

Adam shrugged. "True, but after getting shot and nearly losing his life, Bo might decide to take some of those holidays and spend some time with his family. Once you live through something like that, your priorities change. *You* change."

Captain Peterson knocked to announce his presence. "A minute, please?"

"C'mon in, Cap," Adam said. He offered the donut box. "We got your favorite, right here."

Gavin Peterson stood before the group, took the box, and held it. "First of all, congratulations on wrapping up the Central West End attack. Felix Santos got the bomber and your good detective work resulted in the arrest of the Farradays in their murder-for-hire scheme. The D.A. is salivating at this case, so be sure all your i's are dotted and your t's are crossed in your paperwork. We've got a solid case to give the prosecutor. Let's not have a technicality screw it up." Captain Peterson set the donut box on the table beside Adam's desk. "Second, I want to personally wish you all a safe and happy Thanksgiving. *Hopefully,* it'll be quiet. Even criminals like to enjoy some turkey. If they steal it, it's up to Robbery, not Homicide." The group chuckled at the joke. "Third, I have an announcement."

Samantha and Connor sat up straight to listen.

"I've put in for my retirement. I'll be leaving after close of shift December 31. At this time, my replacement has not been named. Before this goes public, I want to let you know that it's been an honor to work with a team as stellar as this one. I'll miss you, but I'm proud to have known you, and I want to thank you for your service."

Silence followed. Then Connor began to clap as he stood. Samantha and Adam joined him. Congratulations were offered. Captain Peterson thanked them and returned to his office, with two of his favorite donuts.

When they were alone again, Connor spoke. "Yous oughtta be the new Cap'n, Adam. It ain't gonna be the same without Cap, but yous should be the clear choice here."

Adam nodded his thanks. "It's not up to me or Cap. That decision is above our pay grade. We'll have to see."

"If it's based on merit, yous are in, but if it's another stinkin' political decision, yous are screwed—and so are we."

Samantha remained silent. She was too new to the group to voice an opinion, but she felt sad and uncomfortable.

"I'll be seein' Bo after my shift. Should I tell him, or will you?" she asked Adam.

"I'll go see him and let him know," Adam replied. He handed them their assignments. "I'd like you two to work this case together. If you finish early, then go home. You've earned it and can submit your reports to me through e-mail, if you don't want to come back. Questions?"

Connor and Samantha reviewed the case. "Looks pretty cut and dried," Connor said, and Samantha nodded.

"All right. Dismissed. And watch your backs."

12:08 p.m.

Jordan Farraday took the elevator to the sixth floor ICU where Lizzie lay in stillness, kept alive by machines. This time, however, he didn't need to steal a lab coat and fake being a doctor. The police guard was gone and Jordan knocked lightly. He didn't expect an answer, and none came, so he went in. The nurse from last night was right. No change. Jordan noticed that the stuffed animals that had been taken into evidence had been returned. But in case they had not, he'd purchased a white polar bear with a red ribbon around its neck. He pulled a chair next to her bed and sat in silence.

He stroked her hand, avoiding the IV lines. "They got the guys who did this to you, Lizzie. They were after me all along. It's a long story. Can you believe I was a suspect in all this? Like I would ever do anything to hurt you. The office is going to open in another couple weeks. Now that the people responsible have been caught, I don't have to sneak around the guard to see you. I'll come every day. Just get better. Please."

Jordan lifted her hand to his lips. Her arms bore bruises from changing her IVs, and, Jordan supposed, blood draws. The room was still, except for the beeping and humming of the machines. The tube going down her throat had been removed and oxygen tubing was in her nose instead, which told him Lizzie was breathing on her own. The bandage on her head had been changed and he noticed the new bandage covered less of her head, showing more of her skin and hair. Jordan hoped these were good signs—signs that she was healing. Had his father's specialists changed her treatment and she was improving? He hoped so.

Jordan placed the polar bear on the bed, next to the teddy bear and the dog, and gently tucked the get-well gifts around her. Then he froze. Lizzie's breathing changed and her eyelids fluttered. She moaned and opened her eyes.

"Carson?" she asked in a hoarse, weak voice.

Jordan's eyes filled with tears. "I'm here, Lizzie. I'm here. How are you?" *What a stupid question! Why do I always sound like an idiot when I'm around this girl?*

"I've been better," came the tiny reply. She turned her head to look at him. "You were here before, weren't you?"

"Yes!" Jordan answered, astounded.

"I felt it. I knew you were here. I could tell...and it made me happy."

"Yeah? Do you want me to get the nurse? Do you need pain medicine?"

The nurse hurried into the room before Lizzie could answer. "Your monitors showed a change!" she said. "I'll let your doctor know right away."

Right away meant after she took vitals and asked Lizzie a series of questions. Headaches? Pain? Short of breath? Follow my finger. Squeeze my hand. Do you feel this? Jordan was getting antsy and wanted to tell her to just go call the doctor already. His mind raced with excitement. Lizzie was awake!

Finally, the nurse entered the information into the computer and left to call the doctor.

Jordan took Lizzie's hand in his. "I don't want to stay long. I don't want to make you tired." He sniffed and wiped his eyes. "I'm so happy you're awake, Lizard Gizzard."

"Thank you," she whispered. "Thanks for coming." She touched his hand, closed her eyes, and went to sleep.

Jordan left the room as though walking on air. He stopped at the nurse's station. "Did you talk to the doctor? What'd he say?" he asked.

"Are you family?" she asked him.

Jordan was tempted to say he was Lizzie's fiancé, but his better judgment warned him against saying something else stupid. "No, just a friend. A good friend."

The nurse smiled at him. "You know I can't violate HIPAA. Unless your friend gives her express permission, we can't talk to you." She paused and looked down at her notes. In a low voice, she said, "Doctor will be here within the hour. That's all I can tell you." She turned and rummaged through a file cabinet.

Jordan didn't have anything else on his schedule. He'd seen his mother earlier at Heather Hills Memory Home. It was a beautiful facility with a warm, friendly staff. Clean, no bad odors, and a luxurious dining room. Mary Rose Hollister would live her remaining days in as much comfort as the Farraday money could buy. Jordan was saddened that she would have little cognizance of her posh surroundings, but was happy that she would receive the best possible care.

While he was at Heather Hills, he'd stopped in to see his grandfather, Robert Farraday. The senior Farraday's room was similar to his mother's. But his grandfather was completely bed-ridden, and Jordan believed that his father, as sick as he was, would outlive his grandfather. He sat by his grandfather's bedside as the frail old man lay in a hospice bed, nourished by a feeding tube. Kenton had warned him. Jordan felt compelled to remain and stayed by his bedside until just before lunchtime.

At the hospital, Jordan took a seat in the lobby next to the elevators where he had a clear view of anyone walking toward Lizzie's room. He would kill the next hour, reading magazines so old the fashions had returned.

An hour and ten minutes passed before anyone resembling a doctor got off the elevator and turned toward Lizzie's room. Jordan followed, walking silently behind him as the man threw open her door.

Lizzie was awake again. The doctor spoke to her, but when Jordan made a sound, he turned and ordered him out of the room. "I'll be right outside, Lizzie," he told her, before leaving.

Twenty minutes passed before the doctor left her room. Jordan peppered him with questions. "Is she going to be okay? Is she in pain? Is she—"

"Young man, I can only talk to you because my patient has given me permission to do so. I'll also let the nurses' station know they can talk to you. Miss Wise is expected to make a full recovery, but it will be a long road. She'll begin physical therapy in a few days, and we'll have to see how that works for her. I don't anticipate any long-term or permanent damage, save for some scarring, of course. The bullet grazed her head, but did not lodge in her brain. She sustained a concussion when she fell and hit her head, presumably on the desk or floor. Her surgery was minor and involved closing the head wound. She sustained additional cuts, abrasions and contusions, but the concussion was her most serious injury."

The doctor dismissed Jordan and stepped into the elevator. Jordan had heard all he needed to hear. He rushed down the hall to Lizzie's room. "Can I come in?" he asked through a crack in the door. Realizing Lizzie was too weak to be heard, he went in, anyway. The bed had been adjusted to a partial sitting position, and Lizzie's bandage had been changed again to an even smaller size.

Jordan smiled at her, encouraged. "The doc says you're gonna be okay. That's great, Lizard!"

"I do have a name, you know," she reminded him. Her voice was still raspy, but she seemed more awake.

"I do, too, but it isn't Carson. It's kind of a long story, but my real name is Jordan. If I tell you everything, it'll only make your head hurt worse, but that really is my name, I promise. Jordan." His eyes teared again. "And it's my fault you're in here. It's my fault you got hurt. I'm so sorry."

"It's not your fault, Cars—Jordan." She scrunched her nose. "That's weird, you know."

"Yeah, I know. I've been worried about you. Look, Lizzie, if you want me to go away, I will. I don't want to bother you or upset you. It's just that, well, I...I really like you and I thought you were gonna die and I'd never get the chance to tell you and you'd never know I cared for you. Those men—were they asking for me? When they stormed the office?"

Lizzie shut her eyes and squeezed them tightly. "Yes. It was horrible." She opened her eyes again. "They shot Murgatroid. She couldn't believe someone had the audacity to not tremble in fear before her. You know how arrogant she is. I mean *they're pointing guns at her* and she's throwing her weight around! Then they just went crazy shooting. I tried to duck... fall down, but got hit anyway. But yes, they demanded to know where you were. Why were they after you? I...I was afraid for you, too."

Jordan pressed his fingers into his forehead. "It's been a nightmare," he said, avoiding the question. "Why haven't any family members come to see you? I've been your only visitor."

Lizzie looked toward the window and bit her lip. She was silent so long, Jordan thought she'd gone back to sleep. "Lizzie Wise is not my real name either."

Jordan sat beside her bed. "Do you want to talk about it?"

Lizzie didn't answer right away. She pressed the button on her bed to adjust it, raising her feet a few inches. "Would you please pour me some water? I'm thirsty."

Jordan did so and handed it to her, holding it steady while she sipped through the straw. "If you don't want to talk..."

"My name is Haley Elizabeth Wyndom." Jordan thought Lizzie's voice sounded stronger. She took a breath and exhaled. "I'm from Minnesota. When I was twelve, my mom died. She had cancer and wasn't going to get better. When I was fourteen, my dad remarried—she was a real witch. His new wife was horrible to me and my younger brother, Kyle. He was thirteen. After a year, Kyle ran away. I never saw him or heard from him again. I don't know where he is, or if he's even still alive."

Lizzie paused and took a drink of water. "Cynthia, my dad's new wife, was a liar and a schemer. She would do things like leave the television on, leave the refrigerator door open, spill things and not clean them up, and then tell my father *I* was doing it on purpose because I was such a rebellious teenager and I needed to be taught a lesson. My dad and I were never close, but I couldn't believe he accepted everything that woman said about me—never even asked me for my side of anything. When Mom got sick, everything focused on getting her better. There were a lot of bills. The cancer affected the whole family. I tried to keep up with some cooking and housework, but I was only ten when she got sick and two years isn't much time to grow up. Cynthia wasted no time in comforting Dad, and before you knew it, he believed everything she told him. She even planted cigarettes in my drawer and showed them to my father before I got home from school! I was so stressed, my grades started dropping and Cynthia told my dad it was a sure sign of drug abuse. The last straw was when I got home from school on a Friday, that wretched excuse for a human had taken my dog, Jazzy, my best friend in the world, and abandoned her at a shelter. Do you know how many shelters are in the Twin City area? I never did find Jazzy."

Tears streamed down Lizzie's face. Jordan handed her a box of tissues. "I can't imagine the pain that caused. I'm so sorry."

"That was on a Friday," she continued. "Once Cynthia saw the damage she had inflicted, she glared at me with her evil, smug sneer, and announced she was meeting my father for dinner. She told me I was grounded for two weeks and I better answer the home phone when she called to check on me, or things would get worse." Lizzie rolled her eyes and wiped a tear that had escaped. "Huh! Like that was even possible! She left and slammed the door on her way out. I couldn't take anymore. I wrote a note saying I was spending the night at a friend's. I packed everything I could carry, and took all the money I could find in the house. I went through her drawers and found quite a bit of money and took that, too. I cleaned out everything I could fit into my backpack, a suitcase and a carry-on, and I took my mom's jewelry, which Cynthia had the nerve to wear. Mom's jewelry was left to me in her will, but Cynthia didn't care. She took whatever she wanted. That jewelry was all I had left of my mom, and she had no right to take it. Just as I was walking out the door, the phone rang. Cynthia was checking up on me. I could tell by her voice she'd been drinking, which meant they weren't going to be home for some time. I walked to my best friend's house. She knew what was going on and swore to me she'd never say anything to anybody. I'd stuck it out for a year after Kyle left, but I couldn't take one more day. My friend drove me to the train station and I got as far as St. Louis before the fares went up to the next level. I didn't want to spend any more money on travel unless I had to, so I got off and started looking for a place to live."

She leaned back in the bed and closed her eyes again.

"That sounds so terrible, Lizzie. Or should I call you Haley? What do you prefer?"

"I became Elizabeth Wise. Haley Wyndom is dead." She motioned for the water again, and Jordan steadied the cup while she drank.

"What happened after you got off the train?"

"I was wandering around the train station, not knowing what to do next." She coughed a short laugh. "I hadn't thought that far ahead. All I wanted to do was get as far away from home as possible. I was scared and alone. A couple approached me. They seemed really kind and sweet. They started talking to me and made me realize I had put myself in a dangerous position being alone in downtown St. Louis. They offered me a place to stay until I could find a job and get on my feet. I told them I was eighteen." She shrugged. "At sixteen, with my seventeenth birthday in a few weeks, I was close enough."

"Were they safe? Sheesh, Lizzie, you could've trusted an axe murderer for all you know!"

"They never harmed me or asked anything of me. They invited me to church on Sundays and I went with them. The husband was a youth pastor and they had some kind of ministry for troubled kids, so they hung around the bus station and train station. They didn't ask me questions or press me for information. They took just as big a chance on me as I did on them. For all they knew, *I* could have been the axe murderer! I did lie, and told them my wallet had been stolen and I had no identification. They knew someone who knew someone, and they helped me re-establish my identity so I could get a driver's license. I'd never given them any reason not to trust me, so the couple believed me when I told them my wallet was stolen. I started working at a fast food joint, and made enough money to get some nicer clothes and an old car that ran. The wife taught me some basic office skills and I started applying for entry level office positions. MSR hired me, and you know the rest. I stayed with the couple for three more months to save money, and then I got my own apartment. I still keep in touch with them, but they've moved on to help other teenagers."

"Have you ever tried to contact your father?" Jordan asked. He refilled her water bottle.

"No. I'm sure Cynthia filed a police report and exaggerated what was taken. If it was up to her, I'd be in jail for grand larceny or something like that. I was lucky. I made it. I don't know what became of my brother."

Carson nodded. Lizzie's story was upsetting to hear, and made him care about her even more. He changed the subject. "You'll probably be getting a new room soon. Especially if you'll be starting physical therapy. I don't want to intrude or make you uncomfortable, but I can take care of you."

Lizzie shook her head. "That's sweet, but I'll manage." She looked down at her hands. "Besides, I've got some serious trust issues. I'm damaged goods, Jordan. And I may even be a fugitive. Who knows? You don't want to get involved with me." She looked away toward the window.

"Don't you think that might be *my* decision? You trusted the couple who took you in, didn't you? Maybe you could trust one more person?"

"Let's get me well and on my feet first, huh? I'm so tired." Lizzie tried to smile, but her eyelids drooped. Her earlier surge of energy had passed, and her voice was fading. She pushed the button to adjust her bed again, and closed her eyes.

"So that's not a no. I can live with that," Jordan said. "You get some sleep. I'll see you tomorrow." He leaned down and kissed her forehead, but she was already asleep.

1:10 p.m.

On the fifth floor in the same hospital, Samantha Hernandez stepped into Bo's room. His mother was seated by his bed.

"Mama," Bo said, grimacing in pain as he reached for the morphine button. "This is Samantha Jane. She's with my team. Samantha Jane, this here's my mama, Annabelle Whitney, from whom I inherited greatness, brains, and my obvious good looks."

"We've met already," Samantha told him in a flat voice. She shook Annabelle's hand. "It's nice to see you again, Mrs. Whitney."

"Now, I told you to call me Annabelle," she scolded Samantha in her thick Southern drawl. Her eyes sparkled when she smiled. "At least, we're not so worried about Bowman this time. It looks like he's making a good recovery!"

"I was never worried about him," Samantha objected. "He's my partner and I wouldn't be a good partner if I didn't check on him."

"Methinks Samantha Jane doth protest too much," Bo said. "That's Shakespeare I'm quotin' there, little lady. Shows I got culture." He nodded his head at her, sporting a smug grin.

Samantha rolled her eyes. "Annabelle, I'm glad you're here. Would you and JoBeth like to join me and my family for Thanksgiving?"

"Oh, honey, that's so sweet of you to ask! We'll be headin' back to Tennessee as soon as Bowman is out of ICU, and I know I won't have to worry. I've got to get back to my farm and my animals. I cain't impose on my brother forever! But thank you for the kind invitation."

"I understand. If I don't see you before you leave, have a safe trip. I'll leave you and Bo alone, then." Samantha headed for the door.

"Samantha Jane, Adam was by here. He told me about Cap retiring. You gonna come back and see me soon?"

Lord, he's obnoxious! "If you're lucky."

When Bo and his mother were alone again, Bo said to her, "Mama, she's the one. You like her, don't you?"

Annabelle's eyes twinkled at him and the corners of her mouth drew up. "Oh, baby, she's the one all right. You done good, child. Real good."

1:58 p.m.

"Hi, son! Where've you been all morning?" Kenton Farraday was dressed in a suit accessorized with an ear-to-ear grin.

"Mom was moved this morning. I wanted to be sure she was comfortable. Heather Hills is beautiful. Thanks so much for arranging the move. It means a lot to me. I think she'll be as happy as she can be, under the circumstances."

Kenton smiled. "Good, Jordan! Good! I was happy to help. She deserves the best."

Vivienne announced, "Coffee's ready!" as she brought out cups from the pantry.

Jordan poured himself a cup. "I also went to see my grandfather—you know, since he's at the same place."

Kenton sat on a kitchen stool. "That was very thoughtful of you, son. He's not in good shape. I see him a couple times a week. Did he say anything?"

Jordan shook his head. "No. I don't even think he knew I was there." He looked at the floor. "He looked pretty bad, and I sat with him for a while. I've had a lot to think about, and I wanted to see him. He's part of who I am…a part I've missed out on." He drank his coffee. "After that, I went to see Lizzie in the hospital." He brightened. "She woke up while I was there and we got to talk! The best news is the new doctor saw her while I waited outside and he told me she'll make a full recovery. Of course, it'll take a while, but she's on the way! I'm really excited. I know you'll like her."

Kenton's eyes sparkled with life. "I'm sure I'll like her, son! I'm glad to hear your good news! Things are looking up!" He stood. "I'd like to take you to the office, so you can meet Martina and take a tour, see what will be yours soon. Vivienne's laid a suit out on your bed, so go and get changed and we'll get going. My driver will be here any minute."

"What about taking my new car?" Jordan asked, heading toward the staircase.

"We'll take the limo. Your car's a little small for me. I hope you like it."

"Love it!" Jordan called over his shoulder as he ran up the steps, taking them two at a time to his room.

Vivienne met him outside his door after he had changed. "Good," she said. "Everything fits. You look very nice." She lowered her voice. "Your father has had such a glow about him, since he found you. He's waited a lifetime to call you his son."

Jordan shifted his feet uncomfortably. "I can't bring myself to call him dad, Vivienne. Not yet, anyway. I hope he understands."

Vivienne smiled. "Your father is not known for being a patient man. But he's overjoyed that you're here with him, in this house. We weren't sure what type of person you might be but those worries were for nothing. You've had a lot of adjustments and more are coming. Things will come in time. You'll like Martina. Now go!"

Jordan jogged down the staircase.

"You look nice, son. I hope you don't mind that I picked out a suit. I know you haven't had time to shop. You might want to get some clothes before the Thanksgiving weekend is upon us and the stores become a nightmare to navigate."

"I'll do that." Jordan opened the front door and helped his father into the limo.

It was a short ride to the Farraday Building in downtown Clayton. Jordan's eyes were wide as he took in the two-story marble lobby, accented with polished mahogany. Stained glass transoms provided a border around the top of the lobby entrance. Security guards stood straight and tall when Kenton entered.

Kenton introduced Jordan to the guards and the head of security, who had been told to meet them in the lobby. Jordan met the ladies at the information desk before going to a row of elevators. He wondered if he was going to meet every person who worked in the building.

"These elevators go from the lobby to the 15th floor," his father told him, pointing toward the row on the left. "These go from the lobby to the 30th floor, and this one," he said, taking out a key, "goes directly to the Penthouse suites." He inserted the key and the elevator doors opened to an opulent interior of marble and mahogany.

Martina was at her desk, typing figures onto a spreadsheet. She looked up when the glass double doors opened. "Mr. Farraday! How nice to see you! You're looking very well today."

"Thank you, Martina. This is my son, Jordan Farraday. Jordan, meet Martina Gonzales, my right hand in everything."

They shook hands. Jordan had pictured Martina as an older woman, like Vivienne or Colette, but she wasn't much older than he was. Her shiny black hair was pulled back into a tight bun, and she was smartly dressed in a navy blue suit with a pale lavender blouse, a single strand of pearls, and a jeweled brooch on the lapel of her suit jacket.

"Martina, I'm going to show Jordan around, give him a complete tour, and I'm hoping you'll help me train him in all he needs to know."

Martina's dazzling white teeth reminded Jordan he needed to see a dentist. "Of course, Mr. Farraday." She turned to Jordan. "I'm glad I finally got to meet you, Mr. Farraday."

"Nice to meet you, Martina, and please, call me Jordan."

4:52 p.m.

Jenna Trent put a generous helping of her special blend of Parmesan and Romano cheeses over her lasagna, covered it with foil, and slid it into the oven to bake. She checked the clock and set the timer. The back door opened and Amy walked in with Blue following her.

"I'll feed Blue and set the table, Mom," Amy said, unhooking the dog's leash. Blue dashed to her food dish and looked up expectantly at Amy. "Have you ever missed a meal?

You're not going to starve," Amy told the big blue pit bull. She filled her dish and Blue attacked it with vigor.

"Wash your hands first," Jenna called. "Please make the salad for tonight. We're having lasagna." She picked up the new book she'd gotten from the library where she worked part-time, and propped her feet up on the sofa.

"Yum. That's one of Daddy's favorites. Did Gomer say she was going to make her special pumpkin pie for Thanksgiving next week?"

"Yes, she is."

Amy continued chattering and Jenna put down her book, unable to read and talk at the same time. There was much to do and Jenna chided herself for indulging in the guilty pleasure of getting lost in a book, when they were expecting a houseful for Thanksgiving the following week.

"Aunt Kate doesn't cook, right, Mom?"

"What was your first clue?"

Amy giggled. "She brings wine to Thanksgiving and chips and buns to our barbecues."

"Sounds like you're a detective like your dad, honey." Jenna rose and made the salad dressing while Amy tore lettuce. "I think I hear him coming now."

Adam entered the kitchen and inhaled. "Ooohhh! That's gotta be lasagna I smell!" He kissed his wife and daughter. "Jenna, I invited Kate and the boys over for dinner. Hope you don't mind. I'll go and change." He left for the bedroom.

"I heard," Amy said, and set the lettuce on the counter. "I'll set an extra place for Aunt Kate."

"Thanks, honey. Would you also check the fence to be sure it's locked up tight? Boris loves to play, and he'll get Blue all riled up."

"I'll take care of it." Amy finished setting the extra place, and she and Blue left for the backyard.

"Doesn't she sound grown up?" Adam entered the kitchen. "What's she taking care of?"

"Securing the backyard against the onslaught of three large dogs." Jenna studied her husband and frowned. "All right.

What happened at work? Your poker face is broken again." She kissed his cheek and returned to the salad, but kept her eyes on Adam.

"Got a little unexpected news today. I haven't told Kate, yet. Of course, it doesn't affect her—she's with K-9. We can discuss it after dinner while Amy's doing her homework."

Jenna nodded.

"The perimeter is secured," Amy announced as she and Blue walked through the back door. She stood straight and saluted her father.

Adam pinched her nose. "Cute. At ease, corporal."

The doorbell rang. Adam let Kate Marlin in. Blue ran to greet the visitors, elated to see her buddies. "Out in the backyard, kids," Jenna instructed.

Amy shooed the dogs out and tossed out balls, Frisbees, and tug toys.

"I brought dessert," Kate said and handed Adam a bag.

"You cooked?" Amy asked.

"Manners, Amy!" Jenna reprimanded.

"Sorry, Aunt Kate," Amy whispered.

Kate laughed. "Ice cream and store bought hot fudge sauce," she said as Adam placed the ice cream in the freezer and the fudge sauce on the counter.

"That'll work," Jenna said, removing her apron. "Good to see you, Kate. Dinner will be out soon."

"I hope so, Mom. I got a lot of homework and Miss Vandover said it's gotta be finished before Thanksgiving break. Can I just start with dessert?"

Jenna sighed. "I *have* a lot of homework and Miss Vandover said it *has* to be finished before Thanksgiving break, and no, you may not start with dessert."

After dinner, Amy trotted into her bedroom to finish homework, while the adults sat in the living room for coffee and conversation.

Kate began. "Adam. Your poker face still needs work. I know you're chewing on something. Should we play twenty questions, or just skip to torture?"

Jenna giggled. "I asked him the same thing when he got home. Nothing like suspense."

Adam leaned back into the sofa cushions and Jenna stroked the back of his neck. "Nothing like having beautiful, stubborn women gang up on a guy. Why don't you two pick on someone your own size?" he joked. He rubbed his face with his hands and sighed. "Captain Peterson announced he's retiring, effective the end of the year."

"No!" Kate said. "I thought he'd never leave. I pegged Captain Peterson to die with his boots on."

"Well, I'm happy for him," Jenna added. "I bet Melanie's really relieved. The other woman in his life will finally be gone."

Adam turned to his wife and raised his eyebrows. "Really? Do you ever feel that way?"

"Sometimes. Goes with the territory. Like you're fond of saying, it comes with the uniform," Jenna answered. "More than the long hours, it's the constant worry. When you leave in the mornings, I wonder if I've kissed you for the last time. When Amy smarts off, I wonder if those words are the last you may hear and if she'll regret saying them for the rest of her life." Jenna sighed and leaned into her husband. "But that's what I signed up for when I married you. I still chose to go through with it, and I'd do it all over again a million times. You're the best man I know." She reached up to kiss his cheek.

Adam pulled her close and kept his arm around her.

"Has a replacement been named?" Kate asked.

"Not yet," Adam answered.

"I hear a really big *but* coming up," Kate said, leaning closer to Adam and Jenna.

"Cap has recommended me for the position," he began.

The women gasped together.

"You *are* the best man for the job," Kate interrupted. "I hear the dogs at the door." She rose and let Blue, Robo, and Boris in. Blue went straight to Amy's room, leaving the German Shepherds to follow Kate. "Lie down," she ordered, and they dropped.

"It's not up to Cap, though," Adam continued. "It's not his choice, but the powers that be will consider his recommendation."

"How do you feel about this, babe?" Jenna asked him.

Adam's countenance brightened for the first time since coming home. "I think about it. There would be a definite boost in pay, which in turn, would affect my pension. That's the best part. But I could also see an increase in my hours, which takes me away from you and Amy. That's the worst part. I wouldn't be out in the field very often working homicide. Mixed feelings about that. There's more responsibility, less risk to life and limb. There's a hodgepodge of positives and negatives to consider. But it hasn't been offered, so we better not count chickens before they're hatched. Cap's leaving big shoes to fill. It's an honor even to be considered. And by the way, the official announcement isn't being made until after the Thanksgiving holiday, so mum's the word."

"Do you know who else is being considered?" Kate asked.

"Not a clue."

Day 7

8:46 a.m.

Edmond Carmody walked through the lobby of Medical Staffing Remedies and nodded in approval. The first floor had been completely restored, and looked as though nothing had happened. Any hint that only a week ago, the walls were riddled with bullet holes, the carpet stained with blood, and furniture lay broken in disarray, had been obliterated. He listened to the noise of the construction crew on the second story, and climbed the stairs to survey the work.

The foreman greeted him and handed him a hard hat. "Just a precaution, sir. The project is right on schedule." He motioned with his hand, showing the progress made. "When all the work's indoors, it's a little easier to finish on time."

Mr. Carmody walked through the second level, satisfied. "It looks like we just need the floors put in and the furniture returned, right?"

"Pretty much. The flooring is ready to install, but we've still got a few light fixtures to finish hooking up. Before close tonight, we should have all of the old flooring up and the subfloor prepped for the installation of the new floors. You'll be open for business the first week in December."

"Looks good," Mr. Carmody said. "I plan to have the Christmas party in-house this year. I want our employees to see that we will rebuild and we will go on. Downstairs in the lobby where the recessed wall is, I want the plaque we discussed hung as a Wall of Remembrance in honor of our employees who have passed away."

"We'll have that ready for you, no problem," the supervisor assured him.

"And the name plate for the office manager's door. Did you get Jalisa Moore's name spelled correctly?"

"Yes, sir. You'll be ready to roll the first of December."

"Very well. Have a nice Thanksgiving." Edmond Carmody returned the hard hat and left to contact his employees so they would be ready to work when the building was finished. Jalisa would have to find a temp to cover for Elizabeth Wise. Robert Shoemaker was not ready to return, so the other recruiters would divide his client list until he was released from care.

Thanksgiving Day

"**I**t's so wonderful to have all of us together again to cele-brate Thanksgiving! We have so much to be thankful for!" Julie's eyes misted as she looked at each person around the Hernandez dining table. "Su Li, Hanna, and Samantha, this looks and smells wonderful! Sorry about the rolls, guys!"

Sam reached for her hand and patted it. "It's all right, honey. We all understand how challenging it can be to remove the rolls from the bag, put them on a baking sheet, and into an oven for ten minutes. It could happen to anyone. And we got the alarm turned off and cancelled the call to the fire depart-ment before they got here, so we're good. If the smell isn't out of the furniture by Monday, we'll call the same company that took care of the smoke the last time you tried to cook."

"It's no problem, Mom," Samantha added, waving her hand to dispel the smoke and coughing. "If they can't get the smell out—well, this furniture is pretty old. It's time for some new stuff, anyway."

"I just wanted to help," Julie offered. She coughed into her napkin.

"We have plenty of starch. Who needs rolls anyway?" Su Li added cheerfully, cocking her head to the side and shrug-ging with upturned palms. "We've got mashed potatoes, stuff-ing, gravy, and two kinds of sweet potatoes. Nobody's going hungry today!"

"Yeah, Aunt Julie. It's not like we trusted you with the turkey or anything important." Matthew chimed in.

"Matthew!" David said with a stern voice.

"Samantha, do you have a boyfriend?" Hannah asked.

"Hannah!" Su Li said, looking at her daughter with wide eyes and pressing her lips together.

"No, I don't." Samantha replied.

Hannah looked sideways at the others and mumbled, "I didn't think so."

"Then why are you taking him leftovers in the hospital?" Levi asked.

"Because he's my partner and hospital food stinks, and it's lousy to be in the hospital any time, and especially so at Thanksgiving, so can we please eat before the meal is cold?"

"Whatever you say." Matthew couldn't resist adding his two cents worth.

Sam took Julie's hand and everyone followed, joining hands. "Let's thank God for this delicious meal, and for our many blessings, especially for families and friends."

"They're here!" Amy's excited voice echoed through the house. She threw the door open and ran out to hug her grandparents. "Gomer! Oompah! Did you make your special pumpkin pie?"

"Gomer had no idea you liked pumpkin pie, Amy," her grandfather teased. "Emma Jo, you didn't make none of that awful pumpkin pie stuff, did ya?"

Adam helped his parents up the steps and into the house. "Looks like Gomer made two pies, peanut!"

Blue trotted in to greet everyone. "Hey, Blue!" Gomer said. "No chickens around here for you to chase."

"No, but she's smelling the turkey and licking her chops," Jenna said, wiping her hands on her apron. She hugged her in-laws.

Dwayne Trent inhaled. "Mmm. Nothing smells quite like Thanksgiving! The house smells so good, I could eat the walls!"

"We'll eat soon. Amy's already finished setting the table. We're so happy you can be here with us. Have a seat." Jenna helped Emma Jo to the sofa.

Blue started barking and whining at the window.

"Kate and Boris and Robo are here!" Amy ran to the back door to let Blue out and opened the gate for Kate and her German Shepherds.

Kate came into the house from the back door with wine and wished everyone a happy Thanksgiving. "My culinary skills are not exactly the stuff legends are made of," she announced. "Hi, Emma Jo, Dwayne. Good to see you all again."

"I've got the giblets, liver, and other disgusting stuff ready to give the dogs after dinner." Jenna told Kate.

"Don't you want to put that in the gravy?" Emma Jo asked, shocked.

"No!" was the unanimous answer from all but Dwayne.

"Kids!" Dwayne said. "They just don't know what's good, Em."

"Can I say grace for Thanksgiving this year?" Amy asked.

Emma Jo beamed at her granddaughter. "Of course you can, sweetheart."

"Grace." Amy said, giggling at her own joke.

"How original," Adam pinched her nose. "Oompah will ask the blessing."

Jalisa and Malcolm pulled into Aunt Mae's driveway. "What'd Aunt Mae say about your friend you was hidin' from the police?" Malcolm asked his sister.

"I, ah, may have forgotten to mention it, so I see no reason for you to."

Aunt Mae opened the door wide and gave Malcolm a hug so tight, even he hurt. Her home was filled with over a dozen people, most of whom had no place to go for the holidays. "Malcolm, welcome home! Your sister treatin' you good, right? And for the record, it was not my idea to keep you in the dark about her operation."

"Happy Thanksgiving, Aunt Mae. So good to see you. It's great to be back home. No, me and Jalisa, we're good. We've had our talk. The house smells like heaven. How long you been cookin' anyway? I sure hope you got some of your famous pecan pie for me! And I want a whole sweet potato pie all to myself, so I hope you got extras."

Aunt Mae's smile spread across her face, causing lines to fan out from her the corners of her eyes. "You know I do! Come on in and meet our guests. We'll be saying the blessin' shortly." She made introductions while Malcolm and Jalisa tried to memorize names.

Jalisa thought of Jordan as the group sat down to eat. He would be having a meal prepared by a top-flight French chef, which would, no doubt, be delicious. But he would be eating with total strangers in a big, cold mansion, while the mother who raised him and rarely recognized him would eat alone until he could get away and visit. *I should've invited him to join us. He would've loved it.* Jordan might have money and prestige for the rest of his life, but she would always have family, love, and laughter. Jalisa thought if given a choice, Jordan would likely have switched places with her. Funny, she thought, how they used to joke around about winning the lottery and what they'd do if they had all kinds of money. She hoped it wouldn't change him. He wasn't just sweet and goofy, he'd proven to be a good friend.

"Jalisa! Whatcha thinkin' bout? You still with us, baby sister? 'Cuz you look like you're a thousand miles away." Malcolm stabbed at another pile of turkey.

Jalisa smiled. "Just thinkin' bout my friend not havin' as much fun as we are. Pass those candied sweet potatoes!"

The dining room table in the Farraday mansion was decked out with china, crystal, and linen napkins. A rust-colored table runner ran the length of the table, beginning and ending a few inches from the plates at either end, graced with gourds on each side of a cornucopia overflowing with apples, squashes and nuts. Crystal candlesticks lit the buffet and sidebar.

Kenton sat at the head of the table with Jordan on his right. Martina and Vivienne were to his left and Colette would take her seat next to Jordan after the meal was served. Colette filled Kenton's plate and the others stepped to the buffet table to fill their own.

"Delicious, Colette!" Kenton said. The others agreed in unison.

"*Merci,*" she replied. "Save room for the pies. There is pumpkin, of course, pecan, and apple." Colette turned to Jordan. "And there will be plenty of food for you to take to your sweetheart, Elizabeth, *oui*?" She winked at him.

"How is your young lady doing, Jordan?" Kenton asked him.

"She's weak, of course, and shaky. Tomorrow, they're going to get her to stand up and start walking. If that goes well, the nurses will work with her until Monday, and then physical therapy takes over. She should move out of the ICU by Monday, I think. She's going to love this food!"

Colette's eyes twinkled. "I think some love is in the air, perhaps?"

Jordan blushed and the others grinned at him.

"Have you told her who you are?" Kenton said. His voice carried a note of warning.

"I told her my real name was Jordan, but she doesn't know my last name, and I haven't told her anything else."

"And she wasn't curious?" he half-asked, half demanded.

"She'd just come out of a coma and was in pain. We've only talked a few minutes. She needs her rest." Jordan got up to get more dressing.

"Don't tell her you have money. She needs to like you for who you are." Kenton took a sip of wine and a bite of sweet potatoes.

"I've thought of that." Jordan returned to his seat and faced Kenton. "Are you going to trust me? Trust my judgment? If I'm going to be trusted to run Farraday Enterprises, you're going to have to trust that I can pick my own girlfriend."

Kenton leaned back in his chair and studied Jordan. Colette returned to the buffet and began stirring the dishes. Martina and Vivienne remained silent, looking at their food.

"I apologize, Jordan. Of course you're right. I'm just looking out for you."

The women resumed eating their meal.

"I'm not ungrateful. You've done a lot for me and Mom and Lizzie. But I've liked Lizzie for a long time. Turns out she liked me as well, but was in a difficult position and kind of withdrew from the world. Kept to herself. She was happy to see me in her hospital room, and for the first time, we talked—really talked."

"What was the difficult position? Is she in trouble?"

"No, nothing like that." Jordan didn't believe he had any right to divulge what Lizzie had told him. "Let's just say her family doesn't exactly put the fun in dysfunctional."

Kenton nodded but said nothing. Jordan frowned, wondering if his new father would hire Mr. Hernandez to look into Lizzie's past.

"I'm certain she's lovely or Jordan wouldn't be attracted to her. The Farraday men have excellent taste," Colette said.

"I'm looking forward to meeting her, son. When she's better, of course." Kenton pushed his plate forward. "If I eat another bite, I won't be able to enjoy any pie."

"That would be unfortunate!" Colette scolded, feigning offense.

"More for us!" Vivienne joined Colette in trying to lighten the mood.

"That's why I'm not eating another bite! When you slow pokes are done, we'll have some pie."

Barnes Hospital was quiet as Jordan and Samantha walked to the elevators bearing gifts of food. They exchanged a friendly greeting and wished each other well before exiting at different floors.

"Jordan! You came! Is that food? Real Thanksgiving food! Thank you!" Lizzie smoothed her hair and swung her legs over the side of the bed to sit up. She reached for the movable table. "That's so sweet of you!"

"I thought you probably weren't going to get anything good. Thanksgiving was always my mom's favorite holiday. I thought I'd bring you a nice dinner, even if it's not all that hot right now. How are you feeling?"

"Better. A little stronger. I still can't get used to the idea that it's Thanksgiving. I've been asleep too many days. What's that?" she asked, pointing to a long tray Jordan pulled out of a bag.

"It's a warmer. The food's not very hot, but I can plug this in, and in just a few minutes, you can have an almost fresh Thanksgiving meal." He crossed to the window and found a plug.

"You're really kind and thoughtful. I feel bad for ignoring you so long."

"Good! I'll consider you in my debt." Jordan began placing dishes on the tray.

"So are you gonna tell me why you have another name?" She inhaled the aroma. "That smells totally awesome!"

"Later. Long story. First, let's get you well and walking. Jalisa's going to be the new office manager."

On another floor, Samantha brought Bo a large platter of food Su Li had put together. He was watching an old movie on the television and reached for the remote to turn it off.

"Samantha Jane, I believe that looks good enough to eat. Now, let's get something straight. This here does not count for our dinner and a movie. You still owe me the pleasure of your always-sweet company. I had that talk with your Daddy. I can tell he's crazy 'bout you an' me."

"Don't flatter yourself."

"Adam told me Cap's retiring. I hope Adam gets the job. He's most qualified, but…"

"But what?"

"Politics. Adam don't play no games, Samantha Jane. He's a straight up good cop. Plays by the rules, treats people fair and right."

"But that's what makes him a good choice, isn't it?"

Bo laughed, and grabbed his side. "Oh, that hurts! Your youth is showin', Samantha Jane."

"Why do you always call me by both my names?"

Bo's eyes sparkled. "'Cuz I think Samantha Jane's about the purtiest name I ever heard. And it fits you—the purtiest girl I ever knowed."

She rolled her eyes. "Get some rest. See you later."

"You got that right!"

Eleven Months Later

October 29, 2017

Samantha and Bo drove up the long, winding driveway and parked in front of her parents' home for Sunday dinner. Becky and Noah were throwing a ball in the front yard and Wolfgang was trying to catch it. Sam had set up badminton for Matt and Levi, leaving poor Wolfgang distracted and confused as to the proper object he should be chasing. Sam and David sat on the veranda, sipping their beers and discussing football strategy. It was a beautiful Indian summer Sunday, only a few weeks before Thanksgiving. Su Li, Hannah, and Julie busied themselves with final preparations for their long tradition of Sunday dinner.

"I'm glad Bo is able to join us today," Su Li remarked as she measured the vinegar into the salad dressing cruet. "He seems like a nice guy. It looks like Samantha's happy with him." She added herbs to flavor the vinegar, and stirred the green beans.

Julie's answer was light-hearted. "You know, they seem pretty serious. I never thought she'd fall for anyone. She's always been kind of a tomboy and a Daddy's girl, all rolled up in one. Sam and I like Bo, too. He's a little cocky, but he treats Samantha like a queen." Julie filled the water glasses, a kitchen task she could accomplish without difficulty.

"He's cute!" Hannah added. "And that sexy Southern accent! I'm happy for Samantha."

Sam entered the kitchen. "Samantha and Bo are here. Dinner almost ready? We're all starved."

"Funny, you don't look like you've missed any meals, lately!" Julie said, giving her husband a kiss on his cheek.

"Five minutes," Su Li said. "Have everyone come in and wash up." She added the oil and honey to the vinegar and shook it. The women began to put the food on the long dining table as the families took their seats.

David said grace and they began to talk while the food was passed around.

Su Li nudged David. "Tell them," she said.

"Tell us what?" Julie asked, piling brisket onto her plate. "Are you keeping something from us?"

The table became silent as all eyes were on David. "I have an announcement. Effective January 1, I'm leaving the firm and going into business for myself. Matthew and Levi have both expressed an interest in architecture, and when they finish college, they'll join me, and we'll be Jernigan and Sons Architects. A young architect from our firm is also leaving to work with me as a junior partner in my new venture."

"How exciting!" Julie said. "Congratulations!"

David and Su Li talked about the stresses at work and how they had spent months discussing their options and arriving at the decision.

A plate of cookies for dessert was brought in, and Bo clinked his spoon on his glass and stood. "I guess this is a day for good news all around. I, too, have an announcement that just can't wait until Thanksgiving. First, the meal was delicious. My compliments to the chef. My second announcement is that Samantha Jane, after some arm-wrestling, has agreed to become my wife."

Gasps of delight and congratulations rose from the group as Bo took a small box from his pocket. "Today, I'm making this official, before my beloved comes to her senses and changes her mind." He opened the box to reveal a full carat emerald-cut diamond set in platinum and framed by smaller baguettes. He placed it on her finger. "Samantha Jane, you are the most frustrating, maddening, difficult, stubborn, and complicated woman I have ever met in my life. I cannot imagine, nor would I want to, living my life without you by my side." He slid the ring on her finger before she could pull her hand away.

Samantha looked at Bo and pursed her lips. "You cannot possibly think that was romantic in any way, shape, or form, Bo Whitney. You are such an arrogant jerk." She took the ring off her finger and handed it back to him. "Try again. This time, add a little romance, if it's not too difficult." She stuck her nose in the air.

Hannah stifled a giggle. The boys watched in wide-eyed silence. Julie rubbed her temples as though her head hurt, and Su Li shook her head. Sam pumped his fist under the table and David stared at his plate, pressing his lips together until they turned white. Noah, oblivious, stuffed more cookies into his mouth and Becky spoke up in her stage voice. "Don't you like the ring, Samantha? I think it's pretty!"

"The ring's fine, Becky. After all, I did show it to him in the magazine," Samantha answered. "The ring's not the problem. Bo's delivery is the problem."

"Oh. Okay," Becky shrugged and reached for another cookie.

"Samantha Jane!" Bo said, hurt. "I am pledging my life, all my worldly goods…"

"That would be Penelope, your cat," Samantha mumbled.

"I am wounded, Samantha Jane. Truly wounded. Penelope loves you. Not as much as I do, of course. But if it's romance you want, then romance you shall have." Bo pulled his chair away from the table and with a flourish of overly-dramatic gesturing, got down on one knee. Holding the ring in front of him, he continued in his most charming Southern gentleman manner. "Samantha Jane Hernandez, I've been crazy about you since I first laid eyes on you. While I admit, it took you a little while, and me saving your sometimes sweet life, for which I will bear a scar forever, you finally realized what a truly wonderful catch I am. And because you're every bit as smart as you are purty, and we talked about this, and I saved all year, even if I ate rice and beans and black eyed peas for six months to get you this gorgeous ring, you've made me the happiest man on earth. Even if I did have to let you win the arm wrestle. Plus, honey, you said we'd announce this at Sunday dinner tonight. I get that you forgot about that little talk, as you are so love struck you ain't thinkin' clearly, so I'll let that go, seein' as I love you so much. Now I realize the ring was a surprise, but in the most romantic way I can, I am telling you that you are the love of my life, and I don't want to live without you. So would you please do me the honor of granting me the one and only wish I have— that you would grow old with me and spend the rest of your life by my side as my wife?" He inched the ring toward her.

Samantha took the ring from the box and held it up to the light, squinting.

"Was that romantic enough, Samantha Jane?" Bo asked.

"Is this real?" she asked, tilting it back and forth in the light of the chandelier.

"Of course it's real!" Bo stood, rubbing his back and flexing his knees. "Are you gonna marry me or not?"

Samantha put the ring on her finger and admired it. She pointed to her parents. "See my parents over there? As you Southern boys like to say, they didn't raise no fools!" She grinned at him.

The table erupted in wild applause. Julie cried, but wouldn't say whether her tears were due to relief, joy, or simply the strain of holding back laughter. Hugs soon enveloped the new couple, leaving Noah and Becky the plate of cookies to stuff into their mouths. Wolfgang was happy to help with the crumbs.

Kate Marlin, Adam and Jenna Trent, and their daughter, Amy, were finishing the last of the barbecue on their deck. Blue, Robo, and Boris lounged around their feet, ready for clean-up duty, should the need arise. "Amy, why don't you go and toss the Frisbee for the dogs? I'm sure they'd love to play," Adam said.

Amy dug into Blue's toy box and pulled out balls, Kongs, Frisbees, and tug toys. "C'mon guys!" she happily called. The dogs trotted behind her to play in the yard while the adults talked.

"You were robbed, Adam," Kate began. "You were by far the best man for Cap's job, the most qualified and the most respected. I used to think it'd be so cool to work under Gavin Peterson's command, with you and your crew." She dipped a chip into Jenna's bacon horseradish onion dip. "Of course, I'd never leave K-9, but in between jobs, I always loved helping your team out. I guess *that's* a thing of the past!" She dipped another chip. "Man, Jenna, you sure are a fantastic cook! Even your dip is outstanding! Good thing I'm not kissing anyone tonight! Besides Robo and Boris, that is!"

Adam's jaw tightened. "I get that the decision was politics. It always is. But I also know that Cap put in a lot more than two cents worth. He really pulled for me to get the job. I wasn't even given so much as an interview. Not a real one, anyway. I knew when I left the room after that sham of an interview, I wasn't even being considered. But I never guessed it would be Farrell." He shook his head.

"Is your team even going to stay together?" Kate asked. "Farrell's reputation is one of a morale buster. He's broken up partnerships and teams before. Anything to throw his weight around and let you know who's boss. Especially if it doesn't even make sense." Kate poured another glass of wine. "Has he threatened to do that?"

Adam stared at the leftovers on the table, as Jenna began picking them up. "He's hyper-critical of everything and everyone. If he finds out Bo and Samantha are romantically involved, he'll definitely transfer one of them out. They're being smart about it. No public displays of affection, no show at all on duty that they're anything more than members of my team. Connor and I sure aren't going to say anything. The four of us make a great team. Ever since Farrell moved into Cap's office, we've all been keeping our heads down. No joking around, nothing extra, doing exactly our jobs, trying to keep under his radar." He reached for the lemonade pitcher and poured a glass. "You know what Bo's doing tonight?"

Jenna brought brownies out and set them on the table. "I could take a guess," she said.

"No clue," Kate answered.

"He showed me the ring. They're announcing their engagement at her parents' home. They have a big Sunday dinner every week. Bo goes when he's not on call. You should see the rock he got her. He said he's been scrimping and saving for months. But he said she won't wear it at work."

Kate's mouth flew open. "Bo and Samantha? Getting *married*? I *have* been away from the team too long! How long do you think they're gonna be able to keep something like that a secret? Farrell's bound to find out!"

Adam sighed. He took a long drink of lemonade. "You know, Samantha's only a year as a detective and another year and some months as a beat cop. Her daddy's got his own private investigation firm, and that family's got money. Trust fund money, life insurance money on her mom's side, and on her dad's side, an ATF pension on top of the PI firm. Her mother plays in the symphony. If the going gets too tough, my money, what little I have, says she leaves the police department and joins her father's PI firm, which I believe, is what she wanted to do in the first place. But her father wanted her to have some formal police background first. She's not even close to being vested and if Farrell comes down hard on her, I could see her leaving. She's a good detective, and I'd hate to see her go, but it's not like she needs the job."

Adam reached for a brownie and continued. "Bo's another story. He's not quite vested, but he's close, so he'd be dumb to throw that away. He can be annoying, but he's not stupid. Bo's style grates on Farrell and it bothers Farrell that Bo lets his criticisms roll off his back. Connor's vested, but with a wife and five kids, I don't see him leaving. But Farrell's sights are aimed at me. I think he knows Cap recommended me, I was the better choice, and my team wanted me so he's all about breaking me, making me look bad."

Adam rubbed his head. "I've got my family, a mortgage, school tuition for Amy, and in a few years, college. I don't want to put in for a transfer. I want to work Homicide. I'd be a fish out of water any place else. I don't want to leave my team. Just as important, I don't want Farrell to think he's won something by running me out." He sighed again and picked at his napkin. "But I'm not sure how much more criticism, second-guessing, and micro-managing I can take. If Farrell's vendetta affects my paycheck, then it'll affect my pension. I feel stuck. It's bad enough the beating we get in the media and the lack of respect from the public we risk our lives to protect! Now we get it from the very people who are supposed to be on our side." He watched Amy throwing the toys for the dogs. "But he's our captain and we have to deal with it. I have to respect his position, but I can't respect him as a person." Adam decimated his napkin and stared at the tiny pieces of confetti piled on the table.

Jenna stood and moved behind Adam. She smoothed her hair and tucked it behind her ears. Her heart ached, knowing her husband's angst over his work situation, but she felt helpless in the matter. She hugged him and kissed the top of his head. "Kate, you're joining us for Thanksgiving, right?" she asked, upbeat, trying to change the subject, even though it was nearly a month away.

Kate noted the defeat in Adam's voice and that he'd sunk into his chair with his shoulders slumped. "Looking forward to it!" she answered, picking up on Jenna's cue. "Will Emma Jo and Dwayne be joining us?"

Jenna nodded. "Yep! Same as last year. Can we count on you for the wine?"

Kate laughed. "So you still don't trust me to cook? Smart lady!"

October 30, 2017

Kenton Farraday's funeral had been a grand affair, complete with a long motorcade following the hearse, and hundreds of mourners in attendance. Several people had prepared touching eulogies, lauding the man's generosity, vision, and kindness. Only Vivienne and Colette knew of his temper, but each had loved the man in their own way.

Jordan held his father's hand as he took his final breaths at home. Lizzie held Jordan's other hand, and Vivienne and Colette stood on the other side of his bed, weeping. Kenton's hospice nurse was present, but remained a respectable distance from the family. As he closed his eyes for the last time, he put his hands over Jordan and Lizzie's hands and summoned as much strength as he could for his final words. "I'm sorry, but it looks like I'm going to miss your wedding. You've done well, son. Be wise and generous in your decisions. I love you both."

New Beginning

November 21, 2017

Jordan and Lizzie Farraday's three-week honeymoon in Europe was drawing to a close. They had toured England, Ireland, Scotland, Wales, France, and Spain, staying three nights in each country, absorbing the sights, the culture, the history, and the food. One final stop remained before their return home.

Jordan left Martina in charge at Farraday Enterprises, and Vivienne in charge at home. Colette was given a three-week vacation while the newlyweds were gone. Excited to see her friends, she returned to Paris for the duration.

Jordan and Lizzie stepped off the plane in Cluj, Romania and looked for the translator Martina had arranged to meet them. They saw a young woman in her twenties holding a sign that read, Farraday party, and they identified themselves to her. Flavia Sala presented her identification and welcomed the couple to Romania in almost flawless English. She was friendly, excited to show her American guests her country and its warm hospitality. Chin-length dark curls bounced in several directions from her head as she spoke, and her deep brown eyes sparkled, illuminating a bright, toothy smile. "You are my first customers. I am new to the agency, but you will find my translation to be very perfect," she announced with pride. "Do you care to have the meal first, or do you prefer to become settled in your hotel? It is some distance. Soon, we are hopeful, the Baia Mare airport will re-open. The construction, it takes some little time extra. The agency has provided Petru as our driver." She pointed to a young man leaning against the wall, and he waved. "I will assure you he is safe driver. Dumbrava has no hotels, but we will go to Baia Mare for hotel and delicious restaurants."

"I think I'd like to get settled in before we eat," Lizzie said. She looked to Jordan for his input.

"I agree," Jordan said, smiling at his bride. "Is our hotel close enough to Dumbrava that we might go there today?"

"It is, of course, as you wish, but allowing the time to travel from Cluj to Baia Mare, to have you checked into hotel and to eat the meal, by the time we reach Dumbrava, it will be dark or almost dark. You may be some tired, I think. But you are customer, so you are boss! You tell me. I do everything to make you happy!" Flavia's effusiveness was contagious, but they had already flown from Paris to Munich to Cluj, and in spite of their young translator's eagerness to please, Jordan thought Dumbrava could wait another day.

"I think we'll relax in Baia Mare after we eat. Perhaps you can show us around for a little while?" Jordan asked.

Flavia flashed her teeth. "As you wish!"

Petru finished loading the baggage into the tour van. They helped their American charges into the back seat and Flavia took her seat in the front passenger side. She spoke to Petru in Romanian and the four of them started for Baia Mare.

As they drove, Jordan and Lizzie stared out the windows of the van, marveling at the lush scenery that rose to greet them in brilliant fall colors. "I never knew Romania was such a beautiful country!" Lizzie exclaimed. "The mountains, the greenery, the trees! Oh look! Those hills are completely white! They look like they're moving! They *are* moving! What *is* that, Flavia?"

"That is shepherd and many sheep. See over there," she said, pointing. "The shepherd leads the sheep and the dog follows to keep them in the right direction. Many sheep walking close together makes it appear like the land is moving. In a minute, look to the edge of the rocks and you will see the second dog. He will keep the lookout for anything that threatens the shepherd or the sheep and he will attack."

"I see him!" Lizzie shouted. "Up there! This is so cool!"

Jordan smiled at his bride and stroked her hair. "This place *is* gorgeous, Lizard. Who knew? It's like stepping back in time. Here we are in 2017, and everything's still untouched by technology, pollution, progress."

The van swerved around a horse-drawn cart in the middle of the road. "Hey, Flavia, are there a lot of horses and buggies on the same roads as the cars?" Jordan asked.

Flavia laughed. "Some, but not a lot. We are fortunate that we will arrive in Baia Mare before the cows go home. The cows take up all of the roadway and they are not in a hurry to get to their stalls. You can wait long time for cows in the road. But we will be at hotel before that happens. Good thing!"

Jordan and Lizzie looked at each other with wide eyes. "Romania might be my favorite part of our honeymoon," Lizzie whispered to Jordan.

"I can think of my favorite part, and it's got nothing to do with cows!" he whispered back.

Lizzie blushed.

"Will it take long to get checked in?" Jordan asked.

Flavia shook her head. "Not at all. I was at your hotel yesterday and reviewed your room, my room, and Petru's room. Is very nice staff. We need only to show the identification. You have paid the agency and the agency has made all arrangements. It will be less than five minutes to have your luggages in your room. Petru will carry your bags. There are many restaurants in Baia Mare. We can walk to a lot of them from hotel, so you tell to me what food you would like and we choose the best place. Hotel has nice breakfast included for your morning." Flavia gestured with her hands and arms as she spoke. "I may warn you a little about Romanian coffee. Is much stronger than American coffee, yes? You may wish to add the little bit of water." She giggled, causing her curls to bounce. "One of the other tour guides told to me that her Americans say you have to drink Romanian coffee with fork and knife."

"We'll consider ourselves warned," Jordan answered. "Are all the roads this twisty and hilly? Should we be going this fast?"

"We must go through many mountains to get from Cluj to Baia Mare. Is beautiful, yes? Not to worry. Petru is safe driver. We give our best drivers for American visitors. Americans have…um…the weak stomach, no?"

Lizzie was gripping the arm rest, wide-eyed, and pale. She glanced at Jordan and swallowed.

Jordan took her hand and squeezed it. "We appreciate having those safe drivers. Wouldn't want it any other way," he answered Flavia, winking at Lizzie.

"You can relax and enjoy the breathtaking view. There is not much else to note until we are in Baia Mare. Is mostly countryside, but quite beautiful." Flavia smiled at the couple and chatted with Petru in Romanian as the van swerved around another horse-drawn wagon, and wove in and out between slower cars. "If you need to stop for restroom break, let me know. Is about two hours total time."

Lizzie looked at her watch. "Another hour and a half," she whispered to Jordan, gripping his hand with her right hand and digging her fingers into the armrest with her left hand.

"I have some ibuprofen in my carry-on. You can take it when we get to the hotel, unless you want to stop for water," he told her. "Might be too late for a restroom break!" he joked.

"I can wait," she answered in a shaky voice. "Let's just get there in one piece."

"Our driver is the safest," Jordan whispered. His eyes twinkled at her as he grinned.

Ninety minutes of awe-inspiring scenery later, the van slowed as it entered the city limits of Baia Mare. Jordan and Lizzie inhaled deeply as they took in the quaint, old city, nestled in a valley beneath majestic tree-covered mountains. "It looks like something out of a fairy-tale book!" she whispered excitedly to Jordan.

The van pulled under an arched canopy that stretched across the hotel entrance. Petru removed the bags and helped the newlyweds out of the van. Flavia led the way to the registration desk and after Jordan and Lizzie showed their passports, the small group gathered their room keys and crammed into the tiny elevator to the floor on which they were staying.

Lizzie gasped as she stood on the balcony outside their room. A sweeping view of the mountains lay ahead, with a birds-eye view of the city below. "Jordan, it's beautiful! Look!" she waved her hand in a large circle.

Jordan stood behind her and enveloped her in his arms. "It's even more beautiful when you're in the picture." He nuzzled her neck and kissed the top of her hair, pressing close to her.

Lizzie turned and kissed him. "Part of me wishes you had known your parents—that you wouldn't have missing pieces. When I think about it, though, it was the Hollisters who raised you to be the sweet, kind person that makes you... well...you. You might have been spoiled and power-hungry like your birth family had they raised you."

"Can't have that," Jordan said, pulling her close. "You would've never had me." He kissed her passionately and buried his face in her neck. "Our children may not want for anything, but we are *not* spoiling them. We agreed. I just might spoil *you*, Lizard Gizzard, but our kids will work for what they want. A little work never hurt us, and it won't hurt our children, either."

Lizzie laughed. "Let's enjoy our honeymoon before we have kids, okay?"

A knock on the door interrupted them. Jordan looked through the peephole and opened the door. Flavia flashed a broad smile and Petru stood back against the far wall in the hallway. "Are you hungry for dinner?" she asked. "You have thought what you would like to eat?"

Jordan looked at Lizzie, who shrugged her response. "Flavia, we've eaten all over Europe, and it's been wonderful. Lots of great local foods, but they've been different from what we're used to, of course. We'll be here a few days. Is there any place we could get a meal tonight that would be like home? Pizza, maybe? Or pasta? We'll try the local cuisine the rest of the trip, but between the travel, the time changes, and different cuisine, our stomachs are a bit uneasy."

Flavia snapped her fingers and beamed. "I was hopeful you would say such a thing! Follow me and we go to Buonissimo! Italian family moved to Baia Mare and have good restaurant. Pizza and pasta the best. And with homemade real gelato for dessert! Many flavors!"

"That sounds wonderful!" Lizzie answered. "Is it close?"

"We walk. Less than five minutes. Afterwards, I show you a bit of the city. Some shopping? A mineral museum?"

"Sure," Jordan said.

The meal was as good as Flavia promised. Jordan got spaghetti, and Lizzie and Flavia split a pizza. Petru was no longer needed as they would sightsee on foot, so he was dismissed with instructions to be available by noon the following day for the trip to Dumbrava. Flavia led the couple on a short tour.

Jordan and Lizzie found the mineral museum fascinating as they learned about the rich mineral reserves in Maramures County and stared at the unique shapes and colors of the samples in the display cases. The information cards below each specimen were written in Romanian and English, so Jordan and Lizzie could follow along and learn.

"You enjoy our museum?" Flavia asked, as they stepped outside.

"Very much," Jordan said

"The minerals were gorgeous! I've never even heard of some of them!" Lizzie answered with enthusiasm.

"It is getting late. We have many shops here, but one is authentic Romanian. Other shops have the imports, but this shop—you will appreciate the Romanian craftsmanship. We can go quickly to see before returning to hotel. Shops will close soon."

She led them down the main boulevard to a small shop nestled between a restaurant and money exchanging business. Lizzie found intricate, hand-carved wooden boxes, crystal, and hand-made porcelain baskets with hand-painted flowers covering the bottom. One section of the shop carried beautiful tea sets and table linens. Lizzie stared at each item, admiring the delicate detail, unable to choose.

Jordan stroked her hair and leaned close to speak softly in her ear. "Get whatever you want."

"Can we…" she started.

"We can afford anything," he cut her off, and kissed her behind her ear.

"That's right. I do keep forgetting!" Lizzie chose several boxes and baskets, two tea sets, three sets of table linens and a selection of crystal lotus flowers. "Some for us, some for gifts," she said.

"Nice of you to leave something for tomorrow's shoppers," Jordan teased her as they walked back to the hotel.

"Is good for local economy," Flavia told them. "Americans are welcome and appreciated here." She nodded toward the little shop behind them. "Shopkeeper can pay expenses this month with your purchases."

They reached the hotel and Flavia waved to them. "A small bar over here. I will have the nightcap. See you in the morning. Petru will meet us in lobby tomorrow at noon. Give you plenty time to sleep well and have nice breakfast."

Jordan and Lizzie thanked Flavia, said their goodbyes, and a few minutes later, lay snuggling together in bed. "Are you nervous about tomorrow?" she asked.

"I don't know," Jordan answered. He squirmed and drew closer to her, stroking her hair and cheek. "A little, maybe. Dumbrava is where my mother lived. Maybe I can find my grandfather. Maybe there'll be friends or neighbors who remember Tatiana Todoran. My father said that she was an only child, and he was not aware of cousins or other relatives, but I don't think it was important to him to learn that much about her. Kenton Farraday saw what he wanted and he took it. He treated her like she was property, a play toy. By the time he realized he really did love her, she was gone. I hope we can find someone who can tell me what she was like. My father wasn't a nice man when he knew her, Lizard. I just have this need to know about my birth mother. I can't explain it, but I want those missing pieces filled in. Tatiana Todoran was my mother and I have no memory at all of her. Colette told me how much my mother loved me, and that she was a sweet, beautiful woman, but she knew her only a short time. If I can't find answers in Dumbrava, then I can't find them anywhere. One thing I do know," he ran his hand through her hair and over her face. "I know that I will never be like Kenton. The father who raised me—Eldon Hollister—taught me better."

"Kenton turned his life around. I believe he was sincerely sorry...about everything. Having you alive and back in his life after all those years made him come alive, at least for the time he had left." Lizzie brought Jordan's hand to her face and brushed her lips across his fingertips.

"I guess so," Jordan answered. "But I saw a different side of him. I always felt he hadn't told me the whole truth about my mother. I do think he was changed from when he was younger, and I think he was sorry for the bad things he did. But I never thought I could trust him like I trusted the dad who raised me. It always seemed to me like Kenton was hiding something."

"I remember his face as he lay on his deathbed...when you finally called him dad. I know it was hard for you to do that. But it meant the world to him." Lizzie dabbed at her eyes. "I wish he could have held on a little longer—to see us get married."

"Yeah, me. too." Jordan kissed her hand. "He was happy for us. Genuinely happy. I wish he could have seen you in your beautiful gown. You looked like a princess. You're my princess." He ran his finger down her nose and across her lips and pulled her close.

The next morning Jordan and Lizzie slept in late, arrived at the breakfast bar for the last ten minutes it was open, and prepared for the trip to Dumbrava. It would be only a few minutes, Flavia had promised, but the newlyweds weren't sure if that was actual time, or Petru driving time, and decided not to ask.

Dumbrava was a small mountain village situated about an hour from the hotel. The natural beauty of the tree-covered mountains, bursting in fall glory held the couple spellbound as they drank in the scenery, awed at each turn, snapping photos as they tried to capture the magic of Romania. But as they entered the village, they were struck by the bleak poverty of the people walking the dirt roads, planting gardens that would feed them, and feeding chickens that would provide them with eggs, and later, soup. Outhouses in backyards and wells in front yards announced the absence of indoor plumbing. Stacks of split wood piled beside the small homes posed an anemic threat to the impending arrival of the bitter winter. Most of the homes had already shuttered the windows in an attempt to keep out the wind and cold. The gray color of the chipped cement and cinderblock homes blended with the grey sky and dusty roads, mocking the brilliant colors painting the mountains in the background. A wave of sadness swept over Lizzie and Jordan as they thought of the comforts taken for granted back home, where families were busy preparing for Thanksgiving and Christmas, parties and indulgences.

"Welcome to Dumbrava," Flavia announced, with less enthusiasm than her greeting the day before. "Is not Baia Mare or Cluj for sure. Not a lot of sightseeing here, but you asked to come, so I bring you." Her unasked question hung in the air; it was neither in her culture nor her character to be rude.

"My mother was from Dumbrava. She died when I was only a few weeks old. I was born in Bucharest," Jordan told her.

Flavia's mouth flew open and her eyes widened. "Oh! I see! I am sorry. Then we will do some investigation! I understand what you seek. Petru will meet us at the restaurant in the town. They have the modern bathrooms there, so do not worry. Your mission—it is important. I will take care of all. Come and we will see." She marched ahead of them and they followed.

Flavia spent little time finding the center of the tiny village and together, they entered the City Hall building. She spoke in rapid Romanian to the woman at the front desk, who picked up a phone and engaged in conversation for several minutes. When she hung up the receiver, she addressed Flavia, again in Romanian. Jordan and Lizzie had mastered please, thank you, and where is the bathroom in Romanian, but could not follow conversational Romanian. They picked up Tatiana Todoran's name, but understood nothing further.

Flavia turned to Jordan and Lizzie and raised her eyebrows. "It looks like two Americans searching for information about your mother has gotten us a meeting with the *mayor!* I am feeling very important right now! We are to go down this hall to the last door and the mayor wishes to see you. Am I a great tour guide or what?" She grinned broadly, and took long strides as the Farraday couple followed. As soon as they knocked, a young woman opened the door and invited them in. The mayor rose from his desk and approached them. He was tall and slender with dark hair, graying at the temples. He dismissed the secretary in Romanian and pulled chairs in front of his desk for his visitors to sit.

"Please to come in," he said in broken English. "My English is not too good, so if I struggle, I will talk to your translator. Coffee?"

The three declined.

"I am Mayor Constantin Dalca." He offered his hand. Jordan and Lizzie shook hands with the mayor, and introduced themselves. "You are seeking information about Tatiana Todoran? Please to sit." He motioned to the chairs and took a seat behind his desk as his visitors sat. He studied his guests. Mayor Dalca appeared to the group to be a serious man, but courteous. "I was young policeman when Tatiana went missing. Some months pass, we discover her father's…" He spoke to Flavia in Romanian, as he struggled for the right word. "…decomposed body in the woods behind their house."

Jordan flinched, but remained silent, absorbing all that Constantin said.

"We search for Tatiana and no find her. Many months later, a letter was received by Tatiana's best friend. A second letter was sent to her father. This tell us she not know he already dead. Or, she pretend to have the…" he looked again to Flavia for help.

"Alibi." Flavia provided the word Constantin did not know.

Constantin nodded and resumed his narrative. "The letters were posted from Bucharest. After that, trail is cold. This is public record. You can find anywhere, so I am free to tell to you. And now, here you are? All the way from America?

What is your interest in Tatiana Todoran?" Mayor Dalca leaned back in his chair, fingering a pen, cautious, but curious as he studied his visitors.

"Tatiana was my mother," Jordan replied in a soft voice.

Constantin Dalca's mouth flew open and he dropped the pen he was holding.

Jordan continued. "I think I can fill in the missing pieces so you can close your cold case. But, I, too, have a lot of missing pieces that I hope you can fill in for me, if you don't mind."

Mayor Dalca picked up his phone and spoke rapidly in his own language.

Flavia whispered, "He told his secretary to hold all calls and cancel his appointments for today." The young tour guide's eyes were bright with excitement. "I did not realize you were such important people! I thought you were only the American tourists. My parents will be impressed when I tell them!"

Lizzie stifled a giggle and looked away.

"I will answer your questions, Mr. Farraday. You must know Tatiana's case has haunted not only me, but all in Dumbrava who knew her and helped in the search. Her disappearance and her father's murder are the only cold cases in our village. I had given up. You will now tell to me what happened?"

"You said my grandfather was murdered?" Jordan asked. His shoulders sagged and he studied the floor. Blinking back tears, he continued. "I had hoped he might be alive...that I could meet him." Jordan bit his lip. "Do you know how he died?"

"He was struck on his head, and his body left deep in the woods. No one was ever caught."

My father did this. He lied to me. It was the only part of his story he stumbled on every time he talked about my mother. He never came completely clean. Jordan squeezed his eyes shut and Lizzie put her hand on his back. "I am sorry. You have come a long way to be disappointed. But you will please tell me what you know. Is important," Constantin said in a kind voice.

Jordan looked up and nodded. "My father was an American businessman helping with the rebuilding efforts in Romania after the revolution. His family spent a year in Romania. He lived in Baia Mare and sought to expand business there, while his father, my grandfather, rented a home in Bucharest. His brother and sister took the Constanta City territory and there were other people from Farraday Enterprises who were situated in the various regions."

"I was young man at that time, but I do remember hearing of that. The work was in the cities. Our villages are still, for the most part, untouched," Constantin said.

Jordan nodded and continued. "My father got lost one day, and ended up leaving the main road. That's when he met my mother, Tatiana. They began to see each other in secret, and they fell in love. When her father discovered she was pregnant with me, he was furious. My father, Kenton Farraday, went to talk with Ovidiu, to tell him he would marry Tatiana and they would return to America as husband and wife with the baby. Once settled, they would send for Ovidiu to join them. However, when he approached Ovidiu to talk, he heard him ranting and raving, screaming to the sky that he would force Tatiana to have an abortion."

Jordan paused to collect his thoughts. "My father had a terrible temper. He told me that he'd given Ovidiu money and that Ovidiu agreed to allow them to marry and return to America. But now that you have told me of my grandfather's murder, I believe what really happened was that my father became enraged when he heard this abortion threat, and hit Ovidiu in the head. I believe it was my father who hid his body in the woods and left to meet my mother, who was waiting for him in town."

Flavia rose and brought coffee to everyone. It was going to be a long afternoon. Lizzie sat quietly, letting her husband speak without interruption.

"Ovidiu had bad temper. I knew Tatiana her whole life and she loved Ovidiu. She never would have agreed to go with a man who killed her father!" Constantin pressed his lips into a thin line and frowned at Jordan.

"She never knew her father was dead. That's why she wrote him letters," Jordan reminded the mayor. "Not because she needed an alibi, but because she was crying out for help. I believe

Kenton lied to her, just as he lied to me. I think he told her he
spoke to Ovidiu and Ovidiu agreed that she and the baby would
receive better care in Bucharest. She believed her father would
join them in America after I was born."

"Okay." Constantin sipped his coffee and leaned back in
his chair. "Makes sense."

"Kenton and Tatiana left for Bucharest, got married, and a
few months later, I was born. But my father had a cruel streak. He
did not treat my mother well at all." Jordan sipped his coffee and
paused. "She became very sick, and less than six weeks after I was
born, she died. She's buried in a church cemetery in Bucharest."

Constantin buried his face in his hands and was quiet for
several moments. He lifted his head and wiped his eyes. His voice
was solemn. "That explains much. She was sweet girl. Trusting.
Two letters were received from her, begging for help, but we did
not know where she was."

"Kenton told me she wrote twice before those letters, but
gave the envelopes to my father to mail. Instead, he destroyed the
letters." Jordan's voice broke as he told his story. Lizzie reached
to him and gently patted his back. Jordan had thought about what
he was going to say, but as he spoke the words to someone who
knew his mother, and who actively worked on her case, he found
it difficult to relay as the story came to life. "Now that I know the
truth, I believe that my father felt that if Tatiana was found, he
could be prosecuted for Ovidiu's murder. He had dug a hole with
his lies until there was no way out."

Jordan shifted in his seat and took another drink of the
coffee. "Tatiana was held a virtual prisoner in the home in Bucharest. She was never allowed to leave. One day, when the house
was empty, she was able to escape, but she didn't know anyone,
didn't know where she was or what to do. She'd never been away
from Dumbrava before. She mailed her last two letters, the ones
you did receive, and made it back to the house before anyone
knew she'd left. That night, she went into premature labor and
the next evening, I was born. But, as I said, she was weak and had
gotten sick, and died a few weeks later."

"And your father did not have the decency to try to find
family, friends, in Dumbrava to tell them?" Constantin asked. His
gaze bore into Jordan.

"No. My father was a coward, and I'm sure he didn't want to answer questions about Ovidiu. The family's work was finishing in Romania and he wanted to be back in the States, safely away from prosecution in another country."

"And where is your father now?" Constantin leaned forward, his voice as stern as his stare.

"He died last month."

"And you grew up as rich American. Why is this your first time to be interested in your poor mother? Twenty-six years later, she finally means something to you?" Constantin's broken English could not hide the disgust in his voice.

"No! Oh, no, not at all," Jordan answered, putting his hands up. "While my father was in Cluj concluding business before returning to the United States, I was stolen from my home and left in a Romanian orphanage, north of Bucharest. My father was told that I had gotten sick and died. It was an evil scheme, fueled by money and power."

Constantin's face softened and he leaned back in his chair. "That is terrible. I am sorry to hear. It is good you survived. Many did not."

Jordan nodded. "A childless American couple adopted me. I never knew they were not my biological parents, although, I had disturbing dreams about the orphanage. I could never understand the dreams until I found out what had happened to me as a baby. The person who stole me was a Romanian nurse who worked for my grandfather in Bucharest. Somewhere along the line, she developed a conscience and came to America to confess to my father what she'd done. That was late last year. He was shocked, of course, having believed for twenty-five years that I was dead. Anyway, he hired a private investigator to find me, but by that time, my father had developed the terminal illness that claimed his life last month."

"I see," Constantin said. "That must have been very difficult, I think."

"When I learned who I was, I wanted to come to Romania right away, but felt I could not leave my sick father, especially after just meeting him. My wife and I were married three weeks ago. My father died shortly before the wedding, but we'd planned to come to Romania as part of our honeymoon. I had hoped to find someone who knew my mother, could show me where she lived, tell me stories about her, something." Jordan's voice trailed off as he struggled for words.

Constantin relaxed and smiled. "Mr. Farraday," he began.

"Please call me Jordan."

"Jordan. Your mother's best friend was a sweet and beautiful girl, Valeria Ionescu. Twenty-four years ago, Valeria became my wife. She would be most happy to meet you. Her English is much better than mine. Would you do us honor and have dinner with us tonight? At our home?"

Flavia whispered to Lizzie, "Yes. It would be impolite to refuse this invitation."

"We'd love to," Lizzie answered, as Jordan stumbled for words. "Thank you. What time shall we be there?"

Constantin wrote on a piece of paper as he spoke to Flavia in Romanian and she translated. "We will arrive at 5:30." She held up the piece of paper Constantin handed to her. "I have the directions and address."

The group thanked the mayor for his time and left, agreeing to meet him at his home at the appointed time.

Outside, Lizzie asked Flavia, "Isn't it rude to spring four guests on your wife with such late notice? In America, most wives would be furious at the imposition."

Flavia shook her head, tossing her curls back and forth. "You will see. For one, you will find Romanians to be hospitable. These are special circumstances. His wife will be thrilled to meet the son of her best friend. Do not worry!"

They met Petru and arrived at Constantin and Valeria Dalca's home on time. Constantin met them at the door and ushered them into his living room. Valeria came in from the kitchen, wiping her hands on her apron. She greeted her guests with cheerful warmth, but her face bore a puzzled look.

"There are Americans in my home to meet me?" she asked. "Welcome. I am Valeria." She appeared confused, but pleasant, and looked to Constantin for an explanation.

"My love," Constantin held her hand as he spoke. "Look carefully at this young man. Do you see his eyes? Do you know who this is? This is a surprise you could never imagine."

Valeria studied Jordan with furrowed brows, as if she should know him, but could not place him. The suspense was killing Jordan, and the scrutiny with which she examined him made him increasingly uncomfortable. "I am Tatiana Todoran's son, Jordan Farraday. This is my wife, Lizzie."

Valeria gasped and covered her mouth with both hands. Tears streamed down her face as she recognized Tatiana's features in the young man standing before her. She grabbed Jordan and hugged him with a vice-like grip. She held him at arms' length as tears poured from her eyes and then hugged him tightly again. "Tell me of your mother! I must know everything!"

Constantin leaned toward his wife and said, "Valeria, I believe the soup is ready? We will have much to talk about over dinner. I'm sure our guests are hungry."

"Of course! Please, sit, and I will bring the soup. We must talk! Constantin! You told me nothing except we had special guests from America. How could you keep such a secret from me?" She hurried into the kitchen, weeping.

Constantin gave a sheepish shrug to their guests. "She is fine. Those are happy tears."

The group was seated at the small table as Valeria brought in a tureen of steaming hot chicken noodle soup. Jordan repeated the story he had told Constantin earlier that day, omitting the part about Kenton's cruel treatment of his wife. He gave her a copy of Tatiana and Kenton's wedding photograph. Valeria hung on every word, sobbing into her soup, as she learned of her friend's fate.

"Thank you so much for coming to see us. I will tell you everything about your mother. She was my dearest friend since childhood. It will be too late tonight. Darkness will be soon, and the roads are difficult. Tomorrow, after breakfast, you will come back to Dumbrava? I will show you where she lived, where we went to school—oh!—and I must take you to Daria and Adina's home. They are sisters, very old now, but after Tatiana's mother, Sorina, your grandmother died, Daria and Adina taught her the things that mothers should teach to their daughters. They will want to meet you, and again, you must tell them the story of what happened." She dabbed at her eyes, returned the soup tureen and the bowls to the kitchen, and reappeared carrying the main dish. "Here, we have the chicken, some potatoes and carrots with butter." She set the dishes on the table, and the group passed them as she spoke. "When we never heard again from Tatiana, we believed she had gone to America with her husband and baby. I knew she was with child, but nobody listen to me." She shot an accusing glance toward her husband, who nodded in resignation. "But after a very long time, she still did not contact anybody, and we feared the worst. I am sorry to hear you confirm our fears. It is, of course, bad news, the worst! But to see her eyes in you—to know that you cared enough to come and learn of her—it helps to keep her memory alive." She began to cry again, and wiped her eyes with her napkin. "She would have been so proud of you! Such a handsome and kind young man. Please, let me introduce you to Daria and Adina. They must know what happened before they die. They are quite old, but still have the memories of Tatiana."

Constantin talked about the search that had been conducted, the newspaper articles, and everything connected with the investigation. Flavia translated, relieving him of the effort to struggle through English. "Will you travel to Bucharest to visit your mother's grave?" he asked Jordan.

"Yes, I plan to do that. I would also like to travel to Dobrogea to visit Ana, the nurse who stole me. What she did was terrible, but because she had a change in her heart, she finally did tell my father, who then was able to locate me." Jordan began to eat his meal. Lizzie and the others had already started eating. "The meal is wonderful, Valeria. Thank you." Lizzie, Flavia, and Petru chimed in their agreement.

"I apologize for no dessert. I ran out of time," Valeria said.

"No, no, please don't apologize," Lizzie responded. "The meal is delicious, and you had very little time to pull it together. I think we'll all be too full for dessert, anyway."

"And we can always go to Buonissimo for gelato," Flavia added.

Petru and Flavia met the Farradays in the lobby the next morning and headed back to Dumbrava. Valeria was waiting for them and greeted them warmly.

"Would you take us to where my mother lived?" Jordan asked her. "I want to see her house—where she grew up."

Valeria shook her head. "I am sorry to tell you, but after many years, the little shack was torn down. A new home is being built on the land. I can take you there. It is a long walk up the mountain road over there," she pointed. "You can see the land, but the house is, how you say, long gone. Would you like to go?"

"Is the walk too far for you, Flavia? Lizzie and I would enjoy the hike." He looked to Lizzie who nodded her head in agreement.

"I can go or stay," Flavia added. "Is your choice. If you prefer the private moment, Petru and I will wait here on Valeria's bench until you return."

"That's a good idea. I need to get a sense of who my mother was."

Valeria led the way and Jordan and Lizzie followed. The trek up the mountain road proved harder than the couple anticipated. Lizzie got winded first. Valeria smiled at her. "The slope, it is deceptive. I am used to it, but we may stop and rest."

Not wanting to be bested by a woman old enough to be her mother, Lizzie leaned on Jordan and replied, "I'm ready. You're right. It's steeper than it looks!"

They reached the site where the Todoran shack once stood many years ago. A new house of goldenrod-colored cinderblocks had been erected. The windows were cut out, but no glass filled them. The doors, as well, were missing, leaving large, unguarded holes, and Jordan could see inside where thick concrete walls separated the rooms. "It looks bigger on the outside than on the inside," he commented, as they approached the space where the front door would go.

Valeria nodded. "Yes. This home has four rooms, plus, you can see there will be an indoor bathroom over there," she pointed. "Tatiana and Ovidiu lived in three rooms less than half the size of these rooms, and of course, no electricity or indoor plumbing."

Jordan stood on the hill and looked toward the woods in the back, then over the road that wound past the house. He tried to imagine his father, driving his Mercedes, stopping by the well and seeing his mother for the first time, as she drew water for the evening meal. The view was spectacular. Majestic mountains and deep valleys as far as the eye could see, untouched by man, unchanged by time. What was her life like, he wondered, growing up in stark poverty amid such lush, beautiful scenery? She, who possessed no wealth or worldly goods, but was rich in spirit and heart, and he, who had everything, but was emotionally bankrupt? They were both a part of Jordan, but, so, also, were Eldon and Mary Rose Hollister, who instilled in him good values, a work ethic, character, and integrity, raising him as their own child. Had he been shaped more by nurture or nature, he asked himself. Or, did they converge, rendering the final outcome ultimately one of choice?

Valeria and Lizzie approached him. "You okay, honey?" Lizzie asked, stroking his arm.

Jordan nodded. "Yeah. Just thinking. Absorbing it all." He turned and gazed at the woods behind the house, taking hold of Lizzie's hand. "That's where my grandfather's body was found?" he asked Valeria.

"It was found far into the woods. It took the search party hours to find it. I advise that we do not go. We could become lost."

Jordan stared at the dense forest, deep in thought. While his mother had been a virtual prisoner in the home in Bucharest, his grandfather's body lay undiscovered for weeks, and she knew nothing of it. He shook his head and faced Valeria. "Why is this house left open and unfinished? It's a beautiful day to work. Where's the construction crew?"

"It may be years before the house is finished. The owner may have gone to Italy or Germany or Spain to work and make more money and then some more work will be done as money comes to pay for it. Then they will go elsewhere to work some more. At some point, it will be done." Valeria shrugged. "I suppose it is a different process in your country."

Jordan let out a small chuckle. "Yeah. You could say that." He placed his arm around Lizzie's waist and pulled her toward him. "Did you tell those women, the ones that helped raise my mother—Adina and Daria, right? Did you tell them we were coming?"

"Yes. They are expecting us. They will serve some little lunch," Valeria answered. "We must travel back down the mountain and into the village. Easier going down than up," she added lightly.

"I hate for them to trouble themselves. Could we, perhaps, treat them to lunch at a restaurant?" Lizzie asked.

"It is no trouble. They will be happy to welcome you. When they know who Jordan is and hear his story, their hearts can rest. They loved Tatiana. Your translator should come, as the Oros sisters do not speak any English. We will stop and pick her up. Your driver, too."

"That seems like a lot of work for two elderly ladies," Jordan said.

"I will give them the assistance they require," Valeria assured the couple. "It will be a simple meal. Some cheese and bread, tomatoes and cucumbers, and of course, we start with the chicken soup." She pointed to some shacks dotting the landscape in the distance as they descended the mountain road. "You see those places? They are much like the house Tatiana lived in. Three small rooms. Tatiana slept on a cot in the front room, where a small table was. And there was a little shed at the side for farming tools."

Jordan looked toward where Valeria had pointed. He could not imagine living in a place so primitive. He had grown up in a modest home, by American standards. His parents had little money, but they did save for most of his college. That ended, however, when his father died and his mother became ill. If it had not been for Kenton, he would still be paying his student loans. But the Hollister home was luxurious, compared to where his mother had grown up.

"I should have warned you. We need to watch for dogs," Valeria said, interrupting Jordan's thoughts.

"I love dogs!" Lizzie said. "Jordan said once we're settled after our honeymoon, we'll go to the shelter and pick one out. I'm excited about that!"

"These are not pets, Lizzie," Valeria answered. "They are wild dogs that roam in packs. They are dangerous and you must not try to pet them. There aren't as many as there used to be, so we may not even see any, but we must be careful."

They met Flavia and Petru and invited them to join them for lunch at the Oros sisters' home. "They will require you to translate," Valeria told Flavia. "I have some good English, but I will take too long to do the translation, and you will be the better choice. I have to think too much to translate. It will give me headache!" Valeria laughed and placed the back of her hand on her forehead. "Is your job."

Flavia flashed a broad smile. "That is my job, and I love my job! These are my first Americans from my new position with the agency."

The group arrived at Adina and Daria Oros' house, a small, gray cinderblock with a garden in the back. Daria opened the door and welcomed them inside. Her white hair was pinned up, and she walked at a slow pace. Adina, the older sister, appeared ancient to Jordan. Sparse white hair tumbled out from a bun at the back of her head, and matched her pale white skin, so thinned by age her dark blue veins were visible. She walked with a stooped posture and leaned heavily on a cane. But her dark eyes were bright and alert.

A fire burned in the fireplace, providing negligible warmth to abate the chill of Autumn, but the younger visitors, warmed from walking in the cool air, removed their jackets and sweaters as soon as they entered the home. The closeness was stifling. Adina eyed their guests as Daria arranged seats for them. Petru sat on the floor. The small table at which the sisters ate their meals had four wooden chairs. Two armchairs with faded, tattered upholstery faced a television set, separating the living and dining areas.

Valeria and the sisters chatted in Romanian. Flavia leaned toward Jordan and Lizzie and spoke in a low voice. "Valeria is telling them she will help with lunch. Petru will arrange the chairs so we can eat together near the table and talk."

"Can we do something to help?" Lizzie asked.

"No, no. If it is okay with you, I will not translate the trivial matters, such as helping with food or seating, and stick with the important parts of our conversation. Otherwise, we will be here a very long time, and it is hot and...how you say...um..."

"Stuffy," Jordan whispered, finishing her sentence.

"Yes, that is the word. But the sisters are very old and so they are cold. In another week or two, all homes will have the fires going. This is some early."

"When we return to the hotel, I need to discuss something with you, Flavia," Jordan said in a low voice. "It is very important and I need your help. It'll go beyond translating, and I'll be happy to pay you extra."

"Of course!" Flavia answered. She nodded her head in excitement, sending her curls bouncing. "I am at your service!"

"Jordan," Lizzie leaned toward her husband. "Would you like to invite Constantin and Valeria to dinner in Baia Mare?"

"Yes, of course. Great idea. I not only married the prettiest girl in the world, I married the smartest. Yay me!" Jordan stroked her hair.

The visit and lunch with the Oros sisters went well. They were sad to learn of Tatiana's fate, but happy to meet Jordan and his bride. "Daria said they can now be at peace about Tatiana," Flavia told the couple. "They say to tell you thank you to come and meet them."

The group walked Valeria home, happy to be outside in the fresh air. She declined the invitation to dinner. "Our youngest son is home from university tonight. He returns day after tomorrow, so our time with him is short."

"I understand," Jordan said. "Would you allow us to host you at a dinner the following evening?"

"I will first talk to Constantin, of course, but I think we can accept. I will call Flavia and let her know. Will that be okay?"

"We'll wait to hear, then."

The group returned to Baia Mare. "I think I'd like a nap, babe," Lizzie told Jordan in the hotel lobby. "Being a world traveler is taking its toll," she suppressed a yawn. "Not to mention Petru's driving is scaring the living daylights out of me. Why don't you go ahead and talk to Flavia about what we discussed last night?"

"Sounds good." Jordan kissed her and she left for their room. Jordan turned to his translator. "We won't need Petru again today, if you'd like to give him the afternoon off. Can we talk over some gelato?"

Flavia's face lit up at the suggestion of her favorite food. She dismissed Petru and accompanied Jordan to Buonissimo.

Two Days Later

Petru drove Jordan, Lizzie, and Flavia to the center square in Baia Mare.

"We still have thirty minutes before we meet the mayor and his wife at the restaurant," Flavia informed the couple. "I want to show you the clock tower and the square."

She led them to a huge stone tower that stood over one hundred thirty feet tall, erected in 1446. "This clock tower, standing here for over five and one-half centuries, is older than your entire country," Flavia said. "Romania is old. Our culture dates back many centuries, and this clock stands, although, some bad weather has had the effects, but is very beautiful, yes?"

"Wow!" Jordan and Lizzie exclaimed in unison. "I don't think I've ever seen anything *this* old," Lizzie continued. "It's so beautiful." She ran her hands over the stones. "It's like I'm touching history."

Flavia stood tall, smiling. "I knew you would like my country!" She showed them the various shops in the square, and they walked by the fountain. A wedding party was taking photographs in front of the fountain and the group hung back to stay out of the pictures.

"I noticed Petru doesn't talk much," Jordan said to Flavia.

Flavia laughed. "He only knows please and thank you. No other English." She glanced toward the restaurant. "Ah! The Dalca family has arrived some early."

They walked to meet their guests and sat down to order. "The food will take some time. Nobody in Romania is in a hurry," Flavia said. "Shall I tell Mayor Dalca what we spoke of?" she asked Jordan.

"Please."

A prolonged conversation ensued in Romanian. Jordan and Lizzie could only watch, not understanding the language, but Constantin and Valeria were smiling and nodding their heads, and Valeria again cried happy tears.

Flavia turned to the Farradays. "They accept your offer with joy and gratitude. I will arrange for the builder that we met with yesterday to contact them and the work will begin to lay the foundation before the weather turns bad. They thank you with their hearts. It will make a big difference."

Jordan and Lizzie shook hands with Constantin and Valeria as the meal was set before them. "It will be named the Tatiana Todoran Farraday Youth Center and Library, as you wish," Valeria said in English. "There will be inside the library with many books and study areas, the room for games and juice, and the gymnasium for the sports. There will be outside the playground for the little children and football field for the older ones. Is so exciting for our village! It is meaningful way to honor your mother's memory." Valeria brushed a tear from her cheek.

"We'll be back to see it next year. It should be finished by then. Flavia has agreed to act as the middle man between us and the contractor, who is happy that he will keep his men working until the snow comes in winter."

They discussed the plans to stock the building, the playground equipment, and oversight.

That night, as Jordan and Lizzie climbed into bed, she gazed into his dark eyes, holding him captive with her blue-green eyes. "Are you at peace, Jordan? Did you find the answers you were searching for?"

"All is well, my princess." He wrapped her in his embrace. "I feel like I have closure, and that something good will come out of something bad, even if it did take all these years."

Lizzie smiled at him and ran her fingers through his hair. "Something good came out of something bad the day you were born. It just took a while for the rest of the world to catch up to it." She kissed him. "The youth center will make a huge difference in the lives of nearly everyone in the village. It's a beautiful gesture and a wonderful way to keep your mother's memory alive. I'm so proud of you!"

Jordan leaned his head on her shoulder. "Tomorrow, we leave for Bucharest to visit her grave and spend the night. Flavia will contact Ana and see if she will meet with us. Then home, where we start our new life together."

Lizzie closed her eyes and smiled. "Mmm. Yes, home. It's been an incredible honeymoon. I wouldn't trade a moment. But home sounds wonderful."

"Yes, it does."

Coming Soon from Laine Boyd
Way Beyond the Blue

A few years ago, I made a promise to a Vietnam veteran, Colonel Jack Jackson, who I consider a great American hero. At the urging of many who knew this man of integrity, he decided to write his memoirs. It was a great idea. The fascinating story of Colonel Jackson's life *should* be written. The only problem he had was that he was better at telling a story than writing one. Through a series of events, he approached me and asked if I would write his story.

I was honored and humbled by his request, and so began the project. In such an undertaking, I needed to speak with him frequently, but our busy schedules made it impossible. At that time, Unharmonious was almost finished, but I was hesitant to put my own book in front of his. Gracious man that he is, Jack told me his schedule was packed, and I should go ahead and finish my book, and we would get together afterward.

I'm committed to finishing the memoirs of this brave combat pilot. It's time for me to keep the promise I made and do my best to tell his story, so I'm taking a break from writing mystery books to honor my word and try to portray the life and heart of a true hero.

Several more mystery novels are on the horizon, but I am asking my readers to allow me to indulge in a project that simply must be finished with no further procrastination.

Sam, Julie, and the gang will return as soon as the memoirs are published. It is my hope, even though my next book is a departure from my mystery novels, that you will be inspired by *Way Beyond the Blue,* the story of Colonel Jack Jackson, and you will find the upcoming mysteries worth the wait.

Thanks for your patience and understanding.

Please continue to visit me on Facebook, or stop by my website, www.laineboyd.com, or drop me an e-mail at lainejb@outlook.com. I love hearing from my readers.

Laine

62183854R00141

Made in the USA
Lexington, KY
31 March 2017